At last, after being trapped for more than nine months in the colonial Williamsburg of 1767 - 1768, Charles is convinced that the answer to his return to the twentieth century is close at hand.

With Jenny at his side, the mysterious vase in hand and the digsite house nearly completed, Charles is faced with the ultimate decision.

Does he remain in the eighteenth century with Jenny, or return to his own time?

Will he, or can he take Jenny forward in time?

...The story continues...

Francis Street

A Colonial Publishing, Inc. Book

First Printing, First Edition — December 1988

For further information:

Colonial Publishing, Inc.
P. O. Box 233
Timonium, Maryland 21093-0233

Printed in the United States of America

ISBN 0-939435-01-2

FRANCIS STREET

by

M. G. McMANUS

COLONIAL PUBLISHING INC.
Baltimore, Maryland

DEDICATION

To those of us who persevere against the odds, and turn an idea into a dream, and then turn the dream into a reality.

AUTHOR'S NOTES

It is refreshing to realize that so many of you who have walked the restored streets of colonial Williamsburg, have wondered or asked the same questions as I have asked - questions which have inspired the writing of this trilogy.

I extend my most humble appreciation to each and every one of you who has helped turn this dream into a reality. With your support, our Williamsburg story can be shared by readers everywhere.

A special thanks goes out to each of you who has taken the time to write and share your words of encouragement.

FRANCIS STREET

The front door flew open. Charles jumped with a start as the dreary evening silence was broken by the conspicuous entrance of the new post rider. Drenched from head to foot, chilled to the bone and totally exhausted, the rider submitted his mailbags and parcels with a hint of triumph in his youthful expression. This was not only his first week of riding through the Virginia colony, it was his first rainy day, and the resulting muck and mire had rendered him three hours late.

Charles tried desperately not to laugh at the bedraggled apparition before him. "Welcome! Nice day for riding, eh?"

The youth stood motionless for about three seconds, then he noticed the grin creeping onto Charles' face and they both burst into laughter. "Tis a bleedin' mess, I tell ye." Charles was pleasantly surprised by the young man's colorful Scottish accent, the rolling cadence and musical tone which characterized his speech. "Lost muh way on more than one occasion, and I don't mind tellin' ye that your bleedin' river crossins' are the wurrst..."

Charles extended his hand warmly, "Charles Dalton. I work here with Tobias Coulter, master printer of the 'Virginia Gazette'. Welcome to Williamsburg."

"Ian MacClellan, on muh furrst trip into Virginia, and it might ha' been muh last! As ye can see, I'm a wee bit late."

At that moment Mr. Coulter descended the stairwell from his second floor office, "Aha! The new post rider, I presume. Tobias Coulter, here." He proferred his hand and greeted the brawny blond Scot warmly.

"Ian MacClellan at your service, sir."

"Nasty business, this spring rain. I am sure you are in need of food and drink. Charles will see to your comfort, lad, and introduce you all around. Now you must excuse me, a certain item of business requires my immediate attention." This said, the irrepressible master printer hurried out the door and into the teeming rain.

Charles showed Ian to the post rider's room where he could change and dry off in front of the warm fire. "We shall balance the postage books later after you've enjoyed a good meal and a hot drink. Take your time, I've a few things to do before we close up shop for the day."

Charles unloaded and logged-in the mailbags and parcels, pausing as he came across a letter addressed to himself. Excitement gripped him as he recognized the distinctive handwriting. He tore it open enthusiastically, wondering how Thomas would respond to the last letter he had sent him in April describing Jenny's triumphant recovery from illness and their subsequent engagement.

Dear Charles

I have had ill health since I returned to Shadwell. I am, however, considerably better. Your news of Jenny's misfortune induced me to fear for her life and I met with great difficulty in following your story. Present Mr. Coulter with my considerable concern for his daughter as I submit most sincere hopes that all goes well with the good family there.

I hope you have weathered the storm in good mental health for I know you have suffered much through your most trying of recent times. I say it pleased me to read that Miss Coulter has accepted your proposal, for I have your health and happiness at heart and the lady's as well.

I wrote a letter to Professor Wythe recently, explaining the need to come to Williamsburg within the fortnight to report observations regarding a legal matter on which I am presently employed.

I look forward to taking comfort in your presence on more than one occasion. I am anxious to see the gardens of Williamsburg once again. I dare say it will please me to witness the spring display of color.

I have had no letter from our friend John Page since I departed your fair town, I hope he has his health.

To another matter which has occurred to me most recently, I suggest you honour me with the pleasure of your company on my

return to Shadwell for I fear that my stay
in Williamsburg will be a short one. I am
in hopes that Mr. Coulter will oblige me
in the matter of this rather unusual
request. There are many articles of
intelligence I wish to share with you, and
Monticello is a particular matter of
interest. I intend for you to stand on
the very site of its inevitable
construction. Present my compliments
respectfully to Mr. Coulter and his
family, especially to the beautiful Miss
Jenny, and be assured of the friendship
with which I am, Dear Charles, yours
affectionately,

Th: Jefferson

Charles read the letter three times,
savoring the wonder of receiving yet another
letter from the distinguished historical figure
who had become his friend. In truth, this whole
eighteenth century experience was becoming more
and more complicated. One moment he
would feel quite exhilarated, and the next
moment he would be overcome by fear and
uncertainty. He reflected once again on all that
had happened since that shocking day last July,
1986, when he had collapsed on the dig site
while engaged in archeological research for the

Colonial Williamsburg Foundation and awakened in the year 1767. His subsequent meeting with Jenny Coulter, the printer's daughter, and their growing love, had been the lodestar which had guided him through those turbulent times. He shuddered, remembering how he had nearly lost her twice; first through his own reckless passion for the bewitching Alanna Ashton, and then through the deadly illness which Jenny had contracted on her way home from Boston. All was well now, and they were to be married in September, but the very fact of their impending marriage presented problems of its own.

Despite his outwardly calm demeanor, Charles' thoughts were ever haunted by the possibility of finding the trigger which would propel him back into the twentieth century. Now, more than ever, he felt closer to success because the original house whose remains he and his colleagues had been excavating on the Nicholson Street dig site in 1986, was just nearing completion in the current year of 1768. Ironically, Tobias Coulter had built it as a wedding gift for Charles and Jenny. Charles was now convinced that the solution to his inexplicable time travel lay within this house, and he was determined to investigate it at the earliest opportunity.

There was still one problem though. He was unsure of the role Jenny might play in the search for this solution. What would happen if he found his way back to the twentieth century only to find that she could not accompany him? Had he any right to marry her in light of this possibility? They had discussed it endlessly, and Jenny had declared herself willing to marry him under any circumstances, but guilt and his own selfish desire to make her his, warred within him.

It was this kind of nervous worrying that kept Charles on edge during the day and awake at night. He was only able to relax in Jenny's company. Now a new worry had presented itself. Should he stay here with Jenny in Williamsburg and disappoint his friend, or should he accompany Jefferson to Shadwell and invite the risks that such a trip would entail? After all, he was not an experienced traveller, and his riding skills left much to be desired; moreover, the threat of Indians loomed large on the western frontier. On the other hand, he was greatly attracted to the magnetic Jefferson, and this would be a once-in-a-lifetime opportunity to cultivate their friendship in Jefferson's own surroundings where the future statesman and president was at his best.

A lilting voice interrupted his thoughts. "Charles, I'm dyin' of hunger, man. I must get a bite in me or I'll soon be regardin' muh horse with a calculatin' eye, if ye ken what I mean."

Amused at Ian's droll expression and his dramatic declamation, Charles smiled back at the post rider. "Yes, of course, Ian, it's high time. You'll find, I think, that our cook, Beulah, is an angel straight from heaven!"

"So long as its earthly victuals she dishes up, lad, I'm nae too particular."

After locking the shop, Charles escorted Ian to the second-floor loft over the bindery shop where Watson and Billingsley waited patiently for supper. Charles performed the necessary introductions with a mock theatrical bow. "Ian MacClellan, allow me to present Dennis Watson, and Richard Billingsley who share the loft with me. This, my friends, is the new post rider."

"Aye, and an equitable man you'll find me when I'm not perishin' from hunger!"

They all laughed as Billingsley led them down the stairs and into the kitchen house where Beulah reigned supreme.

Every time Charles saw Billingsley, he was vividly reminded of the man's role in rescuing Jenny on that terrible night in Alanna's barn. One memory inevitably lead to the next and he found himself reliving the entire nightmare step by step, ending with the look on Jenny's face as he cradled her unclothed body in his arms. That look would haunt him for

14

as long as he lived.

"It's high time yo' come in heah and get yo' supper. I ben workin' on dis meal for hours, an' I wanto see yo' all get busy an eat!" Beulah's stern expression belied her kind concern as she shooed them into the dining area and began serving up her famous beef stew and large fluffy dumplings. Her mouth-watering gravy filled the kitchen with the scent of freshly harvested herbs and spices. Charles detected the presence of thyme, sage, basil and ground pepper with just a hint of cinnamon. As always, homemade bread was still hot from the oven.

Charles felt he could spend day and night here in Beulah's kitchen. As he ate, his thoughts wandered, and he speculated on the domestic arrangements attendant on establishing a household in the eighteenth century. He and Jenny would be expected to acquire their own staff, including a cook, and it would be difficult to find one of Beulah's caliber. Presumably, Jenny would have received training in such things, and he could leave the decisions to her. He would be busy enough with the logistics of transportation, the stabling of horses, etc. If the marriage actually occurred as planned, and he and Jenny moved into the Nicholson Street house, there would be ample time to settle these questions.

In any case, he would visit the house first

thing in the morning and begin his search for clues both inside and outside the building.

Later that night, unable to sleep in the oppressive humidity of the bindery loft, Charles crystallized his strategy for searching the house. The first item he had unearthed on the 1986 dig site had been a shard from Jenny's Chinese vase, and it was with this discovery that his dizzy spells had begun. The shard had been found in section F 15, in what was now the parlor, or sitting room of the Nicholson Street house, specifically, the hearth. It was here, then, that he would begin.

CHAPTER 2

"Oh, Mist' Charles, heah! Heah's a note from Miss Jenny, I near forgot to give it to ya!"

Charles was hurrying out of the kitchen when Beulah reached into her apron pocket and handed him a small slip of paper. He scanned it quickly.

Dear Charles

Meet me at the new house this morning.

Jenny

"When did she give you this note?"

"Why, first thing dis mawning, before yo' come in heah'.

"Thank you, Beulah," he replied enthusiastically, and out of the door he flew. Walking across the Coulter rear yard toward Nicholson Street, Charles breathed in deeply, taking in the warmth of the early morning sun and enjoying what promised to be a picture-perfect late May day. He suspected the temperature might climb to 75 or even 80 degrees. Spending more time with Jenny would make it perfect. He wandered down Nicholson Street toward what would eventually be called Botetourt Street. Situated on the northwestern corner was their new home -the location of the future dig site. Charles could feel the adrenaline running through his veins and his pulse racing in anticipation. He could see Jenny sitting patiently on the new front steps.

"Sweetheart! I just got your note!"

"Charles, oh how good it is to see you again! I was afraid you couldn't get away." They embraced warmly.

"You, my dear, are a sight for sore eyes." He recalled momentarily how he had stared in awe at her face the first time he saw her in her family's drawing room last summer. It was amazing how the mere sight of her could excite him so. His attraction to her was incomprehensible. After all, his number one objective was to return to his own time, and yet, his effort was encumbered by every thought of Jenny. The threat of losing her had foiled every effort thus far.

Holding her in a lingering embrace, he realized that it was almost impossible to be completely rational and objective in her presence. He longed to be near her, to touch her, to be part of her.

As though sensing his thoughts she looked at him with concern. "Charles, what is it?"

"To be quite honest with you, my dear, I was debating the wisdom of this commitment we are about to enter in view of the fact that we don't even know if we can stay together. Suppose, for a moment, we find the way back to my time. Will it be right for me to take you away from your life and your family and everything you know?"

"Absolutely! We have discussed this before, Charles. You know I will go wherever you take me!"

"But what about your father? What about your mother and our new home here and..."

"It is with you that I wish to spend the rest of my life, make no mistake about that, Charles Dalton."

"I know that, darling, but I still don't

feel comfortable about it."

"What then?"

"I'm not certain of the consequences of your going to my time. What if you got hurt, or..."

Jenny pulled his face down to hers and kissed him tenderly on the mouth. "Whatever is required will be done. Surely you'd not desert your bride even before the wedding? Give us our chance, Charles. Give us our time now." She kissed him again, more aggressively as though to underline her words.

"Jenny, I'm beginning to believe that this house contains the answer to this time travel thing, and though I have determined that we must search everywhere, I want to start in the drawing room near the fireplace. Come, let's see what we can find." Jenny led the way and together they studied every inch of the building, but there was no tangible clue to be found. After two hours of touching the walls and floors and pounding here and there, they still had no idea whatsoever.

Jenny sat quietly on the central stairway next to Charles. Neither had said a word for some time, and she wondered what was going through Charles' mind. He was a complex man, but then he had reason to be troubled. She thought he must feel quite lonely most of the time, having lost all that he had known from his

20

previous life. It had to be more than one could bear. She wondered how he had maintained his composure through so much for so long. Nearly one full year had elapsed since he was brought to her time, and he had done well for himself – with the assistance of her father, of course. There was a strong bond between the two men. Charles was right about one point, she mused. She would certainly feel a great loss if she were separated from her father forever. But if Charles could take her with him, she would go. She knew she would give up everything for their future together.

"No! I can't stay. I won't stay here without you. I will not be separated from you again!"

Perplexed by this outburst, Charles took her gently in his arms. "What brought that on, darling?" He was somewhat alarmed by her aggressive tone. During their last two or three meetings he had noticed an almost hostile tone to Jenny's personality, as though she were greatly disturbed by something or someone. Her recent shock might have contributed to this state of mind, but he was almost certain that it was the result of fear.

Jenny hesitated at first, completely unaware that she had actually spoken out. "Oh! I...I must go with you. I have lost you twice in the last year, once to Boston, and then... I

21

will not lose you again."

Taking her delicate shoulders in his hands and pulling her into a tender embrace he tried to comfort her. "No, you will not lose me again, not if I have anything to do with it." He was suddenly reminded of Thomas' invitation to Shadwell and wondered if he should mention it now or tell her later when Thomas came to town. He chose the latter.

Too frustrated to sit still a moment longer, he stood and began to walk along the front of the house, occasionally pushing on the clapboard or tugging on a windowsill.

"Charles, what are you looking for?"

"I'm not quite sure. Maybe some sort of sign, or possibly something that would have a physical effect on me."

"What are you saying? What kind of physical effect?"

"Well... the same type of symptom I experienced when I touched your vase here on this site in 1986. I became dizzy and sick, and my vision blurred. Eventually, I passed out altogether."

Jenny remembered handing the vase to Charles on the street not long ago with no apparent effect. "When my father brought us here for the first time, I placed the vase in your hands, do you recall? Did you experience any symptoms then?"

"Now that you mention it, no, and I wondered about that. Apparently certain conditions must be met before anything happens. Maybe one must be holding the vase in a certain place or location in the house to make it work. It is possible that you might be involved somehow. I just don't know yet, but I really feel that the answer is in the house. We must find the right combination of ingredients, and then God help us!"

"Charles, do you suppose it could happen to me? Without you at my side? The vase is my property, so it is not inconceivable..."

"I dread the thought! It is imperative that I be with you. Maybe we shouldn't take the vase into the house unless we are together...but no, that couldn't make any difference. You wouldn't know what to avoid anyway."

They strolled back to the rear porch and sat down again. A horse-pulled wagon moved ponderously down Botetourt Street toward one of the taverns on Duke of Gloucester Street and they both gazed idly at it as it passed, the horses clip-clopping along. Charles remembered that sound - it was the first sound he had heard when he awakened into the 18th century. He would never forget the shock and terror of that interminable day. And now, here he was still, after eleven months. He had not only survived, but prospered, and he had found love. He wondered how Jenny would adjust to the 20th century should that ever come to pass. Would it prove too much of a culture shock? Could she adjust to modern conveniences like electrical appliances, plumbing, telephones, radios, television, cars, airplanes, computers, and a host of other things? Modern clothing would be difficult for her to accept, he was sure. But then maybe she would surprise him. After all, I became accustomed to the archaic "plumbing" and lack of electricity, he thought. Maybe she could handle fast food restaurants and the music of the 80's. I can see her now, he mused, a woman of the 80's. The idea began to excite him. It began to seem plausible all of a sudden. "Jenny, I've been thinking about you in the 20th century. If, and I emphasize if, you were exposed to the change in culture slowly, I believe you would adapt."

Her face glowed. "Do you really think so?"

"Yes. But it wouldn't be easy, and it would be nearly impossible if you were alone. Someone would need to be there to explain everything and to protect you from injury or accident. Most of all to protect your sanity."

"My sanity! Charles, you jest. You've not lost your sanity through this experience, however dreadful it has been for you. Why should I not fare just as well?"

He smiled. "You have no idea how close I

came to losing my sanity, dear. We didn't meet until the worst was over for me. At any rate, I was somewhat prepared for 18th century life through my studies of history and archaeology. I was already familiar with the mode of dress, the coinage, the customs to some extent, and oh, so many things. You, on the other hand, are a rank novice. Take clothing, for instance..."

"Yes, do explain, Charles. What would a woman of your time be wearing?"

"Well, ah, it's about 70 degrees or so today which means that it's warm enough for light pants, a light blouse, or maybe even shorts, if a woman wants to get some sun on her legs."

Jenny frowned in concentration. "Sun on her legs, how so?"

"Well, shorts are short pants, not unlike mine, except not so baggy, and they are only this long." He demonstrated with his hands. "Down to here, or maybe even here. Most of the leg is left completely bare and exposed to the sun. Then, more than likely, a woman would wear a short-sleeved blouse which would leave her arms bare as well."

He watched her lovely mobile face as she pondered his words, trying to imagine what such an outfit would look like. Suddenly, a brilliant smile lit her face, and her violet eyes sparkled. "It must be quite strange,

Charles. I'm afraid I should laugh if such a female crossed my path! Though I admit it must be cool in the heat of summer."

He threw back his head and laughed. Her sense of humor was one of the things which most endeared her to him. Yes. she would adjust to the 20th century alright; she would probably love it!

On a more serious note, he continued, "Frankly, women don't need to wear all these clothes," he indicated her ruffled and flounced skirts, "Fashion has changed in two hundred years, but I must admit that it's not perfect in my time either. Many people expose themselves to too much sunlight, particularly at the beach, and cause tremendous damage to their skin. They age quite rapidly in many cases, and some develop a dangerous disease called skin cancer."

"Why Charles, we have always known how dangerous the sun is to one's complexion! Do your physicians not warn against such exposure?"

"Yes, of course, but I'm afraid it's a matter of following the fashion. In my time, the fashion is for a tanned face and body, just lightly browned by the sun. Some go too far, that's all. Ah, I can just see you on the beach, darling. With your figure and that magnificent hair, you'd be a knockout in a swimsuit!" He traced a brief description of a swimsuit for her

26

benefit, enjoying the consternation with which she greeted his words.

"Oh, Charles, I wouldn't be permitted to show my ankles in public without scandal. How do they dare?"

"Well, you will see, if it ever comes to that. We will have to take it slowly, one step at a time."

Jenny jumped up. "I had best return home. Mother will be concerned."

"I suppose you are right. She is in her element just now, helping plan the furnishings, I imagine."

"Oh yes, isn't it exciting? Mr. Haye has ordered the bedroom from Philadelphia, and he is making our table and chair for the supper room. I hope you approve?"

"My dear, as I told you last month. Anything you order will be fine with me, just as long as it makes you happy."

She gave him a quick hug and off they went down Nicholson Street. When they reached the rear courtyard of the Coulter house, Jenny turned to him and said, "Please wait here, Charles, I shall not be long."

Five minutes later she returned, an air of suppressed excitement about her. "My father hasn't returned yet, could you return in one hour?"

"What is it, Jenny? What's going on?"

"I can only tell you that it is a surprise gift for you, and about its particulars I can say no more. Just be here in one hour, now, off with you!" She gave him a playful shove and pulled a wry face as he made her a mock bow.

"Madame, your wish is my command. One hour, no more, no less!"

Five minutes later he sat in Beulah's kitchen trying to coax some information out of her. "What do you know about a surprise gift for me, Beulah? Jenny's acting mighty mysterious."

She glared at him in mock anger. "I dunno nothin' 'bout no surprise, Mist' Charles."

"Well, something is going on.."

"Yah, yo' goin'. Doan go askin' me nothin''bout dis heah surprise. I dunno, and dat's dat!"

"Can I at least have some coffee?"

"Yassir, yo' sure can." She poured him a steaming mug of the brew, then turned away and began to chop vegetables noisily, but not before Charles saw a smile begin to creep across her broad black face.

It was obvious she knew something, but he would never get it out of her, that much was certain. He finished his coffee, threw her a wink and sauntered out into the midday sun. There was just time enough for a short stroll over to the silver smith shop. For he, too, had planned a little surprise for his Jenny. He

sincerely hoped that it would be ready by now.
The gift had been ordered almost four weeks
earlier.

CHAPTER 3

Having collected Jenny's silver locket, Charles found himself standing in front of his new house. He realized that the house was becoming something of an obsession. He thought about it all day. He stood there staring at the site wondering how long it would take to stumble onto the answer which must lie within these walls. Recalling vividly that section F 15 was the location where he had unearthed the vase, he could now determine that this section was located directly in front of the sitting room fireplace. He concluded that the answer must involve being in the sitting room near the fireplace. He imagined some sort of "doorway" into a travel dimension. He knew that the vase was the "key"; what he did not know was the sequence of events which actually triggered the time travel. What minor detail was missing? He concluded that a combination of conditions similar to the principle behind the modern deadlock was essential to solving the puzzle.

Walking back toward the Coulter house, he remained convinced that he was getting closer to his return home. He wondered what year it would be when he returned, and how much time had elapsed since he had been trapped in the 18th century.

Strolling leisurely into the Coulter rear courtyard, Charles heard more than the usual commotion coming from the stables. The raucous clip-clop of horses' hooves on the brick stable floor and the pandemonium of horses neighing in accompaniment to Rogers' shouted instructions made it quite clear to Charles that something was amiss.

Coulter stepped briskly through the back door of the house into the courtyard and greeted Charles. "Aha! Charles, my dear boy!"

"Mr. Coulter, sir," Charles replied respectfully, "what's happening here?"

Jenny ran out to join them, her ebony hair

31

shimmering in the noonday sun. She flashed them a smile that was guaranteed to melt any man's heart.

Coulter placed a companionable hand on Charles' shoulder. "Come, see what I have here, lad." Tobias was obviously thrilled about whatever was going on. "Rogers, bring the beast out to us!"

Charles threw an inquiring look at Jenny who beamed with suppressed excitement. She took his hand and waited patiently. Soon Rogers appeared from out of the stable accompanied by the most magnificent thoroughbred Charles had ever seen. He was a giant, about 16 hands, with a glossy black coat under which every powerful muscle was sharply defined.

"He's yours, Charles," Coulter said enthusiastically.

"I...I don't know what to say!"

"It was Jenny's doing, lad. Fond as she is of the beasts, she wanted you to have the best."

"His name is Jupiter," Jenny added, "isn't he wonderful?"

"Indeed he is. I just don't know how to thank you both!"

"He's fast, my boy. I saw him run this fortnight past, and took to the saddle myself with the greatest pleasure. He's one to be proud of." Coulter's smile broadened as he noted, "Of course, you must be taught to ride him properly.

He needs to know you are his master in every way, and then he'll never give you a bit of trouble."

"I'm overwhelmed, sir. But I can't possibly accept such a gift. I may not be much of a rider, but I know prime horseflesh when I see it."

"'Twas nothing lad."

"But I insist on repaying you for the animal..."

"I'll not hear of it. You have already paid me a hundredfold." He glanced meaningfully at Jenny, and Charles knew he was referring to the two occasions on which he had saved Jenny's life. "Not another word now, Charles. It's settled, then. What say you to a ride?"

"Do you think he'll take to a strange rider? He does look rather formidable."

"You must gentle him a bit, Charles. Let him get used to you, and talk to him. He'll soon come to know your voice and carry you right willingly."

"We shall both be here to help you, Charles," Jenny added. Then she turned to the stable boy. "Rogers, will you saddle Liberty for me as well, please?"

"Yes, Miss Coulter," He turned to Coulter inquiringly, "and Lady?"

"Yes, Rogers, thank you." Tobias placed a hand on Charles' shoulder and one arm around

Jenny's waist. "This calls for a celebratory drink. Come, join me in the sitting room for a moment!"

Comfortably ensconced in the well-appointed sitting-room, Charles accepted a cordial from Tobias and smiled as the older man toasted, "To Charles!"

He responded with, "To Jenny, my destiny!"

"To Father!"

Tobias refilled their glasses. "To our health and happiness!"

Jenny then excused herself to change into her riding attire and Tobias took that opportunity to address Charles confidentially. "With regard to your toast, lad, I must say that I find a great deal of truth in your words."

"How do you mean, sir?"

"We had been acquainted less than a fortnight when I recognized you as a hard-working and dedicated young man with much courage and ambition. Though I had my doubts concerning your extraordinary behavior and unfamiliar ways, nevertheless I continued to support and encourage our relationship. I knew of your intentions toward Jenny at the outset and Jenny's desire as well. Considering the course of events which have recently passed, and the life-saving role with which you have entrusted yourself, I suspect that in some mysterious way, you have been delivered to us for the purpose of restoring to us our daughter. It is as though you were destined to be with her and she with you.

Charles paused to gather his thoughts, raising his empty glass for a refill.

"Right! Another one for the ride!" Tobias attended to the drinks. "What say you, Charles?"

Charles chose his words cautiously. "Mr. Coulter, allow me to speak frankly."

"Pray do so."

"It is true that my original interest in Williamsburg was purely historical." Tobias frowned and raised one eyebrow as Charles continued, "Virginia politics coupled with the uncertain future ahead brought me to your town; however, I must confess that I had vivid dreams of Jenny before we met for the first time in this very room."

"Indeed, I recall your initial reaction at the sight of her."

"Quite so. It was as if I had already known her, and I was shocked at our actual meeting. I must confess that the thought of her presence often distracts me."

"Indeed. She is a remarkable woman."

Charles twisted the stem of his glass, frowning. How could he explain what was on his mind in terms that Coulter would understand? He took a deep breath and plunged in. "Sir, I'm sure you have noticed an absence of customary behavior on my part with regard to this marriage..."

"I suspect that you have reasons for not taking up certain matters of domestic responsibility, in particular, your own residence here in town. If you wish to apprise me of these reasons, that is your affair. I've no wish to meddle. I know my daughter to be secure with you, and happy, and that is my chief concern."

Well, sir, I am still somewhat reluctant to settle here permanently. I feel that much unrest and turmoil is in store for these colonies during the next 10 years or so, and maybe even longer. Virginia will not be alone in her assessment of political and foreign affairs."

"The Quartering Act, eh?"

"Precisely. New York is merely the first to be effected, but soon all the colonies will have to unite in this struggle for independence from parliamentary tyranny."

"I dare say there is much truth in your words, Charles, and it is just this rare understanding which you possess in matters of foreign and domestic affairs which holds my fascination and not a little admiration."

"I suggest that our neighbors in Boston will lead us into the struggle."

"It may be so, lad. However, here in Williamsburg it has not yet come to outright rebellion, and I am more concerned at present with Jenny's and your happiness."

"I know, sir. I wish to assure you that whatever happens, and wherever I am compelled to go, taking Jenny with me, my love for her will always be as strong as it is now, if not greater with time."

The subject of their conversation soon joined them in the parlor looking luscious in her riding habit, and the three made their way to the stables eagerly anticipating their outing. In spite of Charles' reassuring words, Coulter felt a slight apprehension, a vague foreboding which he tried to put out of his mind. Things had been going extraordinarily well of late, but he was experienced enough to know that tragedy could strike at any time, as it had with Adam's death and subsequent events. If only he could keep Jenny at his side forever; but, failing that, he would be content just to know she was near, in Williamsburg...

"Ah, Liberty! Come to me, boy!" Jenny patted him lovingly on the nose and allowed him to nuzzle her shoulder before she mounted him swiftly and effortlessly, her face glowing with anticipation.

Charles, mindful of Coulter's advice, approached Jupiter gingerly. He took some time with the animal, getting to know him, and allowing Jupiter to become familiar with him.

He spoke softly and soothingly, while stroking the horse's neck. Rogers produced an apple from his pocket and urged Charles to feed it to him, which Charles did, careful to keep his palm open as the horse ate from his hand.

"That should do it, sir," Rogers exclaimed. "I've never known a horse yet to reject an apple!"

"Yes, but will he reject me?" Charles laughed.

Rogers remained close by in case Charles should need his assistance, and at first, it looked as though this would indeed be the case, for Jupiter began to sidestep each time Charles attempted to mount him. The others began to laugh in earnest as this courtly dance was repeated several times.

Charles placed his left foot in the stirrup which struck him as being dreadfully high. It seemed as though his knee was almost on a level with his neck. With a sudden agile movement, he was astride Jupiter, right foot set and reigns in hand. Well, he thought, here goes!

Coulter led the way, and Charles allowed Jupiter to follow Lady and Liberty onto Nicholson Street. The rhythmic clip-clopping of the animals' hooves across the courtyard bricks amused Charles, reminding him of old movies he had seen, particularly the original Sherlock

Holmes stories. As they progressed, he felt invigorated. He admitted to himself that he was still rather nervous. After all, he didn't know the horse at all, and thoroughbreds were notorious for their unpredictability.

At that very moment, halfway down Nicholson Street, Jupiter jumped ahead and suddenly took off, running wildly. Taken completely by surprise, Charles nearly fell off, but managed to regain his seat. He crouched over the horse's head and let up somewhat on the reigns as Jupiter ran out into the countryside with Tobias and Jenny in pursuit. He could hear Coulter shouting, "Get hold of his head, man. Pull up, pull up on him!"

"Charles! Charles!" Jenny added her screams to the general pandemonium as Liberty made an attempt to catch Jupiter, but he could only keep an approximate pace and was slowly losing ground.

" Ride him out, man, and keep your seat!" Tobias was gaining, but not by much. Charles took his advice, and Jupiter ran over a mile before Charles could finally pull him up, slowing from a gallop to a fast trot and finally to a canter. The others caught up and gathered around, relief etched on their faces.

"Thank heaven you are not hurt, darling. You frightened me near to death!" Charles reassured her with a weak grin though he felt rather sick. He took several deep breaths and the color slowly returned to his face.

"Now don't give him his head in that manner again, Charles," Coulter warned, "let this serve as a lesson. He could very well have thrown you and done you a serious injury. We would never have caught him, I can assure you."

"I don't know what set him off. One minute he was following Liberty, and the next, he's off and running."

"Probably saw something that spooked him. He might try it again at any opportunity. So remain in control, lad. You may not fare so well on the next run."

"Oh, Father, perhaps we have made a terrible mistake in procuring this horse for Charles. He is difficult to handle, and Charles is not an experienced rider. If anything should happen to him I would never forgive myself..."

Jenny did not add, "or you", but the words hung in the air and troubled Tobias as he couldn't help but agree. He turned to Charles as if to speak, but Charles held up his hand to forestall him.

"You mustn't blame yourselves for my ineptness. I will learn to ride Jupiter, and soon I will be the best rider in the county. I won't let him beat me, Jenny. All I need is practice, and that is where you come in. You and I will practice, and before long, you will not need to be ashamed of me."

"But are you certain you can learn to handle him, Charles? He could be dangerous."

"Only if he feels I am not in control, as I was not just now when he bolted. I'm confident we will make a good pair with practice."

"If you believe it to be so, then it will be so, lad. I'll not contradict you. Are you game for continuing on, now, or shall we scrap it for today?" Coulter's hearty manner belied his lingering concern, but he was determined not to let Charles see this. He would have to have a talk with Rogers at the earliest opportunity.

"By all means, let's continue."

They rode for almost an hour enjoying the late spring beauty of the landscape. It had turned into a magnificent late May day, and the temperature soared. The last trees to develop leaves, the tall oaks, were now in full canopy. The air smelled fresh and clean, and everything seemed wonderful to Charles. He was becoming more used to Jupiter, keeping close reign on him, though the horse behaved beautifully. Best of all, Jenny was nearby, and her presence always worked its magic on him.

Soon they were walking the horses back along Nicholson Street and Charles once more attempted to thank Coulter for Jupiter. It had occurred to him that this gift was comparable to receiving a luxury car from a man who expected to become your father-in-law in 20th century terms. The quality and breeding of the animal was certainly equivalent to a top-of-the-line model, somewhere in the neighborhood of forty to fifty thousand dollars. Where had Tobias found the money?

Coulter tried to shrug off his thanks and pressed Charles to accept the horse as a measure of his affection and gratitude. This done, he refused to hear of the subject again. When Rogers had taken charge of the horses, the older man hurried him off for a private word, and Charles found himself alone with Jenny.

"Will you call for me tonight, Charles? I should love to take a walk through town." Her eyes caressed him as she spoke and his blood quickened.

"Of course, darling. Nothing could keep me away, and I have a little surprise to give you."

"At six, then!" She kissed him tenderly and flew into the house. Charles watched her with his heart in his eyes.

CHAPTER 4

Having just completed his evening meal,
Charles stood in the rear of the book bindery
and packed some fresh tobacco into his clay
pipe. Upon striking his match, the match head
flew off and into the small stream which flowed
through Mr. Coulter's property. Charles followed
the match as it floated down toward Nicholson
Street and as he did so, he imagined it
floating toward the York River and ultimately
into the Chesapeake Bay. He strolled along
considering that all of the water drainage to

the east side, or Nicholson Street side of Duke of Gloucester, flowed to the York River, and all of the storm water drainage on the south side of Duke of Gloucester flowed toward the James River. He surmised that Duke of Gloucester must be the high ridge dividing line between the York and the James. He wondered if Francis Nicholson actually selected the town site for this reason, or whether it was purely coincidental. It was curious, but he hadn't made this observation when he walked the restored streets of Williamsburg in the summer of 1986. Perhaps he, like most tourists, especially first-time visitors, had been too immersed in historical facts and itineraries to notice the actual flow of water throughout the town. Maybe the old Duke knew what he was doing after all when he drew up the plans for the colonial town in 1699 or thereabouts. Charles wasn't quite sure if that was the year when the colonial capital site was moved from Jamestown. He would have to check it out.

Charles knocked on the door of the Coulter house at six o'clock and, to his surprise, Jenny answered it. He quickly stepped inside glancing toward the empty parlor. It was all he could do to keep from crushing Jenny to him in a fierce embrace, she looked so alluring. She read his eyes and blushed.

"Your parents?"

"Father is visiting at the Raleigh with friends, and mother is in her room writing to Aunt Caroline."

"Good!" He kissed her passionately, absorbing the energy which she poured into him. Electricity raced through his veins, as it always did when they touched. When he released her, he looked deeply into her eyes. "Do you feel what I feel?"

"Yes, my love," she whispered. "We must be together more. I feel the lack as keenly as you do, but..." she turned and looked toward the stairs, "not now, not here."

"I understand."

"I shall not be a moment." She snatched up her cape just as Bea came through the rear entrance with a tea tray in her hands.

"Bea, Charles and I are going out for a short walk. Mother already knows, but please tell her we won't be long."

"Yo' can be sure, Miss Jenny, I'll tell her."

"Thank you, Bea." Jenny took Charles' hand and led him out the door into the courtyard. "Shall we walk up to the Palace Green?"

"Fine. You can be my personal tour guide."

"Tour guide?" She pulled him along playfully. "Oh Charles, I suppose I'm meant to inquire into your meaning. But I don't want to think about that now. Let's just enjoy the

45

evening!"

He smiled his acquiescence.

They crossed the little bridge over the trickling stream and climbed the steep stairwell to the street level of Duke of Gloucester. Once out in front of the print shop, they strolled toward Chowning's and the Market Square. Jenny was the first to break the silence. "I have received a letter from Boston. Aunt Caroline is well and intends to leave as of the first of July to attend my preparations for the wedding these months coming."

"She's a dear lady. I wonder what news she will bring from Boston."

"I wonder. I was surprised to hear that she would be coming so soon, during so hot a season. I fear she will suffer terribly from the heat, more than she expects."

"She will survive. She's tougher than she looks."

"I know that she adores you, and she probably can no longer wait to catch up on the latest events."

"No doubt her news from Boston will be equally as exciting." He glanced at Chowning's as they passed the front door and turned impulsively to Jenny. "Let's go in and take some coffee. What do you say?"

"Do you suppose I should go in?"

"I see no reason why not." He peeked inside

one of the serving room windows and saw very few patrons eating. "It is not crowded at this hour."

"Father has never taken me in to any of the inns. I know mother would not approve."

"Why?"

"I do not...I am led to believe that young ladies do not frequent public inns and taverns.

"You will be under my protection."

"Are you certain that..."

"Yes, of course." He took her by the hand to the front porch and into the interior hallway. Glancing into the room on the right he muttered to himself, "Not bad!"

"What did you say, Charles?"

He turned to her in surprise, unaware that he had spoken aloud. "Oh! I was just thinking about the Foundation's restoration of this building, and I dare say the Foundation would be pleased if they could see how closely their efforts match the original." Catching Jenny's confused expression, he sighed. "Don't be overly concerned about me, dear. I make these comparisons all the time. Remember, I have spent some very enjoyable nights sitting in this room with a mug of ale, some peanuts and several good companions. But the best part of it was meeting strangers from every part of the world who had come to see this little town restored, and to take a look into the past - to your time. We have come to recognize in eighteenth century Williamsburg the beginning of something of great value and meaning for the whole world."

"Tell me about it, Charles." She took his hand and regarded him expectantly.

"I will explain more about it later, dear. For now, just look around and take note of how things look, because I will bring you back here when we get to the twentieth century."

"Remember, this is my first time in the inn."

"I haven't forgotten, Jenny. Well, I will say one thing. There is a lot more furniture here than the Foundation has set up. Of course, money may be a deciding factor..."

"What money?"

"You see, the Foundation has a limited budget. They probably couldn't afford to provide the necessary amount of furniture. Furthermore, over a million people walk in and out of these buildings every year...Or, at least during the 1980's. I wonder how many people stay here now?"

"I wouldn't know, but my father comes to this inn with some frequency, possibly once or twice every fortnight."

"Yes, I noticed. He frequents most of the inns about town, doesn't he?"

They both laughed heartily. Charles squeezed her hand and whispered, "Now, let's go into the public dining room for that coffee."

He led the way across the large entrance hall bypassing the stairway to the second floor. It was much quieter on this side of the tavern, as considerably less drinking was going on in the dining room. In fact, Charles could not help but notice that the inn on the whole was more subdued than he expected. Although he heard a musician playing what sounded like a mandolin, the atmosphere was far calmer than the noisy fun-filled rooms he remembered.

Having taken seats at a corner table near the front of the inn, Charles asked Jenny, "Is there something happening in town tonight? It seems unusually quiet in here."

"There is the play at the Theatre."

"Oh, that's right! I had forgotten."

I believe there are two performances. One is 'The Orphan, or the Unhappy Marriage'..."

"Yes, and that is to be followed by a 'Comic Dance'."

"Yes. The Bedlamites."

"I am not too keen on the theater myself, are you?"

"I have only seen two plays, and I did rather enjoy 'A Midsummer Night's Dream' last year."

Before Charles could respond, a pretty young girl served them their coffee. Charles asked how much he owed her and the girl replied,"One tuppence, sir. Thank you." She waited patiently as Charles produced the necessary coin.

"What is your name?"

"Jane Gibson, sir."

"May I ask how you came to be working here at Chownings?" There was something very appealing about the girl who appeared to be about 16 or so, and both Charles and Jenny felt drawn to her.

"I am indentured here for seven years, sir. The owner paid for my voyage across the ocean from England, and I have already served two years." Her voice was scarcely audible and tears filled her eyes.

Jenny sensed her pain instinctively and reached out to take her hand. "What is it, dear? Are you unwell?"

The girl stepped back before Jenny's hand could touch hers. "I...I try not to recall that horrible voyage. I lost my baby at sea.'Twas the smallpox." She broke into sobs and Jenny tried to console her. Charles now regretted prying into the girl's personal life. Her brief answer reminded him that cruelty and disease were an integral part of this life, the cruelties and diseases simply taking different forms as the centuries advanced.

He spoke to her in gentle tones. "Try to be strong, as you have been for so long. Things will be better for you soon. It won't be too long before you are a free woman."

A spark of hope lit her face and she dried her eyes on her apron as she answered, "The proprietor said he would release me one year early, on my twenty-first birthday provided I work very hard for him. He provides generously for all my needs,"she paused a moment and a faraway look came into her eyes, "well, almost all of my needs. Please excuse me, sir. I must be about my work. Is there anything else you'll be wanting? No? Then, I'm off."

Reaching across the table, Charles took Jenny's hand. "I'm sorry I started that, but there was something about her face..."

"I know. I felt it too. She is so young, and has suffered so much already!"

"These are hard and difficult times, Jenny, and things will get a good deal worse before they get better, you may be certain."

"How do you mean?"

"Well, I'm not saying we don't have cases of hardship and difficulty in the twentieth century, we have those aplenty, but when you consider the population now, and what it will be in 1987, one can see that in this country, in my time, every man, woman and child has the greatest opportunity known to all mankind to pursue happiness and live a relatively comfortable life."

"That is indeed a wonderful thought,

Charles. I do wish to see your America."

"One sad thought, however, is that many Americans of my day don't really know how good it is. They don't think in relative terms. I can understand, though, how easy it is to get caught up in the race to have more things, and bigger and better things, always more, more, and never content. Well, I should talk, I was headed in that very direction myself."

By this time, Jenny had become acutely conscious of several men at neighboring tables who were looking at her with a mixture of admiration and familiarity. As she glanced around the room, she encountered some downright hostile stares which made her increasingly uncomfortable. She longed to jump up and race out of the room, but at that moment, the young indentured servant returned to their table. She looked at Jenny apologetically. "Some of the guests inquired about you being here, ma'am. I must admit, you are the first lady I have served here."

Jenny bit her lip. "Perhaps we should leave, Charles. I must confess I begin to feel most unwelcome." She inclined her head in the direction of their fellow patrons who were unabashedly commenting on her presence with laughter and sly innuendos.

"Darling, we will leave when we are ready, and not before. Now, those men are free to go if they find your presence disturbing. However, if any of them find your presence disturbing, they must be sick!" He turned to the serving maid. "Is that not so, Jane?"

"Indeed, you are a beautiful lady, ma'am." She looked around nervously, then curtseyed swiftly and ran to one of the other tables where several young men were banging the table with their blackjacks to demand her attention.

By this time, the noise and activity in the game room had increased considerably, and the music had become quite raucous. It was about fifteen minutes past eight o'clock according to Charles' pocket watch, and he was about to draw Jenny's attention to that fact, when she gasped in dismay as a familiar figure in the entrance hallway caught her eye.

Tobias had already spotted Charles and Jenny and hurried over to their table in the corner. "What on earth are you two doing here? Jenny, have you taken leave of your senses? I should have thought you would have more commonsense than to bring my daughter to a public tavern!"

Jenny defended Charles hotly. "Why not father? Why is a lady not permitted to do as we have done here tonight? I see no harm in it!"

Tobias was taken aback at Jenny's passionate outburst. "Why...uh, look around you. How many ladies do you see? I tell you, it simply isn't done!"

"We merely stopped in for some coffee, sir." He echoed Jenny's objection. "We see no harm in doing so."

"No harm? 'Tis a matter of protocol, man. A gentleman would not bring a young lady of breeding into a public tavern and expose her to the riffraff. It is not accepted custom here!"

Jenny was somewhat subdued, recalling the rude stares and ribald comments which had greeted her only moments before. But her independence asserted itself now and she continued to spar with her father. "When I was in Boston with Aunt Caroline, it was not considered ill-bred for a lady to frequent an inn!"

Tobias frowned. "That was Boston, not Williamsburg. I'll take a course with you later, missy." He regarded Charles with ill-concealed ire. "Drink up, man, and be off before you cause another scandal."

"Very well, sir. I'll take Jenny home at once, you have my word on it. Please do not interrupt your own entertainment on our account."

Tobias was somewhat mollified at this and leaning over, he kissed Jenny's forehead. She smiled up at him and his heart turned over. He could never be cross with her for long.

"Right! Just a few more minutes, then

you're off. Good night!" He saluted Charles briefly and made his way over to the game room to join his friends, muttering as he went. "Daft notions! Don't know what the younger generation is coming to!"

When they reached the Coulter house, Jenny was reluctant to end the evening. "Charles, it's a beautiful night, let's visit the garden! I can't bear to go in just yet."

Charles agreed, smiling. Jenny stood on tiptoes and kissed him teasingly, then she turned toward the gardens.

CHAPTER 5

They strolled slowly and quietly through the formal boxwood garden toward Jenny's favorite circular garden. This was a very special place for Jenny. It was where Charles had first kissed her. She remembered the warmth of his tender touch so vividly, it wasn't possible that all that had happened ten months since. She realized how little time they had actually shared alone since he had arrived. She sat down on the wooden bench and Charles propped up one foot next to her.

Gazing into her pensive face he asked softly, "What thoughts do you ponder so earnestly?"

"Don't talk to me now." She surprised him with her vehemence. "Touch me! I have longed for you so!"

He caressed her face tenderly with his fingers and ran his hands through her long shining hair. Moving swiftly next to her on the bench, he pulled her into a loving embrace. They held each other tightly at first, and then more tenderly. Charles could feel the heat of passion radiating from every inch of her beautiful body. She was overwhelmingly desirable, and it was all he could do to simply hold her close to him and feel the love she so generously poured into him.

At length Jenny broke the enchanted silence between them. "I could go on like this forever, and yet, I feel that we were never meant to experience such joy in this world."

"But it was intended, surely, for was I not brought to you in the most mysterious way?"

"You are right, my love." Every inch of her willing body was ravenous for his touch. She wanted to abandon herself to him completely as she had done once before, in a nearby meadow. She took his hands and placed them over her breasts, and his continued fondling rapidly threatened to bring her to the point of no return. Then, suddenly, she turned abruptly and whispered, "Not now! Not here!"

"What is it?"

"I'm not certain. I...I want it to be right with us, and if we continue, I won't care!" She frowned and drew her hand across her forehead distractedly. Then she stood and began pacing around the circular brick pathway.

"Oh, Charles, I am so tired of this! Why can't we marry at once?"

"Are you prepared to deal with all the myriad domestic decisions such a move entails, my darling?"

"But of course! I know very well how to make all the necessary arrangements. Be certain, my mother has trained me in the arts of wifehood since I was quite young."

"Ah, yes. I had forgotten. But I must make one thing quite clear, Jenny. I will not have slaves."

She was startled by the fervor with which he uttered these last words, and she knew he was deadly serious.

"Why..then...you realize, Charles, that servants are very costly. Can we manage thus?"

"My income will have to suffice for our needs. Do what you will, only I will not have slaves."

"I have a thought! Do you suppose...?"

He loved to watch her face when it was lit from inside with such radiance. "What is that?"

"Jane. The girl from Chowning's. Do you suppose we could buy her indentures and pay her to work for us?"

Charles frowned in concentration. "I would have to make inquiries. She has several years to serve, and I don't know if Josiah Chowning will be amenable to such an offer. Moreover, it would be expensive, I'm sure. I know you were very taken with the girl, but we must wait and see. By the way, have you made any arrangements for a cook?"

"Beulah has been training her neice. But she is a slave, and in light of your objection to slaves, I will have to make another arrangement."

"Please do. Jenny, I was rather upset last week by a very nasty scene here in town, one that I would rather not think about."

"What was it?"

"I witnessed another slave auction at the Raleigh Tavern. I cannot describe the disgust I feel whenever such a thing occurs. I stood there immobile, filled with the greatest animosity towards everyone involved. What disturbs me most is the complete absence of recognition of these people as human beings. I have seen much more personal concern applied to the purchase of horses than I do with blacks. Slavery is a disgrace, and it dehumanizes every one who participates in it."

"But, Charles, you see how our family looks after and cares for our people. Father won't have it any other way. Why Bea and Beulah are all but members of the family! Often Bea or Rogers will sit at table with us. There is no abuse of black people under father's protection."

"I do respect your father, of course, but it still comes down to a matter of property. People should not, and cannot be considered the property of other people simply because their skin is a different color."

Jenny could only remember one other individual who spoke in such a manner. It was one of her father's house guests who spent an evening with them last spring. His name was Patrick something...She aroused herself from her reverie and replied to Charles' last statement. "I understand your feeling on the subject, Charles, and I will respect your wishes in our household."

"Thank you, my darling. I am looking forward to exchanging views on this and other subjects with Thomas next week."

"I was not aware that he was coming to Williamsburg so soon."

"Yes, I received a letter from him projecting his arrival on Monday next."

"He is such a gentle man. I know how much you value his company. We should invite him to dinner at father's home one evening, don't you agree?"

"Yes, that might be arranged. But I am not sure how long he will stay. He did intimate that it would be a brief visit this time. And that reminds me! Thomas suggested that I accompany him on his return trip to Charlottesville for a visit."

"Where?"

"I'm sorry. I mean Shadwell, his mother's plantation on the Rivanna River in Albemarle County. It's a little more than 120 miles from Williamsburg, to the west."

"I am unfamiliar with that part of the colony."

"A lovely town will develop in the foothills adjacent to Thomas' future estate, Monticello, and it will be called Charlottesville. Thomas will design a State University there in the future. Oh my darling, I do ramble on, don't I?"

"I don't mind. I love to hear you speak of the future."

He chuckled. "You would have been a real 'Star Trek' fan in the twentieth century."

"It is only because I am interested in your world, not because it is the future. Although, I must admit, parts of it sound inviting. What is Star, uh...?"

"Don't worry about it now. I'll let you

watch a rerun when we get there - if we get there."

"It makes nonsense of our domestic arrangements here, does it not, Charles? Here we are planning a household when we know we will ultimately be elsewhere. Do you feel the futility of it?"

"Yes, darling, I do," he sighed, "and that explains my reluctance to confront so many of these little details. I know your father has noticed it and thinks it strange. We must simply carry on as though we mean to stay, yet do everything in our power to find the way back to my time. Now, I wish to hear your thoughts concerning my trip to Shadwell. It would mean at least two, maybe three weeks away from you. Would you rather I stayed here?"

Jenny frowned. "I shall certainly miss you, my love." She squeezed his hand. "But I do want you to maintain your friendship with Thomas. You value it so."

"I knew you would say that. The problem is persuading your father to allow me leave from the shop."

"I will speak to him."

"No, Jenny. I will speak to him. He admires Thomas as much as I do, so perhaps he won't object. On the other hand, I feel guilty asking him for leave. I have no wish to stir up petty jealousies among the other employees who already see me as your father's favorite. Perhaps...no, I suppose that wouldn't be advisable."

"What is that?'

"I thought you might go with me on a sort of wedding trip, but the odds are heavily against it."

"No, darling. We would have to be wed first. Moreover, there is much for me to do in preparation, as we discussed. You go with Thomas, darling, and together we will bring father around."

"You are certain?"

"Quite certain. Oh, I nearly forgot! Our sitting room furniture will be delivered within the fortnight together with several additional pieces for the bed chamber. I must oversee the delivery and placement of it. You see how busy I will be? Do not distress yourself."

"I will miss you damnably. And the only piece of furniture I am interested in is the bed."

Jenny blushed and looked down. Suddenly her head flew up and she looked at Charles in dismay. "Are you ready for such a long journey with Jupiter? He did run away from you today, and he is difficult to manage. Perhaps you should borrow another horse."

"I have to admit I will have my hands full with Jupiter," he mused.

"You must also consider the danger of

Indians. There have been reports of several attacks of late."

"Thomas has made the journey often with no ill effects. I doubt he ever saw an Indian, darling. And I won't be alone. I trust Thomas' experience on the road. If it makes you feel any better, I will also be armed."

"It does not make me feel better, Charles. I shall pray that all will be well with you."

"Your trust will not be misplaced, Jenny. I swear it. I promise to return to you safe and sound."

Jenny regarded him with a cryptic smile. "Perhaps it is I who will be in more danger, Charles." He questioned her, but could make no sense of her odd remark.

After a few seconds of quiet, Jenny observed a sudden glow on Charles' face. "What is it, my love?"

Reaching into his pocket, he answered in a soft voice, "I believe this is a good time to give you a little surprise that I had made for you."

"A surprise for me?" She was filled with anticipation.

"Yes." He pulled a small box from his pocket and gently placed it in her delicate hands.

"Whatever could it be?"

"It is a small token of my affection for

you. Why don't you open it?"

Slowly, she removed the lid and lifted the wrapping paper. She gasped with surprise and delight at the sight of a small heart-shaped locket made of sterling silver. It was accompanied by a delicate silver chain. "Oh Charles, it is a most beautiful gift." Her expression was filled with joy.

He helped her open the heart, "Look inside, I had it engraved."

Jenny read aloud, "To my dearest Jenny, from Charles, with all my love." Tears filled her eyes. "Oh Charles, I shall cherish it always." She threw her arms around his shoulders in a warm and affectionate embrace. "I do love you so."

"And I shall love you eternally. Here, put it on. I want to see how it looks." Tenderly, he reached under her wealth of thick hair to the back of her slender neck and attached the chain gingerly. "There, it is the perfect companion for such a beautiful face."

"I love it, Charles. I shall wear it always." She kissed him again and again with tenderness and passion pouring her heart-felt emotion onto him.

CHAPTER 6

Charles had been working quietly for some time in the stationery shop when Tobias entered the room and whipped open the door. "What a glorious day, lad!" He stretched his arms high over his head and sighed deeply. "I hear young Jefferson will be arriving any day now."

Charles smiled. "Indeed, yes. I look forward to it."

"Jenny mentioned it in passing last night, and I agreed to invite him to dine in our home one evening."

"That was a kind gesture."

"I trust that you will join us for the occasion."

"Certainly. It will be a pleasure, sir."

"Right." He paused, momentarily uncertain how to proceed. "There is another matter I wish to discuss with you."

"Yes?"

"I was very distressed to find you with Jenny at Chowning's the other evening. Your behavior surpasses my understanding at times."

"I realize I was mistaken, sir, but surely no harm has come of it."

"Ladies do not frequent public inns and taverns unless a special event is in progress. Please remember it. I will not have Jenny made a figure of fun or scandal. Nor, I should think, would you. Enough said. I understand you intend to speak to Josiah Chowning on the subject of Miss Jane Gibson."

"Yes, sir. The idea was Jenny's and I agreed to investigate the possibility of purchasing her indentures. What do you suppose it will cost?"

Tobias folded his arms across his chest and frowned. "Well, you might buy her freedom from Chowning in which case Miss Gibson would be indebted to you and Jenny for a predetermined length of time. On the other hand, you could, if you so desire, grant her freedom from all debt, and then negotiate her employment with you for a minor wage." Watching Charles' reaction, he continued, "I wager the latter sits better with you, am I correct?"

"You know me too well, sir", Charles laughed.

"Well, I wish you luck with Chowning, Charles. He has a hard head for business, and her indentures may be beyond your means. Still, he might be amenable. I will accompany you, if you wish. He is a personal friend of mine."

"I would appreciate that, sir. I had intended to do this alone, but I believe I will learn more from watching an expert negotiate the transaction." He bowed slightly in Coulter's direction.

"Well said, my boy! We will settle the matter tonight. As for the rest, Jenny has the domestic arrangements well in hand. You are fortunate to have her, lad. Never forget that!"

Charles was glad to see the older man return to the second floor office. He was beginning to feel uneasy about discussing matters pertaining to his future household. He really wasn't looking forward to having his own home and all the responsibility that comes with it. Sometimes he wished things would just stay the way they were - no home, no servants, and no more commitment to the eighteenth century. On the other hand, he wanted to be with Jenny on a permanent basis, and things were not going to stay the way they were for much longer, with or without Jenny. He was quite certain that something significant was about to happen soon, though he hadn't a clue what it would be. Every time he thought about it he became uneasy.

Near the end of the day, a messenger entered the stationery shop with a note for Charles. He knew at once who it was from without even opening it. Thomas had written to say that he had set up lodgings at the Market Square Tavern and would visit Charles tomorrow. It was exciting to know that Thomas was back in town. The long days at the shop often dragged, especially as Charles had been accustomed to a very active itinerary during the past years. Except for the occasional news story from one of the other colonies, or from London, not much was happening in Williamsburg outside the public season.

Suddenly Charles was overcome by a spell of dizziness and weakness. He couldn't understand the unprovoked onset of these symptoms, however, it somehow reminded him of the digsite experience. Soon it was gone, as though it had not occurred at all. Charles pondered the significance of this episode. Could it mean anything, or was it perhaps a quirk of nature? Lacking a basis for drawing a single conclusion, he could only wonder in dismay. For the present time he decided to think no more about it.

That evening, Charles, Watson and Billingsley enjoyed another superb seafood dinner in Beulah's kitchen house. Charles was continually amazed at Beulah's expertise considering the primitive tools she worked with. Tonight's oyster stew was an outstanding example. It was the aroma of this stew which first greeted him when he entered the kitchen, that, and her homemade brick oven bread. He thought he might eat the entire loaf himself.

Billingsley had also made great headway with the stew, and Charles teased him goodnaturedly, "I swear, the only reason you came to work for Mr. Coulter was to enjoy Beulah's oyster stew. Imagine getting paid to eat!" They all laughed heartily.

After the stew, Beulah brought out a hot platter of steamed clams, succulent scallops and steamed shrimp. Charles had forgotten just how bountiful the Chesapeake Bay and its tributaries could be. He had forgotten about the affect of thirty-eight million people with their twentieth century pollution and overharvesting.

One course after the other, each one a masterpiece, and to think that she did it all in a fireplace, and on trivets and small piles of coals from the fire. Charles didn't know very much about eighteenth century cooking, but occasionally he would steal a glance at her as she worked. It was easy to start a conversation with her. All it took was a smile and a compliment. He noticed that she worked easily and surely, whether she was conversing or not, and she often appeared to be doing three things at once. Yes, she was a very special lady.

After two cups of coffee, Charles struggled to his feet. "Excellent meal, Beulah. I'll be sorry to leave when the time comes!"

"I will be sorry to see you go, Mist' Charles. Mighty, mighty sorry."

"I'll miss you, you know."

"I thank you fo' dat, Mist' Charles, but it ain't gonna be all dat bad."

"How so?"

"I be teachin' dis girl heah." She turned toward the oven and pointed to a young black girl of about twenty years who was very slim and well-groomed. "Come heah, girl, and meet your new mastah. Dis is Mist' Charles Dalton, soon to marry Miss Jenny."

Charles was taken aback by the words 'new master'. He could only stare at the girl, stunned. She, on the other hand, seemed quite content to smile back at Charles in a pleasant manner. Obviously she had no problem with her

station in life. In fact, Charles thought he
observed in her a touch of pride at being in
Beulah's kitchen.

Beulah continued, "Dis is Desiree. She will
be yo' cook and Miss Jenny's. I'll see dat she
is ready for yo when yo' new home is all
finished."

"Ah...ah, yes, of course, Beulah." Turning
to the girl, he smiled. "You are in good hands,
Desiree."

"Thank you Mister Charles." She smiled
shyly.

Charles was surprised by the hint of an
accent in her voice. "Where are you from
originally, Desiree?"

"I was born on the island of St. Thomas in
the Caribbean, sir. My father is a native of
that island, but my mother is French." She
raised her head proudly as she spoke.

"I see. And where were you before coming to
Mr. Coulter's establishment?"

"I was apprenticed as a cook for four years
in the South Carolina colony."

Beulah interjected, "Mist' Coulter took her
away from Mist' Johnson at the Raleigh Tavern
jus' las' week when he heard 'bout her comin'
heah. She's a good gal, a very good gal, and she
can cook too, mmm mmmh!"

"Well, I'm sure Desiree will do quite well,
especially with your help, Beulah." He turned to

72

Desiree with a warm smile. "Listen well to Beulah for she is far and away the best cook in the colony, and if you work with her for any length of time, you will more than exceed my expectations."

Beulah beamed at him and began to make shooing motions with her hands. "Now yo gwan and get, we got work to do. Gwan! Get!"

Charles decided to turn in early and made his way back to the loft. He wondered about Desiree and her French background. Troubled by the thought of her becoming his slave, he decided he would have to speak to Jenny about it. It was one thing to free an indentured servant, but he remembered that no one was allowed to free a slave in the Virginia colony. This was going to be a very serious matter and required a good deal of diplomacy. Coulter had already reprimanded him on several occasions for his 'peculiar' notions on slavery, and he had better be damned careful in his future dealings with the man.

He lay restlessly in bed that night anticipating his meeting with Jefferson the next day. He wondered what advice Thomas might give him on the subject of Desiree. During one of their previous conversations Thomas had mentioned something about wanting the right to free one's own slaves. Thomas considered that as the slaves were his property to do with as he pleased, he ought to be able to free them if he so desired. He had questioned the government's right to dictate to the landowners in such matters. In fact, Thomas had objected to quite a number of governmental infringements on the rights of individuals.

Charles often found himself pondering Thomas' words on government and individual rights, but he kept coming back to one major point, one major flaw in Thomas' thinking, as he saw it. Thomas neglected to recognize blacks when he discussed men's rights and liberties. Charles realized that the times in which he lived had a great deal to do with Thomas' thinking, but surely a man as great as Jefferson could transcend such views. Perhaps the colonists, particularly the great landowners were secretly afraid of what might happen if they freed the slaves. Thomas had intimated such a thing when he reminded Charles that slaves were forbidden under law to learn to read or become educated. If the slaves were freed, an entire way of life would perish, as it did after the Civil War. At this point in colonial history the ratio of blacks to whites was something on the order of 50 to 1 at least, maybe higher.

At any rate, he would have plenty of time to discuss it with Thomas during the trip to Shadwell, and while he was there, he would see for himself the state of affairs at Jefferson's mother's plantation. Therein might lie a clue, not only to Jefferson's sometimes enigmatic personality, but to the man's philosophy as well.

CHAPTER 7

Jenny rose later than usual although it was a bright, sunny morning. She wanted to spend some time in the new house arranging a few of the new pieces of furniture and small accessories her mother had given her. She quickly performed her toilet and ran to join her mother in the master bedroom for their usual morning tea, but Anne had already gone downstairs. Jenny soon found her in the parlor with Bea, both busy with their mending. Anne looked up with a smile at the sight of her lovely daughter.

"Good morning, dear. You slept well indeed, this morning!"

"Good morning, mother, Bea. Yes, I did. Oh, mother, will you come with me to the new house this morning? I want your opinion on how to set up the parlor, and also to carry a few things over there."

"Of course I will go, dear. But I do have an engagement with the ladies this morning at eleven o'clock."

Jenny frowned. "That won't give us much time."

"Well, perhaps Bea will accompany you. She may stay as long as you like." Bea nodded her assent.

"Very well. I shall need some time, but I do wish you were there as well."

"Don't fret, child. I shall stay as long as I can. You know I'm as excited about the house as you are!"

"Have you breakfasted yet, mother?"

"Long since, dear. I never expected you to sleep so long."

"Well, I must eat, I'm positively starving. Mother, when do you suppose the furniture will arrive from Philadelphia?"

"It will depend on which pieces are in stock, and which are actually under construction at this time. If all goes well, you should have it by July or August at the latest."

"I hope so."

Anne looked at her daughter shrewdly. "How is Charles bearing up under the circumstances?"

Jenny laughed. "I believe he is as nervous as I am. Oh! I nearly forgot! Charles may travel to Shadwell with Mr. Jefferson for a visit within the fortnight."

"How long will he be away?"

"I am not certain, but it shouldn't be more than a month, perhaps less."

"Do you think it wise for Charles to absent himself at this time?" She looked at Jenny anxiously. Much as she loved Charles, she had to admit his behavior was surpassing strange at times.

"Yes. He discussed it with me and I agreed to it. Charles is very fond of Mr. Jefferson, and their friendship is important to both of them. However, I cannot say I am altogether happy about it."

"That is understandable, dear. Well, the sooner he departs, the sooner he will return, I suppose."

Jenny kissed her softly on the cheek. "I simply must eat! Meet me at the house as soon as you are free, mother. We've much to do!"

When Jenny had finished breakfast she returned to her room to find Bea already waiting there. "Miz Anne told me to help you carry some things down to the new house, Miz Jenny."

"Oh yes, Bea. Here are a few bundles, and several quilts. Is mother nearly ready?"

"Miz Jenny, your mother be stayin' to get ready for her meetin'. She had a note from dat Missus Carmondy sayin' she's comin' early, so Miz Anne stayin' here."

Jenny tried to hide her disappointment. "I see. Well, we shall go on alone, then."

As they approached the front door to the new house, Bea turned to Jenny enthusiastically. "Miz Jenny, you gonna have a whole new life in dis house. You gonna be very happy here with Mist' Charles, I just know it."

"Yes, isn't it wonderful?" Jenny's face beamed with joy as she unlocked and opened the front door. "It is a bit empty now, but..."

"Dat's alright, soon it be filled with joy and laughter and chillun."

Their conversation was punctuated with the distant banging of a hammer as construction progressed at the rear of the house. Jenny went to the back study and looked out of the window. Three men were sawing and nailing what appeared to be a window frame.

"What they doin', Miz Jenny?" Bea had come up behind her and was watching the workmen with curious eyes.

"I'm not certain, perhaps some exterior

trim work." She wandered into the dining room. "Oh look, Bea! They have finished the built-in corner cabinets. Are they not beautiful?"

"Dat fireplace will get right hot too, Miz Jenny. You'all will be warm in hea!"

"Yes, I love our little house already. Come, let's set these odd pieces about in the sitting room."

They unpacked the things from the other house and Bea pulled out Aunt Caroline's vase and held it up for Jenny's inspection. "Wheah do yo want to put dis vase?"

Jenny looked around the room. "Try placing it on the mantle, Bea."

They stared at it for a minute. "No, let's place it off to one side, like this." Jenny moved it several inches to the right. "How is that?"

Bea shrugged. "Dat's fine."

"No, I don't like it there. Let's try it here." She placed the vase on the left side of the mantle toward the front window. "There! That is much better."

Suddenly, Jenny felt an alarming dizziness and stumbled back, nearly falling to the floor. Bea rushed to help her and Jenny sat down shaking her head as though to clear it. "What happened to me?"

"I wuz just gonna ask yo dat, Miz Jenny." She took a piece of the wrapping paper which was strewn about the floor, folded it, and began to fan Jenny briskly. Her mistress' face had gone quite pale and beads of sweat had formed on her forehead. "Yo not catchin' fever, is yo, Miz Jenny?"

"I...I don't know, Bea. I feel dreadful, and there is a ringing in my ears."

"Just rest heah awhile, until yo feel better." She gathered a length of petticoat in her hand and blotted the perspiration from Jenny's face. Jenny's face had taken on a greenish tint and she clutched her stomach in dismay. "Lie still, Miz Jenny, it'll pass."

Jenny closed her eyes and took a deep breath. When she opened her eyes once more her glance fell upon the vase, and all at once she remembered Charles telling her about his experience in the twentieth century when he first made contact with it, and the consequences he had suffered. Her heart began to pound in fear. What if she were transported into the twentieth century right now? What would she do? How would she get back? If only she hadn't touched it! But then, it had never affected her before. Now she had some inkling of how Charles had felt on that fateful day. She must go to him, and tell him at once! She sat up, and the nausea threatened to overwhelm her. No, not yet. She must get back her strength and quiet her stomach before she went anywhere. Obviously, she was not going to go forward in time, perhaps she had not handled the vase long enough. She must discuss this with Charles!

"Miz Jenny? Should I fetch Miz Anne?"

"No, Bea. Do not disturb her, now. You were right, the feeling has passed. But please, would you bring me the vase?"

Bea looked at her in amazement. "What fo'?"

"Oh, just humor me, Bea, please?"

"Yes, Miz Jenny."

Nothing happened. There was no dizziness, no nausea, no faintness. How odd, Jenny thought. It must have to do with the placement of the vase on the mantlepiece. I must find the exact position...

She directed Bea to replace the vase upon the mantlepiece and Bea did so with no ill effect, though she obviously thought Jenny had taken leave of her senses. Maybe the girl had fever after all.

Jenny sat up slowly and brushed her hair out of her face. "Come. Bea. let us get on with our work. I feel much better already."

"If yo say so, Miz Jenny. Dat was a bad turn yo had. And de fever is goin' around just now! Maybe yo should go on home and get in bed."

"No, Bea, I'm much better, and I'm certain it isn't the fever. Stop fussing!"

Bea sighed. Jenny was going to be stubborn about it, and when Jenny was being stubborn, there was nothing much to be done. "If yo say so, Miz Jenny. Now, what yo want me to do next?"

At two o'clock Thomas Jefferson entered the stationery shop. With a sense of mischief he placed himself at the end of the queue Charles was serving and patiently waited his turn. When all those in front of him had been served, Thomas stepped quietly up to Charles and grinned. Charles looked up with a perfunctory smile which broke into laughter when he saw who his next customer was.

"Thomas! You rogue, you are a sight for sore eyes!"

"How good it is to see you once again!" Thomas replied with a hearty handshake. "It appears that the prospect of wedding bells suits you. I've never seen you looking better."

"You are looking well yourself."

"I must admit your last letter alarmed me not a little, but it would seem that all has progressed favorably for you and the beautiful Miss Coulter. And how fares Tobias?"

"Actually, he is just upstairs. Let me run up and tell him you are here."

"Right."

"No, on second thought, come along. He will be happy to see you. Mind your step, the stairwell is quite narrow."

They found Tobias Coulter going through some papers at his desk as usual. Charles had Thomas wait just out of sight at the head of the stairwell.

"We have a visitor, sir."

Tobias peered over his wire-rimmed spectacles frowning in concentration. "How is that?"

"We have a visitor. It is someone I think you will want to see." He smiled broadly.

Jefferson stepped into the room and greeted his old friend.

"Thomas! Why you handsome young beggar, it's good to see you again!"

"And you, sir." Thomas grasped Coulter's hand warmly.

"What brings you all the way from Albemarle County?"

"I have some business with Professor Wythe, a legal matter which gives me no end of trouble, and which I hope to resolve with his aid."

"I see. And how is it with your family?"

"They are all well, thank you."

"You know, we shall want you to stop for supper one evening, Thomas, if that is convenient. What say you to Thursday at seven o'clock?"

"I am unengaged at that time, sir. I look forward to it." He turned to Charles with a smile and a barely perceptible nod.

84

"Particularly as the beautiful Miss Coulter will no doubt join us."

Tobias chuckled. "Can't blame you for that, my lad. She is undoubtedly the fairest lass in Virginia."

Thomas continued, "What I fail to understand is how such a rare creature would bestow her heart and hand upon Charles here."

He winked at Charles who replied, "I don't suppose any of us will ever know the answer to that!"

After a few moments of conversation Thomas excused himself to keep his appointment with Professor Wythe. He and Charles agreed to meet at Chowning's that evening at eight o'clock and Thomas turned to leave, but before he had gone two steps he turned around to address Tobias.

"Mr. Coulter. I would like to ask a favor of you, if I may."

"But of course, Thomas, ask away."

"Hear me out before you agree so readily!"

"Go on."

"I shall be leaving for Shadwell on Monday next, and I would appreciate if you would allow Charles to accompany me on my trip."

Coulter scratched the top of his balding head and frowned.

"I would like to show Charles the site of my proposed estate, Monticello, and there is much to discuss. If it does not create a hardship for your business, I would take it as a gesture of friendship if you would look upon my request favorably."

"Well now, just how long would you be taking Charles away from Williamsburg?"

"I planned a three or four week visit, though there is no set schedule at this time."

"I agree upon one condition, Thomas, that you keep an eye on Charles. I've no wish to lose a prospective son-in-law after all we've been through these past months, and," he winked at Charles, "the young man in question is not noted for his equestrian skills. There is some rough country west of Richmond, as you well know."

Thomas nodded his agreement. "I do, indeed. However, I am well acquainted with the roads and the conditions in all weathers. I have made the journey innumerable times. I must admit, though, to having encountered some difficulties on my trip to Philadelphia last spring."

Charles looked at his friend with concern. "Why? What happened?"

"Actually, I lost my way twice. My horse bolted at the most inopportune moment, and I nearly drowned crossing the Susquehanna in the pouring rain." He laughed wryly. "It was a humbling experience which merely served to remind me that in any contest between man and nature, nature is certain to prevail. I shall not soon forget it."

Charles looked at Coulter and added, "And I have the feeling that I won't soon forget the journey I am about to undertake either."

After Thomas had gone, Tobias asked Charles, only half in jest, "Now what the devil am I going to do without you for four weeks? I do have a business to run, young sir."

"I'm quite willing to stay if you find you can't do without me."

"I do need you; however, the experience will do you good, if you don't kill yourself on that horse. Perhaps you'll know how to ride him when you return, if you return."

"If I return?"

"Well," laughed Coulter, "you had better return or I'll place an advertisement in the 'Gazette' for your speedy recovery. I'll bill you as a runaway, and offer a sizeable reward for your capture. What say you to that, lad?"

"Why, I'll turn myself in and collect the reward myself, sir."

"Insolent puppy! Will you indeed? Go on now, get back downstairs. You've four weeks' work to do in one, so get busy!"

Later in the afternoon, Coulter passed through the stationery shop on his way out. After noting the day's receipts, he remarked casually, "That Thomas! He is quite a young man."

"Yes, indeed," Charles replied, warming to the subject. "You don't know the half of it. He hasn't any idea of what's in store for him. The governorship, then presidency of the United..." The blank expression on Coulter's face alerted him to his error. He'd gone too far this time. Blood rushed to his face, and he began to sweat profusely. What would Coulter think of him now?

Coulter stared back at him dumbfounded. Had Charles taken leave of his senses? "Governorship? Presidency?"

Charles cast about for an explanation, but his answer only worsened the situation. "Ah, Governor of Virginia." Uh oh, he thought.

"Governor of this colony? Thomas?" He lowered his voice significantly. "Charles, if you know something of significance regarding the political future of this colony, why have you not discussed it with me? You must know that anything you tell me will be kept in the strictest confidence. On the other hand, if you are playing with me..."

Oh God, thought Charles, now what do I say? "Sir. I am deadly serious. I do not know more about the situation than you do, I merely speculate."

"I don't believe that for a moment, Charles. This sort of thing has happened before, you know. You know something the rest of us are as yet unaware of. How, I cannot tell, but you know." He looked around the room which was fortunately quite empty and lowered his voice yet more. "For the love of God, if you know aught about the career plans of young Jefferson, tell me. Such information may be of tremendous value to our circle. Need I say more?"

"But...I..."

"Come now, don't be coy. Thomas hasn't indicated any particular interest in politics at this point, at least, not that I could see. In fact, George Wythe has told me that he has tried to encourage young Jefferson to enter the political arena without success. Whence comes your information? From Jefferson himself?"

"No sir. Thomas has not discussed it with me. But I firmly believe that his personality and fine education, not to mention his great intellectual prowess all combine to form the makings of a first-rate political candidate, quite worthy of the governorship of this colony. He is as yet too modest to recognize his leadership qualities, but sooner or later, I feel he will either seek out political leadership or have it thrust upon him and accept it as his life's work. This is merely my own analysis. In fact, I would not be surprised if he decided to run for offfice in the General Assembly, or the House of Burgesses within the year."

"This year, you say? This is excellent

news, Charles! George Wythe will be most gratified to hear it."

Charles clutched his arm in agitation. "Oh please, say nothing to anyone of this. If it does indeed prove true, let Thomas be the one to announce it to his friends. He may not have made his decision yet. In any case, I will see him tonight, perhaps I will know more at that time."

"You are right, lad. I will say nothing." Coulter's mind was racing with possibilities. "You will see him tonight, hmmm. Perhaps you will have some news for us. Well, this trip of yours looks better and better. There is no telling what valuable news you will bring back with you. Do not be reluctant to use your influence on him, Charles. He is a good man, and Virginia needs him. Moreover, he respects your opinion."

This was almost too much for Charles to take in. Jefferson respected his opinion! Good God, what have I let myself in for? "I will do my best", he replied weakly.

CHAPTER 8

The Coulter family was at dinner. This evening an unusual silence reigned; each member of the family, it seemed, was immersed in his own thoughts. Jenny's thoughts were of Charles.

"Father, what did you say to Charles today? Did you have occasion to speak to him at all?"

"Yes. In fact, we had a very interesting conversation concerning Thomas Jefferson. Incidentally, Thomas came into the shop today."

"Oh, he's here then?"

"He just arrived this afternoon."

"I wanted to suggest that we invite him to dine with us one evening, and Charles, too, of course. I would enjoy seeing them together once again."

"It has already been done, lass. I extended the invitation to him today and he accepted for tomorrow night, if that is agreeable to your mother." He looked across at his wife, a question in his eyes.

Anne smiled and nodded her assent. "It will be a pleasure to have a guest in the house again. I will see to the necessary arrangements. Heavens! The last time we entertained was during the public season, I vow. How long ago it seems!"

"I believe you are right, my dear." Tobias responded correctly, but his mind was miles away. His usual brisk manner and hearty tone were conspicuously absent this evening. "Charles is meeting young Jefferson at Chowning's tonight," he continued almost to himself. "I must quiz him tomorrow on the subject of Thomas' incipient political ambitions."

"Thomas Jefferson with political ambitions? 'Tis the first I've heard of it!" Anne was astounded. "Now that I think of it, however, he may do quite well. He is such an intelligent, well-spoken young man. I presume he has his eye on a place in the House of Burgesses?"

"For the love of God, Anne, say nothing

about this to anyone. It is all speculation and rumor at this point. Should he decide to run for office, I would be the first to back him, but nothing definite is known. Charles may discover more tonight. I hope so. By the by, have you heard that Charles is considering a trip to Albemarle County with Thomas next week?"

Anne sighed. "Jenny told me of it. Can you spare him in the shop for four weeks Tobias?"

"I can manage. In fact, it may be to my advantage, though I know you are distressed by the prospect, Jenny."

"I do wish he would stay, it's true, but I know how eagerly he anticipates his time with Thomas. I dare say he is excited at the thought of such a trip across the wilderness."

"Yes, there is truth in what you say, Jenny, dear," said Anne. "Well, the house will not be finished before the end of July, and the furniture will surely not be ready before August. Apart from his work in the shop, there is really nothing much he can do to prepare for the wedding. Let him enjoy his outing, Jenny. He will be all the more eager to see you when he returns."

"I know, mother. But waiting is so tedious!"

Tobias laughed. "Be patient, my dear Jenny. What are four weeks out of a lifetime?"

"Perhaps more than you think, father."

FRANCIS STREET

As he approached Chowning's Charles could hear lively music and animated laughter from within. He smiled to himself, remembering Chowning's in his own time. It hadn't changed much; even the songs were the same. Only the clothing and attitudes of the patrons were different. Two hundred years of progress momentarily forgotten by those who willingly paid to go back in time. Well, he hadn't had to pay, God knew, and he was seeing the real thing.

At that moment he spotted Jefferson at the entrance, strolling back and forth with his hands behind his back, for all the world like one of Charles' philosophy professors back in college. He chuckled. "Well old man!" he called, "What world problem are you dissecting now?"

Jefferson looked up and grinned. "Actually, I was wondering why you were late. I hope you haven't dined?"

"No, I was waiting to dine here with you."

"Splendid!"

The tavern was more active than usual with a large crowd in the game room. Thomas led the way into the public dining room where various groups were gathered discussing the latest news about town. Smoke from many pipes filled an atmosphere redolent of well-spiced food, ale and sweet cider, almost, but not quite overpowering the smell of honest human sweat. Thomas selected

a large table at the back of the room designed
for at least eight people.

"Will this do?"

"At this point anything will do. I'm
ravenous. Thomas, it just occurred to me that we
may not be served a meal at this hour. I hope
I'm wrong."

"Josiah will see to it that we have
something to warm our stomachs, Charles. He has
never disappointed me yet."

"You know, Thomas, although I have lived in
this town for some twelve months now, I have
never actually eaten a meal in this tavern."

"You amaze me, Charles. May I ask why?"

"Perhaps I can lay the blame at Beulah's
door."

"Beulah? Aha, we are in deep waters here, I
fear."

Charles laughed. "No, nothing like that, my
friend. Beulah is the Coulters' black cook, and
a finer cook you will not find in Williamsburg -
in the world!"

"I must confess I am relieved, Charles. For
a moment I feared for the beautiful Jenny. I
must confess I had visions of pressing my own
suit with her."

"Not if you value your life," Charles
laughed.

A young girl in mobcap and apron
approached to take their order and was greeted

enthusiastically by Thomas. "We'll have a bowl of your finest sower punch, and please bring two tankards."

Charles nodded his agreement. He had no idea what sower punch was, but it sounded good. Looking more closely at the girl, he recognized her as Jane. They exchanged pleasantries for a few moments, then Jane hurried away to fetch their punch.

In response to Thomas' smug grin, Charles explained Jenny's plan to buy the girl's indentures from Josiah Chowning and offer her employment in their new home.

"What a splended idea! Have you inquired into her past history, her family?"

"Not too closely. She mentioned losing a child on the trip over, though what became of her husband, if she had one, is anyone's guess. She seems a good girl. I scarcely think she could be a convicted felon, unless she was falsely accused. There is a strong aura of decency about her."

"It might be well to inquire more closely into her past, Charles. You wouldn't want Jenny exposed to any unwholesomeness. The girl may seem decent, but one can never be too sure."

"There speaks the careful lawyer! You are quite right, Thomas. I will make a point of it." He settled back in his chair as Jane returned bearing a large Delft bowl half-filled with a concoction Charles had never seen before and two tankards. Thomas filled the tankards and proposed a toast to "the beautiful young women of Virginia." Charles' first sip was a delight. He could not fail to detect the strong flavor of rum which was sweetened and rendered more interesting with a pungent dash of lime. Glancing around the room, he noticed punch bowls at several other tables as well. Moreover, some men were drinking directly out of the bowl. He was grateful for Thomas' delicacy and decided that eighteenth century etiquette sometimes left a good deal to be desired.

"So Thomas, tell me. What particular Virginia beauty has caught your eye since our last meeting? "

Jefferson's face sobered. "To be honest, my friend, there is one lady to whom I am infernally attracted, and it is, I am sorry to say, an attraction I can neither explain nor justify since she is the wife of a very close friend and neighbor."

"Wife!"

"Yes, and mother, too. She was recently delivered of a daughter."

"Who is this enchantress?"

"Actually, you will be in her company when we return to Shadwell, for though I consider it a dreadful mistake, I have unwittingly taken her under my care and my roof for the duration of the summer."

"She is living at Shadwell with a new baby?"

"Yes. Her husband, John Walker, has joined his father on a trip to the colonial frontier to administer a long overdue Indian treaty, and as he has seen fit to request it of me, I shall indeed take care of his family in his absence."

Charles whistled softly. "You are in a precarious position, if your attraction to this woman is at all strong."

"Can I be of any further assistance, gentlemen?" Jane had returned and Thomas turned to her with some relief. "We would like some supper at this time. What does Mr. Chowning have at hand this evening?"

"He will be serving a cold collation at eight o'clock, but I will see what is available now, sir."

"No, no. We can wait until eight o'clock, can we not, Charles?"

"Of course. It is only twenty minutes away.

"Very well, sir. We will be serving leg of veal with bacon and sprouts, ham, pickled tongue, puddings, mixed vegetables, a selection of sweets and fruit."

"Excellent. Thank you, Jane." She bobbed a curtsey and departed.

"Now, Thomas, tell me about Mrs. Walker." He refilled the tankards, then set down the ladle and studied his friend's face carefully.

"Charles, all I can say is that she seems to me the very epitome of womanhood. I swear I would go to her without a moment's hesitation if the opportunity presented itself. It seems a vile injustice that the woman I desire can never be mine."

"She's not for you, Thomas. You know it already."

"Yes, I know it." He drained his cup angrily, his expression one of confusion and despair.

"Don't take it quite so much to heart, Thomas. We all go through it, sooner or later. Anyway, I dare say with your very special gifts, you will likely have any number of women vying for your attentions."

Thomas laughed somewhat wryly. "Tell me more, Charles." He rubbed his forehead, sensing with dismay the approach of another headache. He was, at times, subject to migraine headaches of such severity that he was forced to take to his bed for the duration, sometimes for several days.

"Well, you are tall, intelligent, kind and sensitive, and you've a fine sense of humor. Women treasure these traits in a man, I've heard."

"Then how do you explain my less than successful history with the fair sex, Charles?"

"Your 'history' as you call it is no less than successful. You have simply not addressed an available woman to date, but you will, and then your luck will change, I'm sure of it."

"Your confidence and your optimism is every bit as encouraging as it is overwhelming. I would like to believe the truth of your words."

"You have a big heart, Thomas, and a generous disposition. You are, by nature, destined to love many women, a certain type, perhaps, but you definitely have the capacity to love more than one woman."

Thomas looked thoughtful. "It is true that I have found myself attracted to a number of young ladies, but I have abstained from meaningful pursuit of any relationship following the botchery with Rebecca Burwell."

"Yes, I believe you mentioned her last spring, Thomas." At this point there was some commotion in the room as men began to gather around one large table opposite the fireplace on which numerous dishes were displayed.

"Come, Charles, let us satisfy our appetites at last."

They sampled all the foods at the buffet table, and Charles found some to be quite tasty, though others were not to his liking, particularly the ham which, in the Virginia tradition, was exceptionally salty.

They continued their conversation with

some others who took seats at their table, and drank with their help, no less than five bowls of punch before retiring a little after midnight.

CHAPTER 9

A cool front came through early Tuesday morning spreading a misty drizzle across the entire mid-Atlantic coast for two days. It was chilly, damp and gray until late Thursday afternoon when the sun finally broke through the low, fluffy clouds. It was exhilarating to see blue sky and feel the warmth of the June sun on one's face again. Charles was always amazed at how a day or two of cloudy weather spurred in him a wild desire to see the sun again.

He was finishing his paperwork in the

stationery shop as usual and preparing to deliver the money box with the day's receipts to Tobias when the front door flew open and Jenny ran in breathlessly. Her thickly lashed violet eyes sparkled like amethysts and she threw him a devastating smile – a smile that could make a good man go bad, he mused. She was wearing a pretty gown of light blue flowered muslin with very full skirts, ruffled lace insets, provocative neckline and closely fitted elbow-length sleeves, all of which emphasized the delectable body within its confines.

"Darling," he greeted her, "you are a sight for sore eyes! What brings you to the shop at this hour?" Charles seized her delicate hand and kissed it.

"After the last two dreary days of rain, I just wanted to walk in the sun again," she replied.

"Is that all?" He teased her.

"Well, no. Actually, I came to see father." It was her turn to tease.

"I see. I was just about to return these receipts, come along, we'll go together." She looked so delicious in her little white cap with her long neck bare except for the small black tendrils which had escaped from it. He longed to grasp her tiny waist as he followed her up the stairs.

"Father, what is this nonsense about you

103

working late tonight? You know we are expecting guests." Jenny tried to keep a straight face, but her mouth involuntarily curved upwards as she watched his droll expression.

"Eh? What...Aha! I see God has not yet forsaken this old man. He continues to shower His blessings upon him with the arrival of the most bewitching creature in Williamsburg!" He winked at Charles.

At this, Jenny laughed outright. "Oh father, flattery will gain you everything, as you well know."

"Fear not, my dear. I will soon be done with this paperwork. You may tell your mother I'll be in good time for supper."

"Of course. Did you know that Professor Wythe will be our guest as well?"

"Will he indeed? I'm very glad to hear it, child. Young Thomas will feel right at home tonight I vow."

The two young people took their leave. Once downstairs, Charles took Jenny gently by the waist, turned her around to face him and kissed her passionately. She melted into him, her mouth opening beneath his. When they finally broke apart, both were trembling. "Until tonight, my love." She turned and ran lightly out the door.

Charles stepped out onto the front porch and watched her go. This must be a dream, he told himself. The whole damned thing has got to be a dream.

It was five minutes before seven o'clock when Bea showed Thomas Jefferson and George Wythe into the Coulter sitting room. They were greeted enthusiastically by Tobias and Charles, offered drinks and settled down in comfortable armchairs to discuss all that had transpired since their last meeting. Anne and Jenny soon joined them, accompanied by Jenny's younger sister, Elizabeth, and the conversation turned to the fast-approaching nuptuals. Charles stood proudly with Jenny's hand in his and received his friends' congratulations and well-meaning banter.

Supper was announced promptly at seven-thirty, and the group paired off to enter the dining room. The meal began with a wonderfully rich turtle soup, and progressed to a main course of English roast beef accompanied by boiled potatoes, oysters on the half-shell, roast fowl, garden peas with mint and asparagus. As always, there was spoon-bread, freshly baked steaming white bread with a crisp brown crust, and various kinds of wine. How Bea contrived to keep the hot dishes hot when they finally arrived at the table was a mystery which always plagued Charles.

Feeling expansive with numerous glasses of wine and Beulah's good hot food in his stomach, Tobias turned to Jefferson. "Tell us, lad, is it true you are considering a move into politics?"

"To be honest sir, I have found it quite rewarding to conduct my own political practice, in all aspects save one. That is simply the lack of monetary remuneration. As you know, I am responsible for the upkeep of my mother's plantation and all the people who serve her, to say nothing of my immediate family. You can well imagine the strain this places on my meager finances. I have therefore decided to consider delegation to the General Assembly, possibly within the year. In the meantime, I shall continue to practice law and hope that the valuable experience I gain in that profession will support me in my proposed political endeavor."

"I am delighted to hear it, Thomas. What say you, George?"

Professor Wythe wiped his lips carefully and returned the napkin to his lap. "I believe he is ready now, Tobias. A year or two of practice amidst the local people can only enhance his reputation and help to gain him a place in the General Assembly. Yes, Thomas will serve us well."

Careful, said Charles to himself, don't let your tongue run away with you again. But the temptation to speak was more than he could bear. "I believe Thomas has a spectacular career ahead of him, if only he can defeat his greatest enemy..."

"Enemy? Oh surely not, Charles," laughed Thomas. "I'm scarcely old enough to have made so dire an enemy. How do you mean?"

"I am referring to the enemy within. You, yourself are your own worst enemy, Thomas. You are a brilliant man, but your modesty can hold you back from the fame you deserve. If and when you learn to conquer it, there is no end to what you can accomplish."

Wythe nodded and glanced at Charles with respect. "Your friend speaks truly, Thomas. Heed him well." He picked up his glass and proposed a toast to Jefferson's new career. The others joined in happily and finished off the third bottle of Rhenish.

At this point Anne thought it wise to retire and rose, signaling Jenny and Elizabeth to do the same. Elizabeth rose at once, but Jenny remained stubbornly seated. "I would like to stay here, mother, and listen to the gentlemens' discussion."

Anne paled, but decided to try again. "Jenny, dear, there is a matter of some importance I wish to discuss with you in the drawing room. I'm sure the gentlemen will excuse you."

Jenny opened her mouth to protest again,

but just then she caught her father's eye. He winked discreetly and motioned for her to join her mother. Jenny understood that he would relay their conversation to her in detail later. With that in mind, she rose gracefully, murmured her excuses and followed Anne quietly from the room.

Some time later Charles excused himself to make a badly needed trip to the privy. He had lost count of the number of glasses of wine he had drunk, and the effect could no longer be ignored. Once outside the necessary, he stretched sleepily and took a deep breath of air to clear his foggy head. He welcomed the stillness of the outdoors and the delightful fragrance of the well-kept garden. Suddenly a figure appeared out of the darkness and nearly collided with him.

"Here, hold on. Who is there?"

"Charles!"

"Jenny? What on earth brings you out here?"

"I needed a breath of air. I thought you were still in the dining room with the guests."

"I was, but nature called, and I had to make a trip to the necessary. Now that I am here..." he embraced her and kissed her longingly. She trembled in his arms and returned his kiss with abandon, all inhibitions drowned by her desire. It had been too long for both of them, and if he could have taken her there on the ground, he would have, but he knew his friends were waiting for him to continue their discussion. Damnation, he ached for her so badly. And soon he would be leaving for a month. A whole month away from her - he must be mad!

Jenny clung to him weakly, fighting her own battle. A sudden burst of laughter from the dining room startled them both and reminded them that they were not yet free to yield to their passion. Reluctantly Jenny disengaged herself from Charles and touching his lips briefly with her fingers, turned and went back into the house.

Several minutes later Charles, too, left the garden to join his host and their friends. They greeted him enthusiastically, and Jefferson announced that he and Charles would leave Williamsburg the following Sunday. The remainder of the evening was spent discussing the hazards and tribulations of travel.

Charles suddenly felt very tired.

CHAPTER 10

Rogers had packed Jupiter according to Charles' instructions and he was ready to go. The horse's obvious high spirits caused Charles a twinge of concern, but he resolutely pushed any thought of disaster out of his mind. There had been no repetition of the unfortunate incident when Jupiter had run amok, and Charles felt the animal was getting used to him.

Charles was waiting for Thomas in the rear courtyard of the Coulter home. He looked around him with pleasure. It was five-thirty on a glorious June morning and the day promised to be a warm one. What better omen for the first day of a long trip?

Jenny came into the courtyard, a somewhat less than cheerful smile on her face. She met him with outstretched arms and they embraced with genuine affection. When they parted, Charles looked deeply into her troubled eyes. "I must be mad!"

She understood immediately, and a real smile hovered around her luscious lips. "You are, that," she teased, "perhaps I should take you upstairs and lock you up with me. I would take good care of you, my love."

Charles laughed. "I know you would, darling, and I would take even better care of you!"

She blushed under his hot gaze. "I trust you will return to me as soon as you can?"

"You know I will, Jenny. While I am away I will see you everywhere, just the way you look right now, in the country, on lonely nights, in strange taverns, and in the face of every woman I see. I swear you grow more beautiful every day."

They embraced again, but soon broke apart at the sound of hooves. Jefferson had arrived.

"Good morning, Charles, Jenny."

"Good morning, Thomas! I see you are loaded down with booty. Books again?"

"I fear so. I can never resist the urge to acquire another volume for my ever growing library. But what have you there, extra clothing? I hope you remembered to bring a cooking pot and a weapon with which you are familiar. Much depends on a swift and accurate aim in the wilderness."

"Everything is here, Thomas." He glanced anxiously at Jenny whose face had paled at the mention of a weapon. Thomas, too, had noted her reaction and realized his mistake too late.

"My apologies for alarming you unduly, Miss Coulter, we always take certain precautions, though they seldom prove necessary. I am in your debt for allowing Charles to accompany me on this journey. Please be assured that I will do everything in my power to bring him back to you safely."

"Thank you, Thomas, but please remember that I am not in a position to 'allow' Charles anything. He is very much his own man and follows his own inclinations."

"Of course. I stand corrected." He turned to Charles. "You are indeed fortunate in your lady."

Charles was too moved to speak immediately, so he merely nodded at Thomas.

They said their final goodbyes and mounted their horses. Charles leaned over to touch Jenny's face gently. "Take care, my love."

"And you, darling."

Soon they were out of town on the James town road. They had passed the property owned by the College of William and Mary and soon found themselves on a lonely stretch of dirt road which seemed to be the only real evidence of civilization in a densely wooded area of native climatic forest.

Thomas led them into an easy gallop, and the horses soon found their own pace. They had been riding for some time in silence when Charles observed to Thomas. "I hate to admit it, but I'm beginning to feel sore. I'm not accustomed to all this riding."

"I shall have to keep an eye on you then. We will make frequent stops along the way to stretch our legs and otherwise relieve ourselves. Perhaps we will reach Shirley by noon, provided Mr. Cole is not preoccupied at the Chickahominy."

"Do you always take the same route when traveling to and from your home?"

"As a rule, yes. However, I often coordinate visits with friends along the way, which create a pleasant diversion. I make it a point to provide myself ample time for travel as one can never be certain of the weather and the river crossings in the western portion of the colony."

"How much time, specifically?"

113

"This journey, for example, may take three days or five days, possibly six, if conditions are particularly unfavorable."

Charles was surprised by this revelation, but after giving it some thought, he began to understand. The two rode companionably for some time afterwards, enjoying the wonders of the woodland and the endemic wildlife. Charles observed the contour of the land carefully. He knew he would have to recognize land references on the return trip. Thomas helped him in this, pointing out certain landmarks by which he navigated the wilderness along the James.

Several miles ahead the road widened, and a small barn and stable appeared on the right. A group of horses was corralled in the stable yard and just beyond stood a two-story clapboard building with a sign hanging out in front bearing the legend 'Cole's Tavern'. As they approached the building, Charles could see a river approximately fifty yards farther along the road. The ground sloped gradually toward the edge of the water.

"Here we are - Cole's Ferry," said Thomas, somewhat unnecessarily. "I hope he is here. He may be on the other side awaiting passengers, or inside entertaining them. Either way, we may be in for an hour's delay." His brow furrowed with concern. "Wait here. I shall return directly."

He rode along the river's edge looking to

see whether Cole's familiar flatboat or raft was moored at the small pier as he had hoped. Two minutes later he was back. "It is as I feared. Cole is not here. However, I could see him crossing the river on his return journey. He should arrive in twenty minutes. Shall we water the horses while we wait? Cole must unload his supplies on the dock before he will take us across. We will just have time for some strong coffee."

"Sounds like an excellent idea to me. I'll be glad to get off this horse!" After watering the horses, they tethered them securely and entered the tavern. It was a smaller tavern than Chownings and contained two rooms on the first floor. The main room reminded Charles of Chowning's game room, but was considerably more primitive, with rough-hewn beams and wooden benches instead of chairs. Charles estimated its construction to be mid-seventeenth century. The center of attention was a large oversized brick fireplace on the left wall. It had a large central chimney which probably served several or all of the fireplaces in the building on both levels.

As they seated themselves at the large wooden table, Charles noticed its worn deal surface and similar signs of wear on the random-width planked floor. A plump, middle-aged, gray-haired woman approached them, grinning broadly. "Well, Mr. Jefferson! I see you are on your way back home already, eh? What can I serve you with, gentlemen?"

"Coffee, please, Mrs. Cole."

"Surely, sir. Won't be a minute."

"Is it just the two of them?" Charles asked Thomas when Mrs. Cole had bustled away.

"No. Cole has five strong sons who assist with the operation of the ferry and on his small farm upriver."

The proprietor's wife returned with their coffee and generous amounts of fresh cream and sugar. Thomas smiled up at her. "Mrs. Cole, this is my friend Charles Dalton. He is returning to Shadwell with me for a short visit."

"I hope you enjoy your stay in the back country, young sir, but I feel I must warn you both. I heard that a group of renegade Indians has been causing some trouble out that way. Yo be mighty careful, now."

Charles gasped. "Indians!"

Jefferson pressed his lips together tightly. "Are you certain this is not merely a rumor, Mrs. Cole?"

"I can only tell you what I hear. Latest word says they were somewhere south of the Green Mountains and heading your way."

"Thank you for the warning, we shall have to be especially cautious once we reach the

Rivanna." He placed several coins on the table. "I suppose we had better be off, Charles. Thank you for your hospitality, Mrs. Cole."

"You're quite welcome, Mr. Jefferson. Good day."

Once outside they spied a fairly tall, thin man unloading a wagon of crated supplies, primarily foodstuffs for the tavern. He smiled pleasantly when he saw them. "Returning so soon, Mr. Jefferson?"

"Yes, Mr. Cole, I completed my business speedily this time."

"Well, you'll be happy to know that young Robert and I will have you headin' across in a few minutes."

Charles turned to his friend. "Thomas, let us wait by the river." They untethered the horses and led them around the wagon and down to the water's edge.

"Appears rather peaceful, doesn't it?"

"It does now. But it was quite another story when I made my last crossing in April. We had had a severe thunderstorm on the previous night and it was three feet deep here on the spot where we are standing now."

"I can believe it." Charles had already noticed the high water markings on the shore line. Obviously. what Thomas had just described was not uncommon in the spring season. Now, however, the river was as tranquil as could be, quietly rolling toward the James to the south. Suddenly. a fish jumped not too far away.

"Thomas, did you see it? You know, I had forgotten completely about fishing. I love fly fishing for trout."

"I fish often in the Green Mountain streams. You will love the Green Mountains, Charles. The views are magnificent. Indeed, I know just the spot on one of the small creeks off the Rivanna River above Shadwell. I have great success there."

"Sounds wonderful. I can still see those cutthroat trout I caught up in Montana a few years ago. Some friends and I stayed in a small cabin a few feet from a huge beaver dam." So caught up in his reverie was Charles, that he did not notice Thomas' confused expression. "Thomas, I swear that beaver dam was a marvel. It was at least twenty feet wide, over a hundred feet long and thirty feet high in the center, and it created a large meadow pond of at least twenty acres. Enormous Douglas firs over one hundred feet tall stood straight up out of the water without a single branch left alive due to the continuous flooding. The water was so clean you could see at least ten to twelve feet down with no effort. Without exaggerating, I tell you I caught a fish with practically every cast. It was a fisherman's dream come true. I will never forget it. I wish you could have been there."

"I wish so too," laughed Jefferson, "it sounds too good to be true. But tell me, exactly where is this place, Montana?"

"Ah... it lies in the far north and west."

"I cannot recall any reference to it."

Before Charles could explain further, Mr. Cole and his son Robert returned to take them across the Chickahominy. Cole's barge was attached to a heavy rope which stretched across the entire river. Charles assumed they would get aboard and simply pull across.

Mr. Cole directed them to bring their possessions on board and tie the horses to the rear of the raft. Large locust poles were used to shove off. The horses followed behind, and when the water got deep enough, they swam along behind the raft. Cole maintained a tight pull on the rope which minimized downstream drift, and in about forty-five minutes they moored the raft at the dock on the west side of the river.

Thomas seemed quite pleased with their progress, but Charles, a child of the twentieth century, could not help reflecting that it had just taken them forty-five minutes to travel about 2,000 feet. He would never take another bridge for granted; provided he ever got the chance to drive across one again. As they busied themselves saddling the horses and repacking them, he chuckled to himself, comparing this experience to a twentieth century travel delay in almost any airport in the country, a nuisance which had become quite commonplace considering overbooking, malfunctioning of equipment, tardy connecting flights etc. Nevertheless, he had learned his lesson. He would be forever grateful for modern modes of travel.

As they continued their journey for the next two hours or so, Thomas pointed out various plantations and riverside estates.

Before long, Charles began to show signs of discomfort resulting from so many hours on horseback. He squirmed on the saddle, trying in vain to find a comfortable position. His friend was not entirely insensitive to Charles' plight, though he couldn't help but be amused by it.

"I have it in mind to stop at Shirley Plantation and visit Charles Carter and his family. If all goes well, we shall have the good fortune to arrive for an afternoon feast fit for the gods. I trust you have worked up an appetite, my friend?"

"Yes, indeed. You'll hear no objections from me!"

Thomas feigned horror. "Surely not! Only a halfwit or a damned fool would decline the famous Carter hospitality."

Between spasms of laughter Charles observed, "I hadn't realized you were possessed of a sense of humor, Thomas. The history books are sadly lacking."

Thomas took this as a witticism on Charles part and continued jovially, "You should see me when I've had more than two pints, my wit would positively dazzle you. I do not take to drink often, but I enjoy the odd refreshment."

"I, too, enjoy the odd refreshment, as you say, but Mr. Coulter, now! That man can drink all night and stand his ground with more sobriety than I can after two pints!"

"In all the years I have known him, and it must be at least six, he has indeed been a prodigious drinker."

"But he is always in control."

"As you say. He is quite a good friend of yours, is he not, Charles?"

"The best. I will never be able to return his generosity and friendship in like measure, but will be forever indebted to him. Sometimes I find myself regarding him as my father."

I can understand that. He obviously regards you as his son, I assure you."

"I don't know what I would have done without him. He has treated me this way since the first day we met in his stationery shop, almost one year ago."

"I believe one of the characteristics which I value most in you, Charles, is your sincere appreciation for practically everything you see or hear. This is a rare trait, and an admirable one, my friend."

Charles was nonplussed. Such praise was welcome as a spring rain, but it embarrassed him, too. "Thank you, Thomas, it was very kind of you to say so."

They continued on toward Shirley in the best of spirits.

CHAPTER 11

Jenny tossed restlessly in the throes of a nightmare. In the dream, she was separated from Charles who had returned to his own time without her and was now trapped there forever. She awakened wet with perspiration, her heart hammering loudly. Rubbing her eyes, she sat up trying to come to terms with her deepest fear. Would it really happen that way? Would it happen soon? Had she seen Charles for the last time?

She jumped out of bed, determined not to be controlled by this thing. She dressed quickly and carelessly, intent on her thoughts. Charles felt that the answer to his time travel lay in their new house. Alright then, she would seek it there and find it before it took him away. She had at least two or three weeks before he returned. That should certainly be enough time, given what she already knew and the reaction she had experienced when she and Bea had visited the house the last time. It was nearly nine o'clock, four hours since she had seen Charles and Thomas off on their journey. She would just have her morning tea, then she would begin her investigation.

Thirty minutes later she unlocked the front door of the new house and entered the parlor. The vase stood there on the mantelpiece mocking her with its normalcy. Jenny approached it with dread. Her heart beat fearfully, and her face flushed with heat. She brushed a few stray hairs from her forehead and took a deep breath to steady herself. Dear God, she prayed, if you can help me, please see me safely through this and protect me in this ordeal. She was now on the hearth, the vase in front of her gleaming in the morning sun. Reaching out with both trembling hands she grasped it and froze. Nothing happened. Still clutching the vase, she backed away several steps. Nothing happened. Why, she thought, why isn't anything happening? This isn't the way it's supposed to be. Last week she had suffered from dizziness and nausea in this very room after handling this very vase, and now - nothing. Why?

She placed the vase back on the mantel and backed away again, staring at it. Some very simple but essential ingredient was missing. What could it be? Perhaps it was the placement of the vase. She moved it to the right. Again nothing. "Damnation!" she muttered huskily. Picking it up once more she was tempted to smash it to pieces on the brick hearth, but she restrained herself with the thought that this was the vehicle through which she would assure her permanent union with Charles, nothing must jeopardize that. Warily, she placed the vase on the far left of the mantel. No sooner had it left her hands than she began to feel the symptoms returning. There was an overpowering dizziness and ringing in her ears. Her stomach was churning and she felt she would faint. The room began to swirl around her, faster and faster, and she lowered heself clumsily to the floor before she lost her equilibrium completely. The nausea was becoming worse. She closed her eyes and put her hand to her forehead feeling its clammy wetness, then she blacked out.

Jenny lay where she had fallen for an undetermined length of time before she slowly returned to her senses. The first thing she became aware of was the soft ba-aa-ing of sheep. She opened her eyes slowly, experimentally. The nausea was gone, so was the dizziness. But where was she? There was a beautiful blue sky above her, and the air was gentle on her face. She was outside. Turning her head slowly to the side, she found herself in the middle of a cornfield. The house was gone. Jenny sat up in shock. She looked around and recognized Nicholson Street, but a different Nicholson Street. There was a small herd of sheep moving slowly toward Anthony Haye's cabinet shop. Slowly she stood up and brushed the dust from her full skirts. She was afraid to move from the spot, afraid to break the spell. Dear God, she thought, is this the twentieth century then? The sounds were different from those she was accustomed to hearing. In the distance was a muffled roar, and a peculiar beeping noise. With every second she became more certain that she had indeed accomplished what she set out to do. This was Charles' time! She was elated, confident and frightened at the same time. I did it! Heaven help me, how do I get back?

Just then Jenny heard a voice cry out, "Move over, come on, move over!" Swiftly she turned to see a young girl dressed in eighteenth century clothing gently prodding the sheep along. The girl saw Jenny and waved casually.

Not knowing whether the salute was meant for her, Jenny turned around to see who might be standing behind her, but she was alone. She turned back and waved at the girl who was grinning at her. Jenny was about to open her mouth when a sudden loud noise caused her to jump back in alarm. The girl was gone, but the source of the noise was very near and seemed to be coming closer all the time, finally stopping right in front of her. Jenny could see some people inside the thing which had glass windows stretching all the way around it several feet above the ground. Before long it moved on, the loud noise was repeated, and a small cloud of black smoke fouled the air in its wake.

Several people were walking down the opposite side of the street. Their clothes were just as Charles had once described them. The women were clad in the most appallingly tight breeches which had been cut off to show the entire length of leg. Jenny gaped in disbelief. What had Charles called them - shorts? She still hadn't moved from the original spot. So far she was unable to summon the courage to explore further.

The people moved on toward Duke of Gloucester Street and she was once more alone. Painstakingly, she studied the field in which she stood and noted the exact spot. As her confidence rose, she marked the spot where she had lain several minutes earlier. There might be some advantage in this. After all, if she was to return to the eighteenth century, this must be where she would do it.

Her curiosity finally got the better of her, and she felt compelled to explore. She wanted to see more, experience more. But where shall I go and what shall I do? Her mind replayed these questions over and over like a litany. She remembered Charles telling her that the women of his time were free to come and go as they chose without an escort. No one would question her. Then she remembered the clothing she had just seen on the women. Her own dress would stand out immediately and mark her as a curiosity. They would think her insane. But no, that shepherd girl was wearing eighteenth century clothing, and she had taken Jenny's dress for granted. What was happening here? Taking a deep breath, she lifted her skirts and made her way out of the field and over to the corner where a sign proclaimed 'Botetourt Street'. That was a surprise. In her experience, this side street was merely an unnamed lane. Walking onto Nicholson Street she was amazed to discover that the road was neither dirt nor crushed oyster shells. It was very hard, smooth and black. Actually, it was quite easy to walk on. She crossed Nicholson Street and proceeded toward Duke of Gloucester Street where she could see people walking in both directions. Wishing to see the main street of town, she walked along noticing an unusual smell in the air. It wasn't at all like the air in her time. No, it wasn't so much a definite smell, as the absence of smell, she thought. There was no animal waste, and the familiar pungency characteristic of horses was absent. Moreover, she couldn't smell burning wood. How did these people cook? Charles had told her once, but she had not fully comprehended. Well, perhaps she would see for herself.

She had reached the corner and walked out into the center of Duke of Gloucester Street. To her surprise it was lined with beautiful tall green trees from the Capitol building, all the way down to the College of William and Mary which she had no trouble recognizing. The trees were a beautiful and impressive sight. The town looked immeasurably better for them, but then, the town looked lovely on its own. Every building was meticulously maintained, whitewashed and repaired. The twentieth century was an excessively clean one, she mused.

More familiar sights met her eye as she came upon the Prentiss house and Tarpley's Store. Here, too, was Wetherburn's Tavern and its sister taverns, the King's Arms and the Raleigh across the street. As she strolled in the direction of the Market Square, she noticed that a large number of people were wearing eye glasses, though they were more like eye shades, and many were carrying strange little black boxes on long straps around their necks. So far, no one seemed to notice anything amiss in her dress, but her beauty had attracted many appreciative glances. Here and there she was relieved to see others dressed in eighteenth century garb - men as well as women - and they all nodded to her in a friendly manner. Looking more closely she discovered that these people were usually involved in some kind of demonstration, and that they were happy to answer any and all questions directed to them. They are like teachers, she thought, perhaps they think I am another such.

Suddenly a small group of people approached her and it was obvious that they were going to speak to her. Before she could evade them, the young man walked up to her and asked, "Would you mind if I took a shot of you alongside my wife and daughter?" He seemed friendly enough, but Jenny had no idea what he was talking about.

"Pardon?"

He responded by raising the small black box in his hands. "Your picture! We'd like to take your picture, if it's alright."

His wife, decided the issue. "Come on, Annie. Stand over here next to the lady." She placed the child on Jenny's left side while she herself stood on Jenny's right. "Ready, Dan?"

The man raised the box to his face as if to look through it. "Okay, big smiles, everyone! Annie, say 'cheese'!" Jenny heard a faint click and the man put the box down again with a satisfied expression. "Thanks, we appreciate that."

Jenny looked inquisitively at the woman and the little girl who were smiling back at the man with the black box. She still had no idea what was going on, but she knew it was harmless, so she smiled back at the man, too. There was a whirring noise coming from the box now, and Jenny saw with astonishment that something was coming out of it. The woman and her daughter moved quickly over and watched as the thing was ejected from the box, then took it into their hands and exclaimed pleasurably over it.

"It's great, Dan!"

The man was happy with it too, and brought it over for Jenny's inspection. "It turned out really well, don't you think?"

Jenny could only gape in disbelief. There, in gorgeous color, was a perfect likeness of herself and the woman with her daughter. "It's wonderful!" she breathed.

The man backed up a few steps and looked through the box again. "One more, for good luck. Smile!" This time Jenny smiled with genuine pleasure. The second picture was as beautiful as the first and she was delighted with it.

"Here, this one's for you for being so patient with us. Thanks again!"

"This is our first visit to Williamsburg. We are from Michigan." The woman was speaking.

"We really love what you have done here." Her husband added. "How long have you been with the Foundation? Do you like the work?"

Jenny was nonplussed. What on earth was the Foundation? She improvised. "No, I have not been here long."

Sensing her discomfort the woman interrupted. "Don't mind us. I'm Gail Johnson, and this is my husband Dan and our daughter, Annie." She extended her hand and Jenny shook it.

"I'm very pleased to meet you. I am Jenny Coulter."

"How long have you been working here?" The woman's husband was persistent.

Jenny knew she had better say something, anything. "I am the daughter of Tobias Coulter, Master Printer of the 'Virginia Gazette'. I have lived here all my life."

After a brief pause, the man grinned. "Oh, I get it. You must be one of the colonial players who portrays actual eighteenth century persons. Your accent is great!"

"Yes, I saw another performer farther up the street. He was surrounded by many visitors.

He was quite good," Gail added.

"Well, I guess we had better let you get back to work. It was nice meeting you, Jenny."

"Yes, thank you very much! Annie, what do you say?"

"Goodbye and thank you!"

Jenny laughed and shook the little girl's hand. "Goodbye, Annie. I hope to see you again someday." The child turned and waved to her as they walked down the street.

They were lovely people, thought Jenny, and they left something quite precious. When I get back home, I can show this to Charles as proof that I visited his time. She was becoming more confident with every passing minute as she continued her walk to the Market Square.

Soon she recognized Christiana Campell's tavern on the left and Holt's general store on the right, but curiously, neither was identified as such. In fact, a number of buildings looked different. Some had different signs, and others were no longer public taverns. Things had changed, though considering the amount of time which had elapsed, it was remarkable how much had remained the same. Then she remembered something Charles had told her. He had said that in his time, the town was maintained and restored to an approximation of its original condition, rather like a living museum, for people to visit and see into the past. It was a marvelous concept, she thought, and very convenient for her purpose.

Good heavens, I am home! She was standing in front of the print shop, and a sudden spasm of homesickness assailed her. Who was in there now, and what were they printing? Many other people were obviously wondering the same thing, for there was a heavy volume of traffic in and out of the building. As she made her way through the crowd, several people accosted her and asked directions to the Governor's Palace. Jenny had no trouble providing directions, and they thanked her, complimenting her on her gown.

She stepped into the stationery shop, half expecting to see Charles standing behind the counter, and more than a little disappointed that he was not. She knew it was ridiculous to feel this way, but the sense of deja vu was overwhelming in this place, and she had to concentrate fiercely to prevent herself from becoming disoriented.

Two ladies in eighteenth century costume stood behind the counter dispensing souvenirs, prints, stationery and postcards. Conspicuous by its absence was the 'Virginia Gazette', for which Jenny searched in vain. She decided not to ask for it, however, since she didn't want to attract attention to herself unnecessarily. Without thinking, she turned to go upstairs and visit her father's former office, but as she stepped out of the room, she saw the door to the lower level standing ajar. She heard voices from down there and decided to investigate. Descending the narrow stairwell slowly, she was surprised to see only two people in the shop. A large portion of the room was roped off to preclude passage from the rear door into the center of the room.

"Can I help you?" A blond young man with frankly admiring eyes smiled at her.

"Oh, no, I merely wanted to see the shop, and..."

Several tourists had entered from the rear door and the young man, a printer, turned from her reluctantly. "Well, if you have any questions, I'll be happy to answer them."

"Are there only the two of you?" Jenny asked, encouraged by the warmth in his eyes.

"For now, yes. Do you work for the Foundation? I haven't seen you here before," he countered.

Jenny wasn't sure how to answer. She didn't want to lie, but she didn't want any trouble either. "No, not exactly. Please go about your work, I'd just like to look around." She smiled shyly at him to soften her abrupt dismissal, and turned to go back upstairs. He watched her go with a curious sense of loss.

Back in the stationery shop, Jenny studied some of the printed materials, one of which particularly caught her eye. It was entitled 'The Declaration of Independence', 1776. She read it carefully, remembering what Charles had explained to her about the independence movement and the creation of a nation, the United States. This small piece of paper brought tears to her eyes as she considered its ramifications. She would have loved to purchase it, but she had no modern currency.

Back on the street, she noticed a small family of blacks strolling along in complete freedom, as though it were an everyday occurrence. Of course, Charles had told her that all the slaves had been freed; indeed, a horrible war had been fought in the process, and now the blacks were finally able to live like white men. Approaching Chowning's, she saw more blacks and some others whom she believed to be of Oriental origin. Imagine, Orientals here in Williamsburg! Jenny had read about them, but she had never actually seen one. Charles' society was a fascinating one, a mixture of many people from many nations. There was so much she needed to ask Charles! When would they be here together? She remembered again the words of the 'Declaration of Independence' and was filled with emotion as she began to appreciate the concepts created and authored by her father's friends, George Mason, Professor Wythe and Thomas Jefferson. The idea was wonderful, a revelation. Before Charles had opened her eyes to it, she had had no idea of what was happening in her own time. Word had not yet spread in 1768, and only a few men like her father had any notion of the rumblings of revolution. Yes, it was profoundly stirring, but it hadn't been carried far enough. George Mason and Professor Wythe and Thomas Jefferson had not conceived of an equality which extended to the Negro. In a sense, she could understand why. Freedom for the Negro in the eighteenth century would have undermined the entire agrarian system upon which the colony was built, as indeed it did a century later, according to Charles. Perhaps the founding fathers felt that although a collapse of the system was inevitable, they would defer it as long as possible. Or perhaps they truly believed the black man to be less than human.

She could scarcely wait to get back home to discuss the issue with her father, if he was amenable. Unfortunately, he was sometimes very reticent with his opinions. Well, she would force a discussion if need be. Charles' society had opened her eyes to a great many issues, and she would never be the same.

CHAPTER 12

"We have company, my friend!"

Charles watched as a wagon rumbled down the dirt path toward them. A lone black man rode in the wagon seat, expertly guiding the horses. "Do you know him, Thomas?"

"Yes. It looks like Joe, one of the Harrison slaves from Berkeley." They pulled up as Joe stopped the wagon. "Well, Joe, where are you bound?"

"'Afternoon Mista Jefferson, sir. I'm for Cole's crossin' to bring Mista Cole across for

138

Massa Harrison. He be goin' to Williamsburg today."

"I see. He's starting a bit late in the day, is he not?"

"Yassir," Joe replied but did not elaborate.

"Well, you had better be off, Joe."

"G'day, gennelmen." He whipped up the horses and disappeared in a cloud of dust.

It took a few moments for Charles to work out that Mr. Harrison's slave had gone ahead to summon Mr. Cole so the gentleman would not have to wait on the riverbank, and so delay his journey even more, possibly an hour. He must have urgent business in the capital, Charles surmised, urgent and unanticipated.

By and by Thomas pointed out the entrance to another estate. "This is the home of the Byrd family, Charles. You may have heard of it — Westover. It really is remarkably lovely." Within several minutes they passed the entrance to Berkeley, home of the Harrisons. In another half an hour Thomas informed Charles that they were at last nearing their destination.

"Thank God, I'm famished!"

Thomas laughed. "Unless I am very much mistaken, you will soon be complaining of an overfull belly. 'Tis a common enough complaint at Shirley."

"Do you suppose your friends will accept me?"

"It is a point of honor with the James River planters to provide hospitality to any and all comers. Charles Carter, moreover, is a generous man, and the size of his household is staggering. He turns no one away."

They soon came upon a particularly lovely stretch of woods dominated by magnificent oaks, some of which were four feet in diameter, and obviously quite old. The dense forest canopy controlled shrub and weed growth on the forest floor leaving it clean, save for the ferns and sparsely located secondary trees reaching for whatever sunlight might pierce the oak canopy. It was possible to see for quite a distance without difficulty, and Charles was enchanted by the sight of several deer on his far right.

"There, Thomas! That is the second group of deer I have seen since we entered this forest. This place is teeming with wildlife!"

"Yes, of course. You are now on the Carter estate and have been for some time. This is a section of his hunting preserve, kept for his own personal entertainment and that of his friends, not to mention for the glory of his table."

"I see."

"Hunting and thoroughbred racing are two important sources of entertainment for the local gentry. This has become a way of life for men of property."

"It is easy to see the influence of your English roots in Virginia. The landed aristocracy is very much the same in the Mother Country, is it not? For myself, that kind of life is somewhat alien. I am too much accustomed to making my own way in life."

"Well, I shall be happy to provide you with a brief education in the ways of the gentry if you wish. I think you will enjoy the experience."

"I daresay I will enjoy it too much for my later comfort! Tell me, Thomas, how is it that you are so comfortable with me? I am certainly not of your station and don't really fit into your circle."

"Come now, Charles, you disparage yourself needlessly."

"No, I really want to know. It is true, you cannot deny that I am not in the same class as the Harrisons, the Carters, and others of your society."

Thomas considered the question in silence for several minutes. Finally he turned to his friend with a slightly sardonic lift of the eyebrows and smiled. "There is about your nature a rather bizarre characteristic which is, to say the least, fey. I suppose that my first interest in you was prompted by your mention of

Monticello upon our first meeting. How you knew
that name remains a mystery to me to this day.
For another thing, and I mentioned this to you
already, I find your appreciation of the natural
world delightful. Your interest is unflagging,
and perhaps I recognize that we are kindred
spirits in this regard."

Charles remained silent, and Thomas
continued. "To return to the first, your mention
of Monticello which I had only just conceived
of the name myself and had told no one of it,
induced me to believe that you were possessed of
unusual powers of the mind, and I must confess,
this intrigued me. This, coupled with your
uncanny grasp of political intricacies, gained
my complete respect. I value our friendship
Charles, and our respective places in society
are of little or no importance, I assure you."

"Thank you for that, Thomas. I will not
speak of it again."

By common consent they spurred their horses
on to a gallop and rode thus until they reached
Shirley.

Nearly an hour had elapsed since they had
left the hospitality of the Carters at Shirley,
and it had been a singularly uneventful hour.
Charles was grateful for the appearance of
riders ahead.

"Look, Thomas. I wonder who they are?"

"I've no idea. But they appear to be in a hurry."

As the horsemen came closer, a feeling of overwhelming apprehension crept over Charles. He was reminded of another incident when approaching riders heralded unspeakable terror for himself and Jenny, and he shuddered at the memory. This pair was leading an extra horse, and they looked innocuous enough. Later, he was to remember his first impression as being the correct one.

When they were close enough to be heard, one of the riders inquired, "Have either of you fine gentlemen set eyes upon two young runaway slaves; one of them a young man about twenty years of age, and the other a girl of about seventeen?"

"We have seen no one but yourselves since we left Shirley Plantation this hour past," Jefferson replied civilly.

"Well, keep an eye out and detain them, if you would. We will pass by this way again. Thank you kindly. Good day to you, gentlemen." The speaker was a middle-aged man with the weathered appearance and leathery complexion of one who spends a great deal of time in the sun. Probably an overseer or an agent, thought Charles. The man was well-dressed, almost a dandy, and accompanied his parting words with a sardonic tip of his hat before continuing on. His companion was not nearly so prepossessing. He was small of stature and heavyset with brutish features and a pronounced squint. He remained silent and appeared disinterested in Thomas and Charles while his eyes slid over the road behind and all around them.

"Good day." Thomas glanced at his friend who was watching the riders disappear toward Shirley with an unsettled expression on his face. He was well enough acquainted with Charles by this time to gauge his thoughts, and was unwilling to raise the question of slavery which never failed to rouse Charles' ire.

For his part, Charles had no difficulty in imagining the abject terror which the runaways must be feeling. He recalled vividly the desperation he himself had felt the night he fled the Raleigh's courtyard after having stolen some food, or the morning he had run from the Waller house on his first day in the eighteenth century, when one of the occupants had caught him stealing clothes. Yes, he knew what it meant to be running scared, with no place to go, and no one to turn to for assistance. There was one difference, though. He was white, and that fact allowed him to lose himself in the crowded town, for the first few days, at least. These two young blacks had no reasonable way to escape. Where could they go? Signs would be posted bearing their descriptions and offering rewards for their capture, and it was only a matter of time before they would be recognized.

Soon Thomas suggested that they stop and rest their horses at a small stream - something they tried to do every hour, if possible. They dismounted and allowed the horses to drink their fill. Thomas had wandered off to stretch his legs, and Charles was filling his pipe when he detected a slight movement about thirty yards farther downstream. He stood dead still and watched carefully, his hand poised over the weapon he had brought along at Coulter's insistence. If Indians were about to attack, they would not find him easy prey. But then he remembered that they were still too far east to make that possibility a likelihood.

Thomas returned, and Charles decided to wander downstream to investigate. "I won't be long, Thomas."

"We've some time yet. You deserve a rest."

Charles had walked about twenty yards downstream when he heard a twig snap. Now he was certain that there was someone or something just ahead. Whatever it was, it did not want to be seen. As stealthily as possible, he picked his way around a thorny bush and various wild thickets which grew along the banks of the stream. He moved closer, and closer still. Then he stopped and stood perfectly still, listening for the slightest sound. He squatted down out of sight and waited patiently, though he knew time was passing and Jefferson would be impatient to press on toward Shadwell. His persistence was rewarded when he heard another twig snap, but this time Charles was able to focus directly on the cause. There, behind a clump of thickets was the runaway slave girl. The whites of her big, brown eyes stared right back at him in fear and anguish. Charles scanned the area for her companion and found him just a few feet to the girl's left behind a large tree trunk. He was clutching a large rock, and the expression in his eyes told Charles he would not hesitate to use it.

Charles got slowly to his feet without taking his eyes from the girl. He knew they could now see him clearly, so he raised one finger to his lips and pointed back toward the horses where Jefferson waited, then he approached them. They eyed him suspiciously. The girl turned to her companion, then back to Charles in growing confusion. Their life up to this point had not engendered trust, and it was difficult to credit altruistic intentions from a white man.

Charles signaled to them again by extending his hands, palms up, in front of him. The girl rose, and the boy came out from behind the tree still clasping his makeshift weapon.

"I want to help you," said Charles softly.

They were still wary and hesitated to answer, but Charles thought he detected a lessening of fear in their eyes.

"Do you know where to go?"

The boy shook his head. "No sah, we have no place to go."

"The way I see it, there are only two options. One, you can go upriver and try to reach the mountains, but keep in mind that you might have to face Indians; or, you could try to go up to Richmond and stow away on a schooner bound for the northern coast. That would be extremely risky, but it could be done. Do you understand?"

"Richmond?" The girl had obviously never heard of the place.

"I knows about Richmond," her companion replied not without some pride.

"It's a long way from here by foot, but I see no other way out of the colony, and you must leave Virginia, surely you can see that."

"Yassir, we knows dat."

Charles wasn't convinced, but he had just about run out of time. "I must be off. God be with you, and remember, travel quietly and stay out of sight at all costs." He pointed toward the river. "Go downstream, and then upriver. You will eventually run into Richmond."

They smiled uncertainly and thanked him,

and he turned away, his mind busy with possible explanations for his absence.

"Charles! I was becoming concerned, thank heaven you are here!"

"I am sorry, Thomas. I spied two deer, and decided to follow them a bit. The male was an eight point buck!"

"There will be ample time to hunt when we arrive at Shadwell," Jefferson returned, a hint of pique in his voice.

"Yes, I know. I apologize, Thomas."

"Right. Shall we be off then?"

Charles wondered if Thomas was aware of the lie. He was uneasy about the necessity for deceiving his friend. Lying was definitely not his forte.

Nearly an hour later, the two travellers stopped once more to rest their horses and were accosted by the same two riders they had seen before, coming from the direction of Shirley.

Charles' heart skipped a beat when he saw that the extra horse was now carrying the two runaway slaves.

The spokesman greeted them. "We got 'em. Caught em' going downstream towards the river, just about where we figured.

In a choked voice Charles inquired, "How did you find them so far off the road?"

The dandy laughed. "That was easy. They left a trail a blind man could follow. But it was the hoof prints of horses that attracted our attention to that particular stream. Probably had nothing to do with it, but we got 'em just the same."

"I suppose you will be taking them back to the farm then?"

"Right enough. We have some lessons to teach them so the others won't get any such notions in their heads." He flicked his riding crop impatiently, and Charles saw the runaways cringe at the sound.

"I see." Thomas frowned and looked at Charles curiously.

"Well, I suppose you are satisfied now." The heavy sarcasm in Charles' voice surprised the man. He raised his brows and regarded Charles with a mixture of suspicion and scorn. "What do you mean by that remark?"

"Just what I said." He locked eyes with the other man, forcing him to look away. Nudging Jupiter with his heels he threw at them a final "Good day gentlemen," and rode off with Thomas close behind.

His emotions were churning, and he felt sick to his stomach. As long as he lived, he would never forget the expressions of betrayal on the faces of the runaways as they sat immobile, quietly waiting to meet their fate.

Having ridden quietly beside him for a while, Thomas finally broke the silence. "Do you know the penalty for aiding a runaway?"

"So you knew all along?"

"You told me with your eyes, though I must confess I suspected as much earlier. I know you Charles, and I know your position on slavery."

Charles lowered his eyes. "I'm sorry I lied to you, but I was afraid you would misunderstand."

"I do not. I have the same feelings quite often, but I school myself to disregard them. However else one approaches the subject, it cannot be denied that they have broken the law in full knowledge of the penalty that entails." He held up his hand to forestall Charles' angry words. "I know, my friend. I know what you are about to say. Perhaps some day the situation will change, but we are constrained to accept it now; we must live in the present, not in some fantasy of the future."

Jefferson's words hit Charles with the force of a blow and he stared at him in amazement. If only he knew!

CHAPTER 13

Jenny stopped right in the middle of Market Square and stared at an unfamiliar brick building. She walked over to the front of it and read the sign: Court House of 1770. So, she thought, it hasn't been built yet; was, in fact, two years in the future. Well, she supposed there were going to be many such surprises. Time certainly didn't stand still. Just then, she glanced beyond the Powder Magazine and saw something that Charles had told her about, but she just couldn't remember what he called them.

151

She remembered his description vividly since she had been aghast to learn that these things had replaced horses entirely as a mode of transportation in the twentieth century. There they were, passing by in both directions on Francis Street. It was curious that there were none on Duke of Gloucester Street. What in heaven's name were they called? She would have liked to walk over toward Francis Street, but the sight of so many unfamiliar buildings intimidated her somewhat, and she elected to remain on Duke of Gloucester where she felt more comfortable.

Soon she reached the Palace Green and the Geddy house on the corner and her gaze fell quite naturally on the Governor's Palace. It looked exactly the same. It was here, in the gardens that Charles had accosted her during the Governor's Ball last year and persuaded her that his affair with Alanna was over, and it was here that he first told her that he was from another time. She sighed. So much had happened since then. Now they were to be married and make a life together in the eighteenth century unless fate or their own ingenuity intervened and cast them into the twentieth century together. What a coil! Her life had become unbelievably complicated since Charles had entered it, but she would have had it no other way.

Deep in thought, she strolled across the

FRANCIS STREET

Green and recognized the homes of Professor
Wythe and Robert Carter. There was Mayor
Everard's house, apparently unchanged as well!
The municipal court building was missing,
however. She wondered if it had burned down, a
common enough occurrence in the 1700s. She began
walking back down Nicholson Street toward the
cornfield, and it occurred to her that something
was missing on the corner. She stopped and
studied the large frame house which had been
augmented by several additions. She seemed to
remember a smaller house which stood on that
particular corner, but it faced the Palace
Green. Could the smaller house have been
appended to the larger one which now faced
Nicholson Street? But why would anyone want to
move a house?

Jenny continued her ramble, passing the
doctor's house and the Randolph house and the
windmill. There was a line of people waiting to
enter the Randolph house, and she wondered why
people seemed to be interested in some, but not
all of the restored buildings. There was no
line in front of Colonel Tayloe's house, for
example, while a large number of people were
going in and out of the cabinet maker's shop.

Until now, Jenny had not thought to visit
her parents' house. It came as a shock, then,
when she was unable to find any trace of it. It
would have been so reassuring just to see it,

but no, there was only a large empty spot where her home had stood. Jenny was suddenly devoid of energy. She had been walking for what seemed like hours and had had nothing to eat or drink in all that time. Weary and disheartened, she settled herself under a large tree near the cornfield and watched idly as another large, multi-windowed vehicle discharged its passengers as before. This time, however, an attractive young man was left standing in the wake of the departing monster, and she was the first thing he saw when he looked up. To Jenny's amazement, he smiled as though he knew her, and waved a casual greeting.

In spite of herself, Jenny was moved to smile back at the stranger. This was all he needed. Before she could utter a word or get to her feet, there he was in front of her – a tall, handsome man with long, exposed legs and bare muscular arms. "Hello!"

Jenny stood up, uncertainly. "Hello."

"I'm Scott. You must be a Foundation employee, but I know I've never seen you before. Or have I?"

Jenny sensed he wanted to ask her name, but was too subtle to ask her outright, and she appreciated his tact. "I'm Jenny Coulter," she replied more warmly than she intended.

"You, ah, do work for the Foundation, right?"

"No, I do not."

"Well, that is quite a costume. You look great!" His eyes held a thousand questions, but he instinctively knew not to push her.

"It is very kind of you to say so."

He stared into her eyes which were the most extraordinary he had ever seen. Violet fire! And what skin! She had to be the most beautiful creature alive. Somehow, he had to prolong this chance meeting and learn more about her.

"Are you busy just now? Would you like to have lunch with me? I know we scarcely know each other, but, well, I thought I'd ask. We could get some pizza, what do you say?" Damn, she made him nervous! If only she would say yes.

She frowned in bewilderment. Pizza, What on earth was that?

"Well, maybe you're not very hungry, just now..."

"Oh yes, I am famished!" It came out involuntarily. Oh dear, she thought, now I shall be committed to sharing a meal with this stranger.

His face lit up, but before he could speak, Jenny stammered, "No. I...that is, I cannot. I'm sorry to have mislead you."

Scott's heart plummeted. He thought it was too good to be true. He wondered where she lived, and if she was a visitor. She had to be English with that accent.

"Maybe some other time, then. Will you be in town tomorrow?"

"I'm not certain. I really must be going." Jenny turned and walked purposefully into the cornfield.

"What are you doing?"

Jenny found the spot she had marked, but realized with annoyance that she could not simply disappear in front of Scott, assuming she would disappear at all. He had to be dispatched somehow.

"Are you looking for something? Maybe I can help." Scott stepped into the cornfield, eager to prolong their meeting.

Damnation, she muttered to herself. She was really losing patience now. "You can help me by going about your business," she snapped. "Really, I am in no difficulty."

Scott looked at her helplessly. This was more serious than he thought. She was nearly in tears, and whatever she was trying to do was obviously not working. He apologized and turning reluctantly, made his way out of the field and down Nicholson Street. He looked back once and was astounded to see that she was following him. Was it possible she was emotionally disturbed? If so, it was a rotten shame. She was the most entrancing creature he had ever seen.

Jenny had decided that she had to be absolutely alone before she attempted to return to her own time. Perhaps she should wait until darkness fell. In the meantime, she was undeniably attracted to Scott who reminded her of Charles. She knew instinctively that she could trust him, and perhaps he could teach her a few things about this strange world. She had not been following him long before he turned around and seeing her, stopped.

"Are you alright, Jenny?" He was looking at her with a mixture of admiration and concern.

"Yes, quite well. I apologize for my rudeness. You've been very kind."

"Okay. Apology accepted. So, would you like to have lunch? We could grab a bite at Chowning's if you like." His heart was racing at the prospect.

"Oh yes, that would be wonderful!" Now that the die was cast, she wondered what Charles would say if he could see her in the company of this attractive man. Would he be jealous, or would he realize that she needed a friend to guide her through this perplexing maze of alien mores?

"Well, let's get on over there and find out what's on the menu. I'm not sure what they serve for lunch."

"We shall soon see," Jenny laughed. Her adventure was just beginning, and she was enjoying it more with every minute.

Scott led her back across Botetourt to

Duke of Gloucester Street and up past the print shop. Encouraged by her laughter and obvious change of heart, he felt free to indulge his curiosity about her. "Do you live here permanently, Jenny, or are you just visiting? I couldn't help noticing your accent"

"You could say that I am visiting, yes." She threw him a devastating sidelong glance, teasing him. She already knew she had the power to excite him, and she had not had the opportunity to enjoy a flirtation for a long time. Not since the Governor's Ball, in fact, and she had been so heartsick at seeing Charles there with Alanna that she had derived no enjoyment from the flirtations she had carried on.

Soon they stepped onto the porch at Chowning's and Scott looked over the lunch menu on the wall. "They serve sandwiches here until four o'clock. I guess I'll have the baked ham and cheddar, how about you?"

"I will have the same", she replied. Whatever a sandwich was, Scott liked it, and she probably would too.

A costumed employee appeared at the doorway. "Two for lunch? Would you rather eat inside or outside in the courtyard?"

Scott deferred to Jenny. "Outside, please."

The waitress led them through the games room and outside where they were seated at

158

a table under the grape arbor. Scott ordered for
them - baked ham sandwiches, and large Cokes
- and Jenny looked around her, enjoying the
view. When the food arrived, she found herself
eyeing Scott surreptitiously to see how he
handled the sandwich, then she followed his
example. She found it quite delicious. The coke
was a delightful surprise. Jenny had at first
been reluctant to try the dark, bubbly
concoction, and was completely at a loss how to
handle the straw. Feigning nonchalance, she
removed the paper, just as Scott did, and placed
it into the drink. She could not hide her
surprise and pleasure after that first sip,
however, and her expression amused Scott.

"Good, huh?"

"It's delicious!" Jenny gasped, having
just disposed of half the glass. "I was quite
thirsty."

"I could tell." They both laughed.

Jenny declined dessert. Thus far, she had
not disgraced herself, but the food and the
sultry air had made her drowsy. New impressions,
feelings, tastes, were flooding her
consciousness, and she desperately wanted to
rest and sort it all out in privacy.

"...you again." She looked up at Scott who
had been trying to tell her something.

"I'm sorry. I was dreaming. What did you
say?"

"I want to see you again, Jenny."

"Oh, Scott, I'm afraid it isn't possible."

"Why? Are you leaving Williamsburg?"

"No, not just yet, but soon."

"Then why? It can't hurt. I promise I will only take you to dinner and we will talk, nothing more. Where's the harm in that?"

Jenny was tempted. She had thoroughly enjoyed their lunch together, but could not lead this young man on. After all, she was about to be married. Perhaps she should make that fact clear to Scott.

"Is there someone else?" It seemed he had read her mind.

"Yes, there is, Scott. Someone to whom I am deeply committed."

"Oh damn. I knew you were too good to be true. There had to be a catch." His face was flooded with bitterness.

Jenny spoke gently. "I should have told you sooner. It is my fault." Then, in a spirit of self-flagellation she added "Perhaps you were best to leave me in the cornfield!"

Scott looked up at her and suddenly burst into laughter. Realizing just what she had said, and how it must have sounded, she laughed too.

"You are the damndest woman I have ever met, and the most eccentric, is that the word? Yes, my mysterious lady of the cornfield. Well, I suppose you will want to go back there now and do whatever it is you do. Are you a witch by any chance?"

She stared at him in horror before she realized he was teasing. "In fact, yes, I must be going. Please forgive me if I caused you any discomfort. I did enjoy our meal together."

"Thank you for joining me. Maybe I will see you again, who knows? I am a student at the College and I'll be here all summer. If you ever want to look me up, just check in with off campus housing, and ask for Scott Baldwin."

Jenny rose and extended her hand. "Perhaps we shall meet again. Thank you." Then she was gone.

He sat at the table a long time, wondering if indeed he would ever see her again.

CHAPTER 14

Charles lit his pipe, flicked the wooden match stick into the water and watched it float away. Nearby, the horses were drinking from the stream and taking a well-deserved rest. It had been nearly three hours since he and Thomas had left Shirley. Charles checked his pocket watch once again. "It's almost six thirty, Thomas. When do you suppose we will stop for the night? We still have another two hours of sunlight."

"We should reach Richmond within the hour. I usually stop at a comfortable tavern near the

162

James which offers good plain fare and clean, comfortable bedding. We have made excellent time thus far, Charles. How are you bearing up?"

"My back, my thighs, my knees, and other parts of my anatomy which shall go unmentioned, are sore as hell. Other than that...!"

"I think I can guess what parts you are referring to," Thomas laughed. "A nice soft bed would not come amiss I gather."

"It would be heaven, not to mention a hot bath."

"Not too hungry, are you?"

"After that meal? Shirley was everything you said, and more."

"Should you change your mind, Mary will take good care of you."

"Mary?"

"She is the handsome daughter of Mrs. Wells, the proprietor of the inn. It should not be terribly crowded on a Monday evening; we will receive prompt service."

"It sounds wonderful."

Before long they came upon another small stream with a swift current and Thomas stopped them at the water's edge.

"Charles, do you see that large rock?"

"Yes, why?"

"Although it appears quite shallow, the water in that area is at least five feet deep, and the current over strong. I suggest you keep a tight reign on Jupiter and do not crowd Jason on his crossing. If I go down, I don't want you to do the same."

"Right."

Thomas started across slowly, speaking softly to Charles who was following him with some trepidation. By the time they had reached the halfway point, Charles was wet to the thighs and was becoming more apprehensive. It was becoming more difficult to control Jupiter and keep him in a straight line. Just when he thought they had the worst behind them, Jason, Thomas' horse, slipped on bottom stone and fell sideways, nearly upsetting his rider. But Thomas kept his seat and managed to calm the nervous animal.

"Stay with him, Thomas."

Charles was pleased that Thomas held on, and he was also very happy with Jupiter's performance crossing the hazard.

Finally, they were both safely across and Thomas dismounted to check Jason's front feet. Charles noticed for the first time that Jason was shod.

"Is he alright?"

"Yes, Jason is very well. I was proud of him back there."

"Jason. How did you come by that name for him, Thomas?"

"Do you remember the story of Jason and the

Argonauts? It was always one of my favorites. He is named for the hero, and he is the best horse I've ever known. I raised him myself."

"How old is he?"

"He was given me by Professor Wythe in '65 as a gift. At that time he was but a few months old."

"By the way, I see that Jason is properly shod. Jupiter is not. Perhaps I should have that attended to. Though it's curious that Rogers would have neglected such a thing."

Thomas smiled. "It is not necessary that horses be shod in Williamsburg where the roads are flat and relatively smooth. In the western counties, shoes become necessary as the terrain grows more rocky. Jupiter will be shod in the morning. Mrs. Wells will see to it."

"I warned you that I had little experience with horses."

"That may be, but I must congratulate you on your performance in fording that stream. You handled Jupiter superbly."

"It was a close call. I expected every minute that he would go down, especially after Jason slipped."

"The gods were with us, Charles."

Several miles farther on they began to see signs of civilization again when the James came into view. Numerous farms and some large

estates dotted the banks as the road widened
into the main thoroughfare of a small town. It
was a charming place, quite a bit smaller than
Williamsburg, with side streets running down to
the banks of the river.

Thomas led Charles down one of the side
streets to a two-story tavern with a sign out
front reading 'Well's Tavern'. The building
faced the water and the harbor. Charles noticed
a number of boats and one large schooner moored
at the docks. Men were unloading barrels and
crates of provisions brought upriver.

The building itself was reminiscent of
Christiana Campbell's on Waller Street. It had a
big front porch with comfortable chairs and
small tables scattered around for the comfort
and convenience of guests. The interior was
typical of the day with its well-worn pine
planking and paneled walls in the dining area.
To the left of the spacious entrance hall there
was a sizeable bar, similar to the Raleigh's
taproom; to the right, a modest crowd enjoyed
the amenities of the game room. Music and
laughter pervaded the place, and Charles felt
his spirits lift instantly.

Soon the proprietress greeted them with
welcoming words and arranged for a comfortable
room which, Charles was relieved to learn, they
would not have to share. Mrs. Wells was a
homely, middle-aged woman in spotless white cap

and apron whose reputation for providing the best was well-earned. She was particularly fond of Thomas, who was a regular patron, and they chatted amiably once the introductions had been made.

"How very good of you both to stop in with us. I hope you enjoy your stay."

"As always, Mrs. Wells, it will be a pleasure," Thomas replied gallantly.

"Might I interest you gentlemen in a hot bath? My Mary will see to your comfort."

The answer was a resounding "Yes, ma'am!"

"But we will have a drink first," put in Thomas.

"...and something to eat, as well," Charles added. He never thought he could be hungry again so soon after that meal at Shirley, but he suddenly found himself famished.

Mrs. Wells beamed. "Certainly, come this way." She led them down the hallway into a large public dining room half-filled with hungry patrons and seated them at a table whose three boisterous occupants had already consumed one bowl of sower punch.

Soon their own bowl arrived, borne in by an attractive young woman with flaxen hair and flawless complexion. Her green eyes sparkled in the candlelight when she saw who it was she was serving.

"Good evening, Mr. Jefferson." She favored

him with a ravishing smile.

"Good evening, Miss Mary. I trust you have been well?"

"Quite well, sir. Will you and the gentleman be eating tonight?"

"The sooner, the better," interjected Charles provoking laughter all around.

"You look quite charming tonight, as usual."

Mary blushed. "Thank you, Mr. Jefferson. It's kind of you to say so. I'll just bring your supper now, sirs." After another shy glance at Thomas, she glided gracefully away.

"Ye be the fortunate one, young sir!" One of their table mates observed with a wink. "There's no mistakin' yon lassie's set 'er cap fer ye." His companions exploded with good-natured laughter.

"I'll drink to that," Charles said mischievously, raising his blackjack.

"Aye, aye! We'll all drink to that!"

Jefferson reddened and withstood the banter with good grace. Nevertheless, he was relieved when the other three men finally took their leave.

"So, Thomas, you have made a conquest."

"Please Charles, I beg you, don't start."

"It's true. Listen, when she returns, look deeply into her eyes, and you will see for yourself."

Mary soon returned with a large covered serving dish, plates and utensils. This time, Thomas paid more attention to the girl. She was quick to see his change of attitude and returned his glances warmly, though with a degree of shyness which Jefferson found enchanting.

After she left, Thomas turned to his friend eagerly. "I believe you are right about Mary."

"Of course."

"She appears to be rather sensitive and shy."

"Not so. She may appear shy here in a public room, but when you get her off to yourself, you will probably find a different reaction altogether."

"Too often you astound me in the matter of your experience with the fair sex, Charles. I must confess I have as little experience with regard to this subject as you do with riding, perhaps less."

Charles burst into laughter. "I am not accustomed to hearing confessions from a grown man. But rest assured, Thomas, I am no expert where women are concerned."

"Come now, Charles, I and half of Williamsburg know that you enjoyed the favors of the notorious Mrs. Ashton last fall. Need I say more?"

At this juncture, Mary returned looking

more fetching than ever, and informed them that she would prepare a hot bath for each of them. Thomas thanked her courteously and they smiled into each other's eyes. Charles could have ceased to exist for all they knew.

"Tell me, how long have you known this girl?" Charles asked when they were alone again.

"We have been acquainted for several years now. When Mary's mother received her license to operate the inn in '64, I was still in attandance at William and Mary. It was then that I first met her. She was but fifteen, a sweet and lovely girl."

"Do you think you could care for her seriously?"

Thomas frowned. "Insofar as a lasting relationship is concerned, I fear not. I value her too highly, however, for a casual seduction."

"You are right about the last. I have my own thoughts about the first, Thomas. But tonight I am too weary to debate the advantages and disadvantages of class distinction. Let's make it an early night, shall we? I am looking forward to my bath."

Thomas sat back in his chair, replete. The punch had made him drowsy, and he, too, was looking forward to his bath. In spite of his words to Charles, he could not help being stirred by Mary. If she should come to his bed tonight...? No, it would never happen. What disturbed him the most was the realization that he wanted it to happen.

CHAPTER 15

Jenny's frustration mounted. Once again, she stood on the spot which she thought of as the doorway through time, and once again she had failed to return to the eighteenth century. Why? In the middle of the empty cornfield where her house once stood, she prayed to return to the past - her present.

It suddenly occurred to her that she had been lying down when it happened the first time. Maybe she would try to position herself exactly as she lay then, and see what happened. Once again, he effort was fruitless. Dear God, she thought, what am I going to do? I must get back to Charles, I cannot remain here alone! She jumped to her feet, and without warning, or conscious effort, it happened. The earth tilted, and she slipped down again, nauseous and trembling. Once again she blacked out.

Opening her eyes, she saw with relief that she was safely back in her own house, the vase in place on the mantel exactly as she had left it. The world had stopped spinning, and she felt quite normal. One thing was certain, she was not going to get near that vase for a while. If it needed to be moved, she would have Bea do it. The vase presumably held no adventures in store for Bea.

When she returned home, Bea was standing in the courtyard. "Wheah yo' been, Miz Jenny? We been lookin' all ovah for yo!"

"I can well imagine, Bea. Where is mother?"

"In her chamber."

"Good. I shall see her now. I know she will have worried about me."

Jenny lifted her skirts and started into the house. Halfway up the stairs she saw her mother's figure above her. She sighed deeply.

Anne's face was the picture of concern. "Jenny, my dear, where have you been? You look dreadful! Come child, come to my chamber and sit down."

"I am exhausted, mother. I suppose I did too much at the house."

"Will you have tea, darling?"

Jenny's eyes were falling shut. "No, thank you, later perhaps."

"I shall call you at four, then. Lie down and rest."

"Yes, mother." Jenny stumbled to her own room and fell across the bed like a lifeless rag doll. She was asleep instantaneously.

"Jenny! Jenny! Come, dear, it is time for supper. I didn't have the heart to wake you for tea. You were sleeping so soundly."

Jenny sat up and smoothed back her hair. "Mother? Oh, I had the most horrible dream."

"Tell me about it."

"Our new house had caught fire, and I couldn't get out. I was trapped upstairs, and Charles could not come for me because he was far, far away." She shuddered, remembering her feeling of panic and complete helplessness.

Anne put her arms around her daughter and held her close. "You have been under a tremendous strain, darling. A girl's wedding often precipitates such fears. Once Charles returns and you are happily settled, there will be no more nightmares, I warrant. Come down now, and eat. Surely the hot food will cheer you and help return you to normal."

174

"I am hungry." She rose and went over to her vanity to freshen herself with cologne and brush her hair.

"You must not overtax yourself in that house, Jenny. Bea was to carry all the heavy parcels and boxes. What exhausted you so?"

Jenny pinched her cheeks to add color. "Odd jobs, nothing in particular, mother."

Anne regarded her daughter thoughtfully. "I shall feel much relieved when Charles returns."

Jenny turned around and smiled at her. "And I, mother. I think you have diagnosed my ailment perfectly." They went down to supper arm-in-arm, in complete accord.

Later that evening the family gathered as usual in the parlor. Anne and Elizabeth sat with their embroidery while Jenny and her father were enjoying their second game of chess. Tobias was in excellent spirits because he was about to declare a checkmate.

"Mind your game, lass! I'll not have you dream it away like the first one."

"Dream it away? I nearly won!"

"Never, you weren't even close!"

Elizabeth looked up from her embroidery and addressed her mother eagerly. "I, for one, shall be glad when Aunt Caroline arrives. She promised to bring me some new pieces for the harpsichord, just published! Boston must be a wonderful town. I believe they have everything there!"

Anne laughed. "I believe they do, from what your aunt tells me. How good it will be to hear the latest news and have another woman in the house to converse with!" She gazed in mock reproach at her husband. "You, Tobias, are always so involved with your journals, I swear you are quite useless."

He looked up and winked facetiously. "With Caroline in the house, there will be an overabundance of conversation, of this you can be sure."

Jenny had extricated herself from her father's imminent checkmate while he was speaking and laughingly tweaked his nose. "Oh father, you love to have her here just as much as we do."

"Quite." His face fell when he saw the board. "How did you squeak out of that, lass?"

"I had a good teacher," she replied demurely.

Tobias turned to Anne. "You had better see to it that we've enough to eat when my sister comes. Eating's her favorite pasttime - after talking."

Elizabeth giggled and even Anne laughed at this. "Poor creature, and she your own sister. I shall be hard put to feed you both!"

"You cannot stint on the child's wedding

feast, woman."

"Never fear, Tobias, we will do well by Jenny and Charles."

"I wonder where he is just now," Jenny said wistfully.

"At Shadwell, no doubt, barring any delays on the road."

"I don't even want to think about that."

"You, lass, should be thinking of your wedding fripperies. I vow you'll make a pauper of me yet before you've done."

"I am to be married in mother's gown. It was her idea that I wear it, but I shall be sorry to see it cut down. It is magnificent."

"I remember it well. Your mother looked like an angel on our wedding day." He looked at his wife tenderly. They were still very much in love after all the years they had shared, and the death of their son the year before had drawn them even closer. Adam had been killed in a freak carriage accident, and the family had no sooner adjusted to the tragedy when Jenny arrived from Boston seriously ill with pneumonia. There had very nearly been another tragedy.

Jenny yawned. The game had been a stalemate, and she was ready for a breath of air. She excused herself and went out into the garden.

FRANCIS STREET

Jenny strolled across the rear courtyard toward the boxwood garden. She loved the smell of boxwoods. They somehow reminded her of Beulah's fresh coffee, a pungent smell she associated with the vigorous growth of the warm season. She continued along the brick pathway toward her favorite circular garden. There was much to think about tonight. Reaction from her day spent in the twentieth century was only beginning to make itself felt. She still had difficulty accepting it as reality.

She sat down on the bench where she and Charles had first declared their love, silently, last summer. She remembered with a thrill how he had run his hands through her long, black hair and her own passionate reaction. It was just such a night as this, she thought, the sky sparkling with stars and the half moon rising slowly above the eastern horizon. If only he could be with her tonight, but no, it wasn't to be.

Too agitated to remain seated, she wandered around the garden pondering the extraordinary events of the day. Her life could never be the same again, for all her eighteenth century dreams were now reduced to insignificance by the wonders she had experienced in the new age, two hundred years removed from all she had ever known. It was almost too much to bear, even though Charles had prepared her somewhat for the experience. She smiled, remembering the kind family who had spoken to her and reached into her apron pocket where she kept that precious memento, her "picture". It was a marvel. No artist could possibly reproduce such a likeness, and all in just one minute. She stared at it in the dim moonlight. The people of the twentieth century dressed most peculiarly; even the men exposed their legs in a most unseemly manner. As for the women, they seemed to think nothing of exposing the greater part of their bodies, yet kept their bosoms well covered. Why a woman's bosom was an asset to be admired and displayed as alluringly as possible! Jenny concluded that twentieth century people placed more emphasis on shapely legs. Why else would men as well as women be so cavalier about exposing them? Twentieth century women scarcely looked like women at all. Very few that she had seen wore dresses, and most of those who did were Foundation employees in eighteenth century costume. It must be very comfortable however, to dispense with stays. Obviously women of the future wore little or nothing beneath their outer clothing. This would be a distinct advantage in the Virginia heat. She wondered how she would look in those curious short pants. Reaching down, she pulled up her voluminous skirts to just above the knee. Not bad, she thought with a grin. Charles would not be ashamed of her should she ever have occasion to don twentieth century clothing.

Charles would look wonderful in such clothing, just like Scott. Jenny decided she didn't particularly care for men in ruffles and loose fitting pants now that she had seen the men of Charles' time. She didn't care much for stockings either, and giggled as she remembered Scott's hairy legs. It was exciting to see so much of a man's body, and oh, how good it was to see men without wigs! She had always thought them faintly ridiculous, even on formal occasions. The gentlemen always held themselves so stiffly, as though afraid they would fall off at the first sign of exertion. Thank heavens she wasn't required to wear one. And twentieth century women? So many of them wore very short hair - and the colors! Some were positively bizarre! She resolved never to cut or change her own hair in any way. She liked it just the way it was.

Her hand strayed toward her pocket and she drew out the picture once more. "What shall I do with this?" She whispered to herself. Certainly, no one must see it but Charles. Where could she hide it? Perhaps the best place would be in her new house. But no, Bea might find it on one of their decorating excursions. Distracted, she looked up and caught sight of the book bindery. Why, that would be perfect! She would put it under Charles' pillow in the loft where he slept with Billingsley and Watson. No one would ever find it there.

Jenny returned to the house and went straight to her mother's chamber and the elegant chinoiserie writing desk where he mother kept the household stationery. She pulled out an envelope and inserted the picture, sealed it, and raced down the stairs and into the sitting room.

"Mother, I must deliver something to Billingsley. Do you mind if I go there now?"

"Now, child? It's quite dark already."

"I know, but I won't be long."

"Can't it wait until morning?"

"I really want to deliver it tonight. It's a surprise for Charles. I want him to find it the minute he returns."

Her parents exchanged amused glances. Young love! "Well, be quick, darling."

"Oh I will. I shall return directly!"

Soon Jenny was standing below the rear window of the bindery loft. Placing one cupped hand to the side of her mouth, she called Billingsley's name.

There was no answer. She searched the ground for a small pebble and tossed it at the window. Her aim was bad, and the pebble rolled off the roof and back onto the ground. She selected a larger pebble and tossed it up. This time it went right through the open window and landed on the floor of the loft. In minutes, Billingsley's head appeared.

"Miss Jenny! Is that you?"

"Yes."

"What's amiss?"

"Billingsley! Please open the door, I need to come in!"

"In here? Now?"

"Yes, please hurry!"

"I'll be right down. Come around front."

The door opened and Billingsley bid her enter. "It's a good thing I was still up, Miss Jenny. I'd never have heard you otherwise, nor Watson. He sleeps like the dead."

Jenny smiled affectionately at the giant. "Were you reading again?"

"Yes, and I was just about to blow out the candle. We nearly jumped out of our breeches when that stone flew in!"

"I'm sorry I startled you." She gave him the envelope. "Will you place this under Charles' pillow? It's a surprise. I want him to find it immediately when he comes home."

"Certainly, Miss Jenny."

"Under no circumstances must you open it! It is for his eyes only. Will you promise me?"

Billingsley drew himself up to his full height, which was considerable. "You know you can trust me, Miss Jenny."

She took his hand and squeezed it. "Yes, of course. Thank you. Remember, place it under the pillow!"

"It will be done."

She gathered up her skirts and whirled away so quickly, Billingsley was almost tempted to believe she hadn't been there at all. Shrugging his massive shoulders, he turned and bolted the door. Then he climbed the narrow stairs to the loft and placed the envelope gently under Charles's pillow.

"Wot's 'at?" Watson had been in a fever of curiosity ever since Jenny's pebble had hit the floor beside his bed. "Can I see?"

"A love note from Miss Jenny to Mr. Charles most likely. And no, you may not see. 'Tis for Mr. Charles' eyes only," replied Billingsley to his slow-witted friend. "Come, douse that candle. It's been a long day."

Watson obeyed grudgingly. He would have loved to see the contents of that envelope, but alas, he couldn't read. With a sigh, he rolled over and snuggled down into a comfortable position. Aye, it had been a long day.

CHAPTER 16

"To return to the subject of your vast experience with women..."

"A vast exaggeration, as I already told you."

"Nevertheless, I wish to hear your philosophy. What, in your opinion, makes a man a great lover?"

Charles was momentarily at a loss. A long day in the saddle had taken its toll on him and the delicious meal he had just shared with Jefferson had engendered the desire to do nothing more vigorous than sleep the night away. But Mary was preparing baths for them, and Jefferson seemed eager to talk. How could the man pursue a serious discussion after all they had been through today? He sighed, ordered a pot of coffee, and addressed himself to the question.

"I presume you have a special reason for asking, Thomas?"

"Frankly, Charles, I have never discussed the subject of women with anyone in my life. After my father died, there was no other man who could, in any wise, replace him, or with whom I would have felt comfortable pursuing the subject. There was Professor Wythe, of course, but I esteemed him too highly to burden him with my insecurities in the matter."

"I suspected as much. How is it that learned men are given training and instruction in the arts, literature, science, mathematics, the classics etc. and yet, when it comes to the subject of relating to women in a meaningful way, men are fobbed off with half-truths, jests and hidebound aphorisms by the score?"

"You have put it very well Charles, I can certainly attest to the truth of your words."

"If one assumes that a woman is born to be loved - as I do - then men such as we, must do the loving, and men such as we, must develop the proper attitude." He paused to finish his coffee and pour another for himself and his friend.

"And that is...?"

"To give! Give of yourself generously and completely."

"I begin to see why you are so popular with the ladies." Thomas grinned facetiously.

"Well, one lady in particular, at least. Seriously, Thomas, we must not approach a woman in order to take, but rather to give to her, for there is no greater pleasure for a man than to make a woman happy, to strive for her pleasure first and foremost, and thereby gain his own. Believe me, there is no greater fulfillment."

Thomas pondered these words in silence while he drank the rich, freshly brewed coffee. "I appreciate what you say, Charles, but I fail to understand why our society has not yet recognized it. It appears so obvious."

"I suppose the answer lies in the fact that few learned men have actually experienced and accepted the secret. They are, for the most part, preoccupied. The women in their lives are all too often victims of an alliance intended to weld together great estates and beget heirs, or, in the case of the lower classes, provide brute labor and beget more of the same."

"You are, of course, absolutely correct in your assessment."

"And, I might add, prominent Virginia

186

families have no monopoly on this practice. Anne Coulter objected most strenuously to my courtship of her daughter. She was hoping for a well-connected son-in-law. It was only after Jenny's illness that her attitude was reversed."

"I remember it well, Charles. And there is no doubt that Jenny could have made a splendid match."

"None whatsoever. She received scores of proposals after the ball last year, some from very well-connected gentlemen indeed."

"I must confess, I feel most confoundedly attracted to young Mary, but as I explained, there is no hope for anything there. I wouldn't know how to approach her."

"Certainly not the way you approached Miss Burwell when you pursued that relationship."

Jefferson's face paled, and he looked at Charles reproachfully.

"Don't look at me that way, Thomas. You know it's true, you told me so yourself. After your failure to speak to her at the ball, you retreated to Shadwell and remained there for more than nine months until you received word of her engagement. Why do you suppose you remained in hiding all that time?"

"I daresay I was protecting myself from further rejection and embarrassment."

"Precisely. You were not thinking of giving to her, or at least, not in a generous way. You were thinking of your own embarrassment, fearing her rejection. This attitude was largely responsible for your failure as a suitor, do you see?"

"I have been aware for some time of my foolishness in that affair. I shall not repeat the mistake."

"Do not be too hard on yourself, Thomas. Sometimes it simply isn't meant to be, however generously you want to give."

"The situation was rather different with Rebecca, however. She was a woman I wished to marry. Though I would like to pursue a relationship with Mary, it would not have marriage as an end. Is this not a selfish attitude?"

"It would seem so, as you are only thinking of your own convenience. What would Mary desire from such a relationship? What would she expect? Is she genuinely in love? Are you? It is never simple, my friend. The answers are not written in a textbook."

"I am not a religious man, Charles, yet I try to live my life in a moral way, according to my own lights. As you say, it is not easy."

"Ah, there is Mrs. Wells. I believe the bath is ready. Will you go first, Thomas, or shall I?"

"You go, Charles. I"ll just finish my coffee."

"Right."

The water in the wooden tub was hot and felt as wonderful as Charles knew it would. He hadn't had a bath in more than a week, and after today's long ride, his muscles craved the benefit of the hydrotherapeutic heat. He had just made himself thoroughly comfortable when he heard a knock at the door. He had been expecting Jefferson, but it was Mary who entered bringing several large towels which she placed in a stack next to the tub.

"Will you require anything further, sir?"

"No, Mary, I think you have seen to everything."

"Very well, sir." She departed as quietly as she had come and Charles was once more free to relax. He put his head back against the edge of the tub and let his thoughts wander. When he caught himself dozing for the third time, he decided to get down to business. He scrubbed himself vigorously, rinsed, and vacated the tub. He was wrapping the towel around him when Thomas entered.

"You look quite refreshed, Charles."

"I nearly fell asleep. I'm all done in. Mary should soon be returning with fresh water for your bath, Thomas. I daresay she was disappointed to find me in here instead of you!"

"Mary was here?"

"Yes, she brought me some clean towels."

There was a faint knock, and Thomas and Charles both bid Mary enter. Charles was fastening his breeches and she blushed, her eyes moving quickly to Thomas.

"Will you be bathing tonight also, Thomas?" He nodded. "We shall be ready for you in ten minutes then."

"Thank you, Mary." Her eyes glowed at him in the candlelight and he felt the full force of her desire. Before he could move or say a word, she was gone.

Charles had not missed this interaction and now he saw with a sinking heart that Thomas had turned to him with an unspoken question.

"Don't ask me, Thomas. Only you know what is best for you, and for her."

He sighed. "I know only too well."

Charles put his hand on his friend's shoulder in a wordless salute. "I'm off to bed, Thomas. I really can't keep my eyes open."

"Good night then. Sleep well."

"And you."

Mary supervised as two young black boys filled the tub with fresh, hot water. Thomas had already begun to undress. After all the punch he had consumed, he was in a very relaxed state, and far less inhibited than usual. Thus, he had not even waited for Mary to vacate the room before he began to shed his clothes. He stepped into the tub and eased himself down. The heat of the water combined with the steam in the room relaxed him even more and he leaned back gratefully with closed eyes. Mary approached him from behind and began to massage his shoulders and neck, easing the tension in his stressed body.

"That feels wonderful, Mary. Please don't stop!"

"You just hush up and relax, Thomas."

"With pleasure."

He abandoned himself to the feeling while all sorts of erotic imaginings flitted through his mind. If only...

"Shall I go now? Will there be anything else I can do for you, Thomas?"

Her voice was so soft, it was nearly inaudible. The candles were burning down, some were already extinguished, and the steamy half-darkness was like a womb he had no wish to abandon. The two of them here, together, were somehow divorced from time and the cares of the world outside. How lovely she looked with her soft golden curls gleaming under her cap, and her red mouth curving into a smile just for him.

He took her hand...

To his disgust, Charles found he could not

sleep after all. After tossing back and forth in the unfamiliar bed for an hour, he dressed and went out. Thomas, he noticed, had not yet come in.

He stepped off the front porch and out on to the main street. Was it possible Thomas was still with Mary? Perhaps, though it seemed unlikely. Time would tell.

He walked down to the small wharf and was met by a combination of odors from the wet bulkhead and piers and from the river itself which was not unpleasant. The night air had cooled considerably and Charles found it refreshing. A large schooner was moored at the wharf and the crew was unloading her cargo. The dock was lit by cressets situated along the piers, their light reflected in waves in the water below. This was a small town, still in its infancy, yet it was destined to become the new capital of the colony, and eventually the state. Charles knew it would grow to become a major port on the James, but for now, in 1768, it was still just another quiet landing spot on the river, content to sleep and dream until destiny remembered and transformed it to comply with her eternal plan.

In this case, destiny was a handful of the landed gentry who would direct the growth of the town in direct proportion to their growing interest and success in land speculation. Thus the town grew as a means of protecting the investment of the wealthy and powerful few. After all, there was nothing particularly significant about the little town. It was just like hundreds of others nestled along the banks of any river.

Charles wondered why more small towns had not developed adjacent to the huge plantations along the James, just as small villages or hamlets adjacent to many of the large English manor houses throughout the British Isles had developed and continued to grow. It could be argued that the practice of slavery was responsible for this, Charles thought. Since the work force in the Virginia colony was largely composed of slaves who couldn't own land, or build their own homes, opportunities for town growth and development were restricted to the minority of wealthy landowners. And since many of the gentry practiced law, like his friend Jefferson, and served in the General Assembly, most of the land transactions and estate auctions were controlled by the same aristocratic few. The system must be riddled with corruption, he thought disgustedly. As long as taxes and duties are paid to the crown, the governor is content, and all is well with the colonial community.

After nearly an hour, Charles returned to

the tavern. As he climbed the front porch steps, and turned around at the top step to see the landing once more, he was suddenly overcome by an attack of dizziness and vertigo. It was the same as the attack of the previous week. Carefully, Charles stumbled over to one of the nearby chairs and sat with his eyes closed. Everything whirled around in his head which throbbed with pain. He was frightened by this second episode of symptoms. It was exactly like the experience on the dig site, and this time it was more severe, like his last day in the twentieth century. He wondered if he wasn't about to faint and wake up in some other time, perhaps his own time back in the future.

After sitting still for a short while, the symptoms began to subside and Charles was reasonably certain that he wasn't about to travel off to another time. He took a few deep breaths and tried to gain control of himself for he felt exhausted as though he'd just completed a marathon race on a hot summer day. He was sweating profusely and his pulse was racing. Now he thought he'd never get to sleep. He was totally bewildered by this event. What did it all mean? Two episodes within a week really had him worried that something was amiss. What on earth could be happening?

Charles returned to his room to find Thomas

still out. Too tired to speculate about his friend's whereabouts, he climbed in and pulled the covers up to his chin. His last conscious thought was of Jenny.

CHAPTER 17

Charles had no idea how far they had travelled, but he was painfully aware that they had already been in the saddle for better than eight hours on this, the second day of their trip. His lower back and thighs still ached from yesterday's prolonged exercise, and by now, he felt as though the entire lower half of his body was on fire. Though it was only about four o'clock in the afternoon by his reckoning, with plenty of daylight remaining, he had had enough.

"Thomas, I don't know about you, but I have

got to get off this confounded horse!"

Jefferson grinned. "What, already?" This was met with such a fierce scowl that he hastened to add, "We shall soon arrive at Dawson's Ferry Tavern. It won't be long, now."

"Thank heaven for that."

For most of the afternoon, signs of human habitation had grown fewer and fewer. Most of the land consisted of undisturbed, seemingly primeval forest. Wild life was prolific, and the travellers saw plenty of deer, all kinds of fowl, coons, rabbits, beaver and muskrats. The most significant change was in the general topography. During most of the day, Charles watched the coastal plains change into picturesque rolling hills dominated by many species of hardwoods instead of the typical coastal pines. They were approaching the Blue Ridge now, and the wild beauty of the scenery was breathtaking.

"Thomas, what are the chances that we might meet Indians on this stretch of the trail?"

"That is difficult to say. My friend, John Walker, is going to the western reaches of the colony to administer an Indian treaty within the fortnight. I have heard that small bands of young renegades have attacked settlements west of the Green Mountains recently, but I have not been informed of any incidents in this immediate area."

"That is reassuring."

"Do not misunderstand me. That is not to say that we may not encounter them, only that it is highly unlikely. These savages are unpredictable at best."

"What do you know of them?"

"What I know is mostly the result of stories my father and his friends told me when I was a young lad. There was, however, one encounter which I personally experienced at the age of thirteen. My father and a friend took me hunting up Doils Creek to the headwaters of the Rivanna River at the foot of the Appalachian Mountains. We were in pursuit of that elusive creature, the turkey, just prior to the Christmas season."

"Go on." Charles leaned forward in the saddle, listening intently. Here was one experience of Jefferson's he had never dreamed of, let alone read about in a history book.

"The excursion was rather successful - we shot no less than four turkeys. My father was no mean shot. On our way home, we were set upon by a small band of Indian hunters. I was terrified, but curiously enough, I learned something about Indians that morning. They arrived in our camp at daybreak. My father's friend, Mr. Frye, was able to speak their tongue and so served as an interpreter for my father."

"What happened? Were you threatened?"

"I do not know to what extent we were in actual danger, but my father made them a gift of the four turkeys in exchange for our continued safe conduct. I believe the savages were rather impressed with our hunting skills. In fact, our freedom was probably due, in part, to their respect for my father's prowess."

"And what of your holiday turkey?"

"After the Indians had gone, we shot two more turkeys on our way home. Make no mistake, Charles, my terror on this occasion was abject. In fact, I thoroughly disgraced myself by losing control of my bladder. I shall never forget my shame at behaving in so cowardly a manner. Fortunately, my father did not tax me with it."

"And what was it you learned about Indians on this occasion, Thomas?"

"The natural law of respect for a man's achievement. It was that which bought our freedom. Those Indians could very easily have killed us, or taken us captive. Instead, we were treated with respect, even though we were intruding on Indian territory, or so they claimed. It was a sobering experience, Charles."

"I should think so. Pray God we have no such experience on this trip."

"I doubt it. Ah, here we are. I know you will be glad of the respite!"

Just ahead Charles could see a rather

primitive clapboard two-story building with a brightly painted sign reading "Dawson's Tavern".

"How is this place, Thomas?"

"There is good food and drink and fair lodging. I cannot complain, for I must admit that I am usually too weary after the day's ride to expect much more."

"As long as the food is plentiful and hot, and the bed soft. I'll not complain either, my friend."

"You can be assured of hot, plentiful food, but as for the bed, well, you shall be the judge. I must admit that one's animals receive the best of care at Dawson's."

Charles stared at the building as they dismounted. It was an unpretentious place with no trimmings, and only a small front porch similar to Chowning's in Williamsburg. He leaned back and stretched his aching muscles. "Oh God, I don't know how you do it, Thomas."

"What is that?"

"Riding. It's so damned uncomfortable."

"I have been riding this distance for more than six years. I have become accustomed to it. Perhaps you should ride more frequently, Charles. Your muscles would soon adapt, and you might become quite fond of the sport in time."

"I suppose you are right."

"One never knows when long distance travel will become necessary. It is an important skill."

"I am beginning to see that. But I dread the return trip to Williamsburg."

Jefferson scanned the horizon with a practiced eye. "I should add that the weather conditions may become a factor to consider."

"We have had beautiful weather these past two days."

"Yes, and I hope the weather holds for tomorrow so that you may see the Green Mountains in the morning sunlight. It is a sight which never fails to enchant."

"Don't be too concerned. This high pressure system should hold for several more days."

They made their way slowly, and in Charles' case, somewhat stiffly into the little tavern which closely resembled their last lodging place in Richmond. It was snug and functional, but crude. In the taproom they placed their orders with a tall, plain-featured young woman whose charming smile bid them welcome.

"Now Charles, please explain. What is this 'high-pressure system' you spoke of some time ago?"

Damn, thought Charles. I let down my guard and what happens? Thomas was looking at him intently, an avid, questioning expression on his face. Oh well, he shrugged mentally, maybe I can finesse it.

"I shall try to answer your question. But

bear in mind, I am no expert. As you probably already know, large masses of air travel under the influence of the prevailing westerly winds, from west to east. The air pressure can be defined in terms of relative pressure. Some are higher pressure; usually cooler, dryer air with clear blue skies. A lower pressure air mass on the other hand, is generally associated with moisture and rain or precipitation of some kind." He watched Thomas' face carefully as he spoke, but his friend appeared enthralled.

"Please, go on, Charles."

"The circulation of air around a high pressure system moves in a clockwise direction. The flow of air around a low-pressure system, however, moves in a counter clockwise direction. In this way, it is possible to follow the progress of a system as it passes over Virginia."

"Fascinating. Now, how would one explain the current weather conditions?"

Their punch arrived and they swallowed their first draught thirstily. Charles poured another measure for both of them and addressed himself to Jefferson's question.

"Remember last week's rain?"

"Yes, indeed. It continued for two days."

"In that case a low pressure system with a trailing cold front moved across the area very slowly. Sometimes these fronts pass through much more quickly and produce nothing more than evening showers or overnight rains. Now, these past two days we have been under the influence of a strong high pressure system. If you will recall, on Thursday it was fairly cool with strong northwest winds."

"Yes."

"Then on Friday, the winds subsided and it became a little warmer. By last Saturday the temperature was approaching 80 degrees, and the winds began to blow from the southwest, as they are today. The wind direction can tell us where the center of the high pressure system is generally located, and approximately how long it will continue to dominate our weather."

Charles paused, but Thomas was eager to learn more. He was totally engrossed in the subject, and his face glowed with enthusiasm.

"The clockwise winds around a high first come in from the northwest, bringing in the cooler, dryer air as we enjoyed last Thursday. At that point, the center of the high was to our west. As the center of the clockwise flowing air mass approaches us, the winds continue to diminish until the center is directly over Virginia, and then the winds are usually calm for a day or so. As the center moves east, the winds come from the southwest bringing warmer air. Eventually, the moisture-laden air brings with it the possibility of more rain, and a low pressure system may develop and repeat the whole cycle again. I must admit that there are numerous variations on this theme, and prediction and calculation can be difficult or impossible at times."

"Please continue."

"I must mention that local factors have a great influence on weather conditions."

"What factors are those?"

"Well, land or water, the topography, even the use of the land can cause air currents and flows which may affect cloud formation. It becomes rather complicated when one considers regional versus local influences."

"Yes, I understand that much."

"Let me say that, for our purposes, we can at least have a good idea of what to expect provided one of the unusual variations doesn't interfere."

"If I understand correctly, we are still under the influence of high pressure which must be to the east of us..."

"Yes, that is quite right."

"...consequently, we have warm winds from the southwest."

"Yes, bringing in moisture..."

"...and setting up the next cycle."

"Perfect assessment! Now, let us take it one step further."

"Pray continue."

"This is our fourth day of southwest winds, and I do not see any build-up of cirrus clouds or horse tails, as they are sometimes referred to. Therefore, I do not expect any precipitation tomorrow. At least, it is highly unlikely."

"I agree with your forecast."

"Right. Now, let us agree to eat. I am famished, and if I consume any more of this punch, you will be carrying me off to bed, senseless."

When the food arrived, they set to with hearty appetites. Charles loved the taste of meat cooked in the eighteenth century style, that is, char-broiled, then cooked in liquid dishes such as soups and stews. This practice lent an indescribable richness to the dishes as did the freshly ground seasonings with which they were laced.

They had not quite finished supper when Charles heard a familiar voice in the entry hall and glanced up eagerly.

"Ian MacClellan, so it is you! Come and join us if you've time!" He turned to Thomas and explained, "This is our new post rider."

The brawny Scot greeted them cordially, his face wreathed in smiles at seeing a familiar face so far from the capital. "Aye, I've time enough and I'll join ye with pleasure. A nice warm supper'll nae come amiss."

Charles introduced him to Thomas and they

exchanged pleasantries as Ian settled down to eat his supper. But he had barely taken two bites of his cornmeal muffin before the other two inundated him with requests for news.

"Waters' plantation burned to the ground last week. 'Tis said there's nae a board remainin', only a pile of bricks to show for it." He shook his head sadly.

"How did it start?" asked Charles.

"Word has it that the master was smokin' and fell fast asleep in his chair. Fortunately, no one was injured."

"Fortunate indeed!" exclaimed Jefferson. "I venture to say that fire is one of the most feared disasters to be visited on man, along with the devastation of draught and similar natural catastrophies. Any of these can ruin a man overnight."

Charles glanced at him with sympathy, recalling that in about two years fire would level his mother's plantation, that same Shadwell that they were about to visit, and destroy Thomas' most valued possessions - his 3,000 volume library.

"A cousin of mine lost a cabin in the Green Mountains last year during a dry spell," Thomas continued. "It was dreadful. They lost everything. My mother was kind enough to provide them the necessary funds to rebuild."

"'Tis a fine thing to do, if ye can afford

it." MacClellan pushed his empty plate away and lit his long clay pipe. "If ye don't mind my askin', where are ye bound?"

"I am accompanying Thomas to his home, Shadwell, on the Rivanna River. Do you know it?"

"Aye. 'Tis at the foot of the Green Mountains is it not?"

"Yes."

"I deliver the post in that part of the country frequently. 'Tis a bonnie stretch of hills and dales, to be sure."

Jefferson smiled at the description. "I find it so."

The candles were burning low, casting long shadows on the rough-hewn walls. Charles tried unsuccessfully to stifle a yawn, and before long, his complaint became contagious. He and Thomas agreed to make an early night of it and set out at dawn. Ian, it seemed, was to return to Richmond the next morning, and Charles scrawled a loving message to Jenny which the post rider swore to deliver the moment he arrived in the colonial capital.

When they were finally alone in their chamber and resting as comfortably as the lumpy rope beds would permit, Charles steeled himself to ask the question which had plagued him all day.

"Thomas, ah, I trust you enjoyed your bath

last evening?"

Thomas smiled to himself in the darkness. It was all too obvious what his friend wanted to know. He decided to have some fun. "Quite," he replied noncommittally.

"I must have been asleep when you returned to our room."

"Yes, you were quite soundly asleep."

Charles had had enough. "Dammit man, you know what I'm asking. If you don't wish to tell me, so be it, I will respect your privacy."

Thomas yelped with laughter. "I am sorry, Charles, I couldn't resist. It's not very often I have you at a disadvantage. As for last night it was all a man could wish for, and more. You were right, and I am happy to say that I took your advice."

"So, that accounts for the happy glow on your face all day. I am happy for you, and Mary too."

"I owe you a debt of gratitude for your kind assistance in this matter, my friend. I shall take your words under advisement in all future relationships as well. I can now understand why the beautiful Jenny is so completely committed to you."

"Thank you for that, Thomas. But does the delightful Miss Mary understand the terms of such a relationship? Will she be content to see you only infrequently in the future?"

Jefferson sighed. "There can be no future for us, Charles. Mary is to be married next month to a man for whom she feels little or no affection. Perhaps our coming together was in somewise a rebellion on her part. Do you understand now?"

"Yes, I believe I do. She wanted to feel loved for the first and perhaps last time before being committed to a barren marriage. With you she experienced a joy she will never forget. As for you, you must search elsewhere for your great love."

"That is true, but now I shall search with more confidence." He turned over and plumped up his pillow. "Let us rest now, so we will be fresh for the journey. With luck, we should arrive at Shadwell before noon."

CHAPTER 18

Jenny lay restlessly in bed, unable to sleep. Since Charles had gone, she had not had one peaceful minute. When she was able to sleep, nightmares haunted her, and when she was awake, terrible premonitions invaded her consciousness. She had absolutely no idea what the trouble would be, but she was convinced of the inevitability of it.

It had been five days now since she had stumbled into the future, and in the nightmares that followed, she and Charles were invariably separated - forever. The dream was always the same: a vision of Charles fading away into dense fog until he was out of sight, then dead silence. She was left standing alone in that terrifying, suffocating mist. Over and over again she tried to penetrate the significance of the nightmare, but the only logical conclusion was that Charles would eventually be lost to her. Now she lay in a tangle of sweaty sheets, too afraid to sleep. Her heart hammered in anticipation of the dreaded nightmare.

She threw off the clammy sheets and sprang to her feet. After donning her long nightgown and mules, she made her way downstairs and found that her father was still sitting up reading in the parlor. She approached him eagerly.

"My God, you gave me quite a start, child." He dropped his journal and stared at her, noting her dishevelment and the anxious expression in her shadowed eyes. "What is troubling you, Jenny?"

She sighed in frustration. "I cannot sleep. This past hour has been a misery."

"Come, talk to me, child. What is it that upsets you so?"

"Oh, everything!"

"Everything? Surely, it cannot be that bad!"

She sat down on the floor with her arms around her knees and folded her long nightgown over them. "On the contrary, since Charles has gone, I continue to dream that I have lost him forever, and I am helpless to stop it!"

"Aha. I thought it might be something of the kind. My dear, you needn't fear that Charles will desert you. I know him too well. He loves you with all his soul."

"It isn't that he will desert me, father. I know he wouldn't do that. But there is some...some power which draws him away against his will, and against which he can do nothing! It is as though fate is determined to separate us."

Tobias lit his pipe and drew on it gently. "Now, let me tell you something about your Charles, my dear. This is no ordinary man. I have known for a long time that he possesses extraordinary qualities. I have no knowledge of his destiny, nor his background, but I can tell this much: wherever he goes and whatever he undertakes, he will be successful. He will accomplish his goals, of this I am certain, and you are a permanent part of his future."

"But how can you be so confident?" She looked up at him for reassurance, amazed at his perception. Fleetingly, she wondered how it would be if she and Charles should disappear into the future together, leaving him behind. Could she do it, knowing how he would suffer? Was she willing to trade one love for another?

"I am convinced that Charles Dalton has come here for you, that you are the sole reason for his sojourn here in Williamsburg. It may sound absurd, nevertheless, I become more convinced of it as time goes on."

She took his hand and pressed it to her cheek. "Yes, father, I believe it too. From the moment our eyes first met, I knew he was the man I had been waiting for. But...suppose Charles' destiny takes him far from Virginia?"

"Why, then you will go with him, child."

"But suppose we were never to return?"

"You must do what you must do. Your happiness will depend on being with Charles."

"But..."

"Let there be no mistake about this. He is your life, your future. Now let us not hear any more about it."

"I would miss you so dreadfully, and mother..."

"Try to see it this way, my dear. One day you shall be without me in any case, no matter whether you remain here in Williamsburg. No, you cannot plan your young life around your mother and me. So long as you are happy, we will be happy and at peace."

Tears lingered on her sooty lashes as she considered the significance of his words. With a swift, graceful motion she stood and embraced him. Her heart was too full for words, but he understood that she was groping for her own peace, and that it would be difficult to find.

"Will you sleep now, my dear?"

"I shall try, father. Thank you."

"Good night, child."

"Good night."

That afternoon Coulter closed up shop early. The paper was running on schedule, and he showed his appreciation by allowing his men an hour of unexpected freedom.

He entered his house through the back door, startling Anne who was unaccustomed to seeing him at such an early hour. "Tobias! Is something amiss?" She looked at him with tender concern.

"Not at all, my dear." He grabbed her small waist and planted a firm kiss on her mouth. "In point of fact, I have letters here for you and Jenny. They arrived just this afternoon." He handed them to Anne.

She examined the postmark curiously. "It's from Boston!"

"Caroline, no doubt."

"It appears to be her handwriting."

"Where is Jenny?"

"She has gone down to the new house. In fact, she should be here by now, it's nearly teatime."

"I shall walk down and see what is keeping her. I have no inkling what she does when she is in that house."

"I should like to know that myself.
although, as I recall, she has not been there
for nearly a week." As he started out of the
room, Anne took his arm. "Tobias, have you
observed any change in Jenny's demeanor this
past week or so?"

He paused. "Yes, I have. I should mention
that she came to me late last night, unable to
sleep. She has been suffering from recurrent
nightmares about losing Charles. The poor child
was greatly disturbed."

Anne bit her lip in dismay. "She told me
nothing of this. But she has been looking quite
pale of late. I had begun to fear a summer
fever."

"We had better keep a close watch on her
until Charles returns. She is quite capable of
making herself ill with worry. Well, I'm off. I
shall return directly."

"Please do not delay. We shall dine upon
your return."

"Hmmm." He barely heard her, so busy was he
groping about in his pockets.

"What on earth are you doing?"

"I can't find my blasted pipe," he mumbled.

Anne burst into laughter. "It's in your
mouth!"

"What? Oh...blast if it isn't." He wiped
the foolish grin from his face. "I seem to be

doing this more often of late. Ah well, it must
be old age, my dear."

Anne shooed him out the door. "Be off with
you, Tobias, and mind, don't be late!"

Coulter opened the front door of the new
house quietly. Stepping into the central
hallway, he glanced into the sitting room and
was amazed to see the figure of his daughter
sprawled out on the floor before the fireplace,
apparently sound asleep. She had rolled up her
apron and was using it as a pillow. He elected
not to wake her, remembering her insomnia the
night before. Rest was exactly what she needed.
He entered the room silently, and seeing that he
had not aroused her, he sat down on a storage
carton and looked around the room in an idle
attempt to find just what it was that attracted
her to the place so often and encouraged her to
stay so long. Nothing arrested his attention
until he spotted the Chinese vase on the
mantelpiece. He stared at it in puzzlement for
some time. He had really never given it much
consideration when it had reposed in Jenny's
chamber. But now, for some inexplicable reason,
it held a curious fascination for him. Seeing
that Jenny still lay in peaceful slumber, he
walked over to the fireplace and gently picked
it up. He studied it for some time, admiring its
intricate brushstrokes and the fineness of the

porcelain. He knew it was very old and that there was some superstition attached to it; exactly what, he didn't know, arrant nonsense to be sure. At length, he placed it carefully back onto the mantel and turned toward his daughter. It was growing late, and she would have to be awakened for supper.

Suddenly the room began to spin, and Tobias clutched at the mantel for support, but he was already too far away to grasp it. He felt himself fall to the floor beside Jenny, too weak to stand. Someone was calling to him from a distance, who was it? He was rapidly losing consciousness, the black spots which danced in front of his eyes were merging into a wall of darkness. He was going...

"Father! Oh my dear God, father! Come back!" Jenny was awakened by the commotion and knew at once what he had done. She held his head and slapped at his cheek firmly as she had once seen her mother do with one of the slaves who had become hysterical. She didn't know what else to do. Tobias remained senseless, and in desperation she began to shake him. "Father, please come back, don't leave me! Father!" Then, to her horror, she saw his body begin to fade and disappear, inch by inch. Beside herself now, she continued to shake him, screaming, "You can't go, you are not ready! Father, come back!"

Jenny closed her eyes in an agony of despair, and when she opened them again she saw that the process had unaccountably begun to reverse itself. Her father's bodily form materialized slowly until it regained its normal shape, and soon he opened his eyes and looked up at her in amazement.

She was watching him with horror in her eyes, her hand pressed against her mouth as though stifling a scream. He propped himself up on one elbow and asked weakly, "What happened?"

"I...I'm not certain," she stammered. "I awakened just as you were falling to the floor. You...must have been taken ill."

He sat up slowly and wiped the moisture from his forehead with his sleeve. "It is most peculiar. I was admiring your vase, there on the mantel," he motioned weakly toward it, "and then, when I turned to wake you, I...became quite dizzy, and queasy. I couldn't stand up...Jenny, what is going on here?"

She averted her eyes from his probing gaze. "You collapsed, father. We must call for a doctor, I fear you are ill."

"No, no, I am much restored. It was only a momentary thing."

"Perhaps you simply need rest. You have been keeping late hours..."

"It isn't that. There is something curious about this place, Jenny. I can sense it."

Jenny gathered all her resources in an attempt to sound normal. "Nonsense, father. I suspect we are both in need of a good meal, and a hearty glass of port. Come, let us get home, mother will be worried."

He struggled to his feet with her assistance. "Very well, child. But don't think to diddle me with red herrings. I shall keep a close watch on you hereafter."

As they walked along Nicholson Street, he peered at her shrewdly. "You lack color still, Jenny. Tell me now, what is it that you do in that house all alone for so many hours?"

"Oh, I don't know, think mostly."

"Only that?" He smiled. "And what do you think about, pray?"

"I think about my life with Charles, and what a house of my own means to me. I think about children, and what I shall name them, supposing I survive childbirth."

He frowned, and grasped her arm forcefully. "You are not to dwell on such things. It isn't healthy."

"I am merely being realistic. So many girls my age have succumbed, why should I be different?"

"Humph. I'll wager there is something, or someone else who commands a greater portion of your thoughts, is it not so?"

"Of course. You know I think of Charles

constantly."

"Charles, yes...that reminds me. There is a letter for you at home from Charles. Ian brought it in just this afternoon."

When they got home, Jenny's first action was to open the letter. It didn't tell her much, as Charles had not yet arrived at Shadwell, but at least she was reassured that he was well and in good spirits. More importantly, it reminded her that he loved her, and missed her as much as she missed him.

"Oh father, how could I have let him go away for such a long time?"

"Well, 'tis done, and there's no use crying over it now, child. Besides, he'll soon be returning. Come now, your mother is waiting, and Elizabeth." Before they entered the dining room, he took her arm and bent over to whisper softly in her ear, "I needn't tell you that what happened in the new house is to remain between the two of us. I've no wish to worry your mother. Promise me?"

She smiled reassuringly at him. "I promise." She would never breathe a word to anyone. Only Charles must know, and pray God he could tell her how to extricate herself from this coil which grew increasingly complex. Charles, Charles!

CHAPTER 19

"Mountains, Thomas!"

Jefferson looked up with a soft sigh. "At last! We are nearly there, Charles. It is beautiful country, is it not? You'll find plenty of wildlife and game for the table. The land is wild, and the soil rich."

Charles observed the gradual elevation of the land above sea level as they travelled further west. The Rivanna, which came into view regularly as they advanced along its flood plain, became smaller and more manageable for

221

crossing. No longer were there wide areas of wetland adjacent to the stream tributaries of the James, as was the case in the coastal flat lands east of Richmond. Here in the west, the land rose quickly out of stream beds and off river flood plains. As they approached the Green Mountains, wetlands became more and more scarce, and travel became easier, at least from the standpoint of crossing waterways.

Charles tried not to remember that Interstate 64 would have reduced this two-and-a half day trip to a mere two-and-a-half hours. It was all relative, he mused. Thomas would probably not appreciate modern modes of travel. He had been riding all his life, and in spite of the discomforts associated with such travel, he would probably prefer its slower pace to that of a car barrelling down the highway at 65 miles an hour. Thank heaven he would never have to deal with such a change; he would have problems enough in the next fifty or sixty years! It exhausted Charles merely to think about the vicissitudes of Jefferson's life. This extraordinary man would rebuild and change Monticello more than once; he was destined to become a widower at a fairly young age and never remarry, though he would eventually find a lasting love; he would serve his country loyally as minister to France, Secratary of State, and later as President, but would never find complete fulfillment away from his beloved home in the Virginia mountains.

"There is the gap in the mountain, and Shadwell is but a short distance ahead," Thomas observed. Charles could detect the suppressed excitement in this brief statement and knew that his friend was once more in his element. He pointed out to Charles several small farms along their route, and it was obvious that he knew everyone in the area.

Soon they came to a bend in the Rivanna at the foot of the eastern slopes of the Green Mountains and Thomas pointed. "There it is, Shadwell!"

To Charles' surprise, the house was a rather modest two-story white frame dwelling. Although he found it unpretentious, the house possessed a certain charm not unlike many of the restored buildings in Williamsburg. A young black boy greeted them at the front entrance to take their horses. Jefferson was met with squeals of delight from a pair of lanky youngsters, twin boy and girl, with Jefferson's red hair and freckles. "Thomas! Thomas!"

Jefferson dismounted hastily and took them into his arms. "And how are my dear twins? Have you missed me as much as all that?" He hugged them warmly.

Charles dismounted and stood by patiently, unwilling to intrude on the pleasant domestic scene.

"Charles! Come meet my twins!" Turning to the boy, he introduced him as his brother Randolph. "And this charming young lady is my sister Anna Scott."

Charles smiled at them and acknowledged the introduction. Jefferson had already turned to greet a slender young woman who emerged from the open door. "Lucy! Come meet my friend Charles!"

Lucy was a dark-haired, serious person with intelligent eyes and a mobile mouth which turned sharply upward at the sight of Charles. "So, the conquering heroes return!" Her light tone belied the envy in her eyes. "I am most pleased to meet you at last, Mr. Dalton!"

"You know my name?"

She laughed in earnest now. "But of course! Thomas speaks of you all the time."

"I am truly happy to make your acquaintance, Miss Jefferson."

"What, no greeting for me, dear sister?" Thomas put in. She flew into his arms. "I'm so glad you have returned, Thomas. Things are always dull here without you."

"How is mother?"

"Engaged in vital conference with the overseer. Mother takes her duties very

224

seriously, as you well know."

"Ah, yes, I do know."

Charles thought he detected weary resignation, even a hint of bitterness in his friend's tone. But this was short-lived. Jefferson quickly took his arm and Lucy's and led them into the house after the twins who were busily regaling their brother with news of their latest musical accomplishments.

Though Charles had met Mrs. Jefferson briefly earlier in the day, the supper meal afforded him the opportunity to observe her more closely. He was most curious about who she was, and what kind of relationship she maintained with her twenty-five year old son who would help shape a new nation and preside over it's young government.

Charles observed that she kept a handsomely appointed house. Much of the furniture appeared quite old, but it was well cared for, and while it was not the least bit extravagant, it did seem to suit the house very well. He was particularly fond of the Queen Anne dining room suite with hand carved scrolled legs and ball and claw feet, all superbly crafted in solid walnut.

225

After two days at Shadwell, Charles became rather disenchanted with the slow pace of life, and began to long for Williamsburg. By now, he readily admitted to himself that he regretted leaving Jenny for so long. He planned to remain with Thomas a few more days, however, before returning. The anticipation of that grueling two-and-a-half day journey on horseback held little charm, but he would endure it gladly this time because Jenny would be waiting for him.

He was walking through Mrs. Jefferson's gardens on a particularly bright and sunny late morning in mid-June when Thomas accosted him with a lovely young woman in tow.

"Charles, I wish you to meet someone. This is Betsey Walker, the wife of my close friend and neighbor, John Walker. Betsey already knows much about you, Charles, and she is eager to make your acquaintance."

Charles bowed slightly and murmured his pleasure. "Your servant, Mrs. Walker."

"Please, address me by my first name. We don't stand on ceremony here. I presume I may call you Charles?"

"Of course, please do." He was somewhat taken aback by her lack of feminine reticence and studied her more closely. Betsey Walker was not a beauty according to the standard of the day, but she possessed a rare charm and animation which was most attractive. In her smile was a sensuality which reached out and touched a man, drawing him to her like a powerful magnet. Now that he had met Betsey, Charles could easily understand Jefferson's infatuation.

"Betsey will be staying at Shadwell until her husband returns. He is currently at Fort Stanwix with General Lewis and the Virginia commission who are negotiating a treaty with the Indians," Thomas explained.

"Ah yes, I remember you mentioned something of the kind. How long will it be until the treaty is concluded?"

"It could be a matter of two or three more months. We have received no intelligence from John of late." Betsey's soft voice betrayed her concern.

"Post from the western territories is sporadic at best, and long delays are not necessarily a bad sign," Charles said softly. He could sympathize with her, for after only one week, he missed Jenny dreadfully. "Surely, Thomas and his mother have provided for your every comfort. I understand that you have a young daughter?"

"Yes, she is still an infant, and Thomas' mother has kindly arranged for a wet nurse. The child is growing at a prodigious rate; I vow John will not know her upon his return." She flashed a brief smile at Thomas as she spoke and he returned it warmly.

Charles watched this interplay with dismay. Though Thomas had already confessed his hopeless attraction to Betsey Walker, Charles had not regarded it as the prelude to a serious affair. Now he was not so sure. A great deal depended on Betsey herself. How strong were her feelings for her absent husband? Three or four months was a long time for a new bride to be left alone, especially one with Betsey's sensuality. Would a sense of abandonment, or mere pique be enough to lure her into Jefferson's arms? It was difficult to tell, but the conditions were certainly ripe for it.

Later that afternoon, Charles accompanied Jefferson into one of the back rooms of the first floor where he kept his vast library. Walls of shelves housed many hundreds of neatly cataloged leather-bound volumes on a myriad of subjects. There were books on law, mathematics, gardening, painting, history, philosophy and natural history in addition to the classics and a large collection of English literature including works by Shakespeare, Milton, Dryden, Chaucer, Pope, Smollett, Sterne, Richardson and Prior. Hume's 'History of England' was there, as Charles knew to his discomfiture. This was one of the works

Jefferson had recommended he read last fall, but Charles had found it heavy going, and finally abandoned it altogether. So far, Jefferson was unaware of his failure, and Charles had no wish to remind him of it.

In front of one of the windows stood a long table on which were scattered architectural drawings and drafting implements. The drawings were done with remarkable precision, and it was obvious that the master of Shadwell devoted a great deal of time and thought to them.

"This is remarkable, Thomas. How many volumes have you altogether?"

"Some 2500, I believe, and I have read nearly all of them."

"Where do you find the time to study as you do, maintain a law practice and still oversee the plantation?"

Jefferson chuckled. "In truth, I have very little to do with mother's planting operation. She has an excellent staff and has, since my father's unfortunate demise, managed quite independently. She needs no assistance from me; consequently, I am free to pursue my reading and the practice of law."

"Speaking of which, how is the practice coming along?"

"Actually, there is more work than I can attend to; however, many of my clients cannot afford my fees which, I might add, are quite modest by most standards. In fact, I have been unable to provide my mother with the degree of financial assistance I had hoped, hence my decision to establish an office in Williamsburg. Professor Wythe assures me that the practice is needed in town and that the clientele will be capable of paying my fees. Our friend Mr. Henry has encountered similar problems with accounts, and he, too, professes to find a healthy climate in Williamsburg."

"It sounds to me as though you have made a sound decision. It makes good business sense to provide your services where payment is most likely to be forthcoming. When will you come to Williamsburg?"

"My presence here is not pressing, and I have begun clearing the home site for Monticello; there is no reason I cannot come to Williamsburg by late summer. Professor Wythe is even now searching for a suitable location for my office, and I shall be ready to depart upon receiving word from him."

"This is good news indeed." Charles wandered over to the drawing board against the wall in front of the window which overlooked the Rivanna River and the little mountain on which Thomas would build his glorious mansion. "I see you have the Palladio collection."

"You are familiar with these volumes?"

"I know of them. I have never studied them

in depth." He picked up one of the volumes and perused the title page, 'Palladio's Four Books of Architecture', Leoni's edition, 1742. He closed it gently and picked up another volume entitled 'Select Architecture' by Robert Morris. Yet another book which bore the title "Rules for Drawing the Several Parts of Architecture' by James Gibbs, lay alongside the others. "I had nearly forgotten that you were one of the finer architects of your day," mused Charles. He was thinking aloud and his voice was barely audible, but Jefferson caught it and looked up in surprise.

"Why do you speak in the past tense, Charles? You frighten me at times, most particularly when you take on the aspect of seer."

"Oh, forgive me, I...uh...was lost in thought. Please pay no attention to my mumblings." He turned and went over to Thomas with the 'Select Architecture' still open in his hand. "Is this where you have taken your ideas for the preliminary elevation of Monticello?"

"In fact I have." Pointing to the first drawing which he opened for Charles, he explained. "It is a classic design, two stories, two-story portico and arcaded first floor."

"Yes, it is an elegant and stately design, just the right combination for your mountain."

"So I believe, Charles. It will be magnificent if I can realize my dream of it."

"And the gardens? Have you sketches for them as well?"

"I have many ideas, but have only drawn plans for the rear terrace. Just now, I am clearing the hilltop. We shall visit the site tomorrow if you are amenable, and don't mind the climb."

"I look forward to the adventure." Pausing a moment, Charles inquired, "Thomas, how long will it take to build this mansion?"

"I would venture to guess anywhere from five to ten years, perhaps more. With this in mind I have decided to build a small outchamber which will serve as temporary living quarters during construction. You shall see that as well tomorrow."

"It will be my pleasure, Thomas."

During the evening meal, Charles found himself opposite Betsey Walker, and once again he was caught up in the radiant sensuality she projected. This time, however, he could not help but notice that she was paying him an inordinate amount of attention. This troubled him, and he tried to avoid her eyes, but found it enormously difficult due to the seating arrangement. He therefore directed much of his attention to

Thomas and his mother, and refrained from addressing Betsey directly. What kind of game was she playing anyway? Thomas had already taken note of her flirtation and signaled as much to Charles with his eyes. Charles shrugged and threw him a puzzled look.

When supper was over, family and guests gathered in the parlor where drinks were served in elegant crystal glasses and Thomas joined Lucy in song at the harpsichord. They performed admirably, but vocal music of the day did not exactly inspire Charles. What he did find entertaining was Betsey's continued interest in him. Though she was trying to be discreet about it in front of the others, she made it perfectly clear to Charles that she was interested.

Soon Charles excused himself for a walk in the estate gardens and Betsey begged to accompany him. He glanced toward Jefferson for guidance, but the latter was oblivious to them, content to indulge his passion for music. Alright, thought Charles, let's get to the bottom of this. He was curious to see just how far she would go with her flirtation.

Once outside on the brick terrace overlooking the modest but beautiful boxwood garden, Charles turned to her. "Let us walk along the Rivanna, I would like to see it from this elevation."

She stared boldly into his eyes and smiled that certain smile which most men find very effective in stripping them of their defenses. "If you like," she replied. She gestured for him to lead the way. Charles strolled through an alley of trees which led down to the water. He stood there quietly, marvelling at the motion and sound of the Rivanna as it rushed toward the James and ultimately, the Chesapeake.

"Water has always held a fascination for me, especially running water," he began.

"For me, as well." She turned to face him directly.

"It's beauty cannot compare to yours, however." Now it's her move, he thought. Let's see if she picks up the gauntlet.

She looked fleetingly into his steely gray eyes and her message was quite clear. "You are too kind, Charles," she murmured, dropping her lashes with feigned modesty.

He pulled her into his embrace and kissed her passionately. Damn, she was hot! He could feel the heat raging in her body like a roaring lion desperate to escape the confinement of his small cage. He was sorely tempted to accept her offering and pulled her more violently into his body to absorb some of her explosive passion. She thrust her tongue into his mouth demanding yet more, but all too quickly he let her go.

Betsey's eyes snapped open in amazement,

her generous breasts rising and falling quickly with every ragged breath. "What is it?"

Charles raised his eyebrow in amusement. She had told him exactly what he needed to know. "Not a thing," he replied calmly despite his own aroused state.

"Why did you stop?" She was genuinely hurt.

"Do not think for one moment that I do not want you; you are a very desirable woman. In fact you nearly made me forget the fact that I am pledged to another." He tactfully forebore to remind her that she was in the same position herself, but he could tell by the way she was biting her lip in agitation that she had just remembered it.

"Believe me," he continued kindly, "I would love to give you the tender loving you desire, but it is not for me to do so." He took her once more into his arms and kissed her gently. "That was goodbye, and that is all there can ever be between us."

"I..."

"Be assured that I can not return your affections."

"Please take me back, now." She turned swiftly and smoothed her disheveled hair, surreptitiously wiping her teary eyes with the back of her hand. God, she almost hated him! He appeared the perfect gentleman, but as far as she was concerned he was the very devil. Pray

God he would not speak to anyone of this encounter. Her good name would be ruined, and John would never forgive her. As for Thomas.....well, that was another matter altogether.

CHAPTER 20

Early the next morning, Thomas made good his promise to show Charles the Monticello site. The bright summer sun had just cleared the tips of the trees from the east as they started out, and it promised to be a glorious day.

"Does not this fresh, clear air raise your spirits, Charles?"

"Absolutely." Charles regarded his friend fondly. Jefferson looked invigorated. A happy smile played about his lips as he led them down to the banks of the river. Soon they reached

Thomas' boat and shoved off. The water was not running high, but Jefferson handled the boat with aplomb and it took them less than five minutes to reach the southern shore of the river.

"This way then!" called Jefferson, and he led Charles across a flat, lowland field of crops before starting up the fairly steep hill to the top of the knoll. Here, it was obvious that a good deal of tree removal was in progress. Two teams of horses and twenty-five or thirty men were busily clearing, removing and hauling massive tree trunks down the entire south face of the hill.

Charles' guide led him over to a large tree and sat down to rest. "This is one of my favorite spots. Oftentimes I read and meditate here. In the past, I was wont to bring my fellow students up here to study when I was home from the college."

Charles lay back against the tree trunk and watched the hardworking men as they pulled another stump free from the clinging earth. "Tell me Thomas, have you given any thought to our last conversation regarding slavery?"

"Indeed, I have pondered your words concerning a free society on more than one occasion."

"And...?"

"I am ever drawn to the same conclusion;

the General Assembly will not have it. It is impossible to induce the members to give even the slightest consideration to such a proposal."

"I was afraid of that."

"Even if one or two members would agree to a compromise, I could never rally enough support to achieve a majority vote, and even those few would be reluctant to speak out publicly on the matter. No sir, it hasn't a chance in hell."

"Yes, I am afraid I see your point."

"Furthermore, it would be the last proposal I would ever have the opportunity to submit; in truth, I would become the laughing stock of the colony." Jefferson's face twisted into a mock-comical, rueful expression as he considered this contretemps.

Charles smiled. "Yes, I dare say you would." He lit his pipe, grateful for the shade of the majestic oak which would live on to witness the construction of Jefferson's Monticello. It was difficult to envision the final design of the mansion with its large, white dome on the top, and the long wooden walkways over the slave quarters and service buildings. When completed, it would be considered an historic monument to Jefferson and one of the finest examples of eighteenth century Palladian architecture. Two hundred years later it would be engraved on every common nickel in the country, and there, totally oblivious to his great destiny, sat the prospective master of Monticello, chewing a blade of grass. It boggled the mind to dwell on it, and Charles quickly changed his pattern of thought in order to maintain his composure.

"What are your feelings, Charles? Surely you have considered domestic service in your new home? How will you fare without slaves?"

"Actually, Jenny and I have given the matter a great deal of thought, and we have decided to purchase the indentures of a young bondswoman currently in the service of Josiah Chowning. Did I not mention this once before?"

"Oh, yes, of course, admirable solution."

"Mr. Coulter has already selected a cook for us. Beulah is training her now. She is originally from the Caribbean islands, but I am not certain whether she was purchased as a slave or an indentured servant. I have made it clear to Jenny that I will neither buy nor own another human being, and she has accepted my position."

"You have the courage of your convictions, Charles, and I applaud that. Unfortunately, I am not in a position to do likewise here at Shadwell."

"I suppose that everyone of the landed gentry would look upon such behavior with the greatest disfavor."

"Yes, and serious charges would be

proffered against the poor unfortunate who dared such an action. I, for one, could ill afford to undertake such measures while actively pursuing a law career. We are speaking of nothing less than treason, Charles."

"Of course. No one could expect it of you."

"To return to a more pleasant subject," Thomas jumped to his feet, "I have determined that the house will stand just about here, facing the Rivanna River valley, thus." He gestured with an outstretched arm. "I wish to look toward the James and to a rising sun from my bed chamber and the study. I am something of an early riser, you see."

"It will be an absolutely splendid house. When will you actually start building?"

"As soon as possible. I wish to complete one of the garden buildings first to serve as an office and temporary living quarters while the main building is under construction."

"Ah yes, you had mentioned that. Where will the office be located?"

Thomas walked across the top of the hill toward the southeast. "Right here, and the gardens will stretch across the entire hilltop after we clear and level."

"I suppose the walkways will connect to the main building and provide shelter for the service buildings?"

"Exactly."

"And your garden, stretched all along this slope, will reap the benefit of maximum sunlight; moreover, you will have excellent drainage."

"Yes. My foremost difficulty will be finding an adequate supply of water."

"That is a problem. I suggest you find water before you break ground for the main building."

"Of course."

"..And a secondary supply as well. I'm sure you know how dry our summers can be here in the mid-Atlantic states." The words flew out before he could stop them, and he wondered how Jefferson would reply.

"Yes, drought conditions are not uncommon. Why last summer we received only one-and-a-half inches of rainfall in the whole of June and July."

"There it is."

"What was that you said?"

"There it is?"

"No, before that, something about 'mid-Atlantic states'?"

"Oh that. Well, that is a geographical charting system that I have realized to identify several vast areas of the country." He looked hopefully at Thomas and paused.

"Please,tell me about it."

"You may find it foolish, and I haven't

discussed it with anyone yet. Let me know what you think."

"Go on, then."

"Right. I have imagined that one day the population here in the colonies will grow and expand to the west. In fact, we will occupy all the land between the Atlantic and the Pacific."

"I, too, feel that that will be the case."

"Eventually, the entire land will be divided into separate, but united states of which Maryland, Delaware and Virginia are located in the middle Atlantic region. So you see, it follows logically when giving consideration to weather conditions which prevail from the west, that I make reference to regional conditions as well as local conditions."

Thomas listened attentively while he strolled back over to his favorite spot under the large oak tree. "I suppose your system could have some merit."

"I haven't mapped it out yet. You see, I can't draw. Someone else will have to draw it up for me."

"That is unfortunate. You have some fine ideas."

"Thank you, but truthfully, I haven't the inclination. Perhaps later in life. I have all I can do working for Mr. Coulter."

"Yes, I had forgotten your...position with

Mr. Coulter. I find it difficult to accept who you are, and your place in Williamsburg when we are together in this fashion. There is always something bothersome about knowing you in the way I do."

"How do you mean?"

"I cannot find the words to describe it precisely; however, I have it in my heart that you are out of place here."

Charles' heart leaped and his breath quickened. "Go on!"

"For one thing, you are much too learned and expressive of thought merely to ply the trade of a printer, no disrespect intended to Mr. Coulter. Indeed, Profesor Wythe expressed the same sentiments the day you met last fall, did he not? Our relationship has induced me to believe that you have attended college and studied as I have, just as the professor surmised, though for reasons of your own, you wish to suppress this. I confess I am at a loss to understand what these reasons might be."

"Allow me to confess more about my past, Thomas. Yes, I did attend a university, the name of which I will not mention at this time, and I have earned a degree in the very specialized field of archaeology."

"Then the professor and I were correct in our surmise!"

"Yes. All in all I had just completed my

nineteenth year of formal education before I came to Williamsburg one year ago in June."

"Please elaborate on your field of study. I confess I am not familiar with it."

"You may not be familiar with the name as such, but informal study in the area is not new. My colleagues and I examine the earth for relics of men and civilizations in ages past all over the world. We search for clues to how these men lived, how they died, how they used the land and animals, what tools they employed and so on."

Jefferson became quite animated upon hearing this explanation. "How delightful! I should love to pursue such a study myself. I am inordinately interested in fossils, particularly those found here in Albemarle. Tell me, did your work bring you to Virginia?"

Charles hesitated, choosing his words carefully. "Yes...and no. What I am trying to say is that, ah...Williamsburg and the eastern coast of Virginia, are rich in a history which goes back over one thousand years, but I would rather not discuss any more about this project. I will tell you that I have worked on dig sites in South America, on the continent of Africa, and of course, here. There remains much work to be done, and there is much to learn from our predecessors."

Thomas frowned. "But why waste so much time with Tobias Coulter? Obviously. you are not engaged in research at this time."

"It is a very complicated story which I will not try to explain now, but Jenny is the reason that I am here. In fact, she is the only reason I am in Williamsburg, to be completely honest." Charles sighed. This was becoming more complicated by the minute.

"Were you acquainted with her before coming to Williamsburg? I was under the impression that you met here."

"If you must know the truth, I will tell you, but please do not laugh." He took a deep breath and began. "I had been having peculiar dreams and visions of Jenny for days before we actually met. I was literally brought to her by some force of fate difficult to explain. Now that I have her, I can not bear the thought of living without her. She has a power over me which transcends rational thought. More than this I cannot say."

"But what of your work? Surely you will not be content to spend the rest of your days in a print shop?"

"No, of course not."

"What will you do after you are married?"

"Do you remember that evening last fall in the Raleigh Tavern when I told you it may be necessary for me to leave some day and never return? I told you then that I was a transient at best, and that we could not even exchange letters once I was gone."

"Now that you mention it, yes, I do remember."

"Well, to be perfectly honest, after Jenny and I are married, we may go away and never return. It could even happen before the wedding for all I know."

"I asked you then, and I will ask you now, why will you never return?"

"Because my work will take me away and I will not return during your lifetime. Nor can you write to me, because there will be no post in the place to which I am going."

"Jenny has agreed to this?"

"Yes. It will be difficult for her never to see her family again, but she is willing to pay that price to be with me."

"This is grave news indeed. I shall miss you immensely; however, if you must go, then so be it. I have lived with the loss of loved ones for many years; my father, the governor, Dr. Small, my sister, and now you."

"If it is any consolation, Thomas, I shall miss you equally. Much as I love Jenny, there are certain things I would be reluctant to discuss with her. You hold a very special place in my life which no one else can ever occupy."

"Thank you for that, Charles."

As they made their way back to Shadwell, Charles turned and looked back at the crest of

the hill where Monticello would one day stand.
"I am sorry that I will miss the construction
and completion of your home, but I already have
a very good picture of what it will look like. I
can imagine walking the exterior wooden walkways
overlooking your gardens even now."

"I believe you can. Are you telling me that
this may be the last time we will meet?"

"I do not know exactly when I will leave,
but I will certainly inform you of my
departure. Perhaps we shall meet again in
Williamsburg when you come to see your new
office."

"I do hope so. I encourage you to stay on
for at least the duration of the summer, if not
the full public season."

"We shall see, Thomas. We shall see."

They had just stepped out of Thomas' boat
when the cries reached them. "Help! Help! He
can't swim! Please someone, help!"

Charles raced up along the shoreline with
Thomas right behind him. A young boy, who had
been struggling furiously in the river,
just went under for the second time, while his
friend looked on in horror. Without a second
thought, Charles dove into the water and brought
the youngster ashore. The commotion had
attracted a small crowd of onlookers who

anxiously awaited the outcome of Charles' apparently futile rescue.

"He is dead!"

Charles shook the water out of his hair and eyes and regarded Thomas with dismay. "What?"

"He is not breathing, and I cannot find a pulse."

"He's unconscious, that's all. Here, let me see."

Gently he extended the boy's head back to open the airway, then he listened to his chest for any sign of a heartbeat. There was none. The crowd gathered closer around Charles who was kneeling down alongside the lifeless body."

The child's friend tugged at Charles' wet sleeve. "Is he really dead, sir?" he asked tearfully.

Before Charles could respond, the boy's mother arrived. At the sight of her child's body sprawled awkwardly in the sand she screamed, panic stricken. "Oh dear God, no! Oh don't let him be dead!" Falling to her knees beside him she took him in her arms, rocking back and forth in anguish.

Charles tried to comfort her. "Please, allow me to try something. I may be able to revive him. May I?"

She nodded, unable to speak. Charles laid the boy flat on the ground, then closed his nostrils with one hand while blowing air into his mouth. The youth's lungs began to expand conspicuously. Charles placed overlapping hands on his chest and pushed down four times, expelling the air and trying to induce the heart to recommence pumping, then he began the entire process once more. "Damn! Come on son, breathe!"

There was still no response.

Charles continued patiently blowing air into the boy's mouth and pumping his chest. Some of the onlookers were beginning to be disturbed by the unconventional treatment. They called out in angry voices for Charles to stop. Jefferson quieted them to the best of his ability, but he, too, was disturbed. The boy's mother was sobbing bitterly, her face buried in her apron.

"It is useless, Charles. He cannot respond. Can you not see he is dead?"

After another minute of intense work, Charles sat back on his heels to rest. Then, to everyone's amazement, Charles included, the boy began to cough, bringing up water and phlegm. Gleefully, Charles put his ear to the boy's chest. "We got him! He's going to make it! Come on now, cough up that water, son."

He sputtered and coughed, and his mother gathered him into her arms, but this time her tears were happy ones. She kissed Charles' hand in gratitude for saving her only son.

"Mother, what happened?"

"My darling, you nearly drowned. But this

kind man has saved you. You will be safe now."

Jefferson looked on in utter amazement. "I would never have believed it. By God, you did save him!"

The crowd cheered; already Charles was gaining a reputation as a miracle worker. There were cries of "He must be a saint!" and "'Tis a sign from the Almighty!".

The hero gave them a tired smile. "It's a simple procedure. Any of you are capable of learning it. Please, go on about your business." He turned to the boy's mother. "See that he gets some rest, ma'am. He should do well now."

"I shall pray to God for you, sir. I cannot express my appreciation and great indebtedness to you." She gazed at him adoringly.

The crowd finally began to disburse as Charles and Thomas made their way back to the plantation. Charles explained the theory of cardio-pulmonary resuscitation to Jefferson who listened eagerly. "I vow, Charles, had I known you four years ago I would never have had need for a university education - a little law, perhaps, but otherwise...!"

"You flatter me unduly."

"Is this a skill which you acquired during your many travels abroad?"

"You might say that, yes."

"I always heard that travel broadened the mind. I can see now its educational value has

251

not been underestimated." He clapped Charles on the back and they were both laughing when the plantation finally came into view.

CHAPTER 21

Jenny stared into her teacup, unable to give her mother the slightest attention. Anne repeated her question.

Suddenly, Jenny returned to her senses. "I am sorry, mother, I was off in another world, daydreaming as usual."

"Yes, I can see that. I wished to know what your plans are for today, dear. I have just received word that the parlor furniture will arrive any day now."

"Oh, that is wonderful! I shall go to the

house and plan the layout as soon as possible."

"Very well, but do not stay there all day as you did the last time."

Jenny looked at her mother reproachfully. "But mother, I haven't been near the house in almost a week."

"Yes, but you have been acting most peculiarly ever since you returned from the house last week. I am beginning to worry about you."

"Whatever can you mean?"

Anne regarded her daughter critically. She had grown quite pale and there were mauve shadows under her beautiful eyes. Tobias had told her of Jenny's nightmares, and Anne knew the girl had been sleeping poorly. Perhaps this would all right itself when Charles returned home. She devoutly hoped so.

"You simply haven't been yourself, dear. Can't you tell me about it?"

"Mother, I assure you, I am quite well, a little tired perhaps, but otherwise in reasonably good health."

"Your father mentioned that you were sleeping when he found you in the parlor of the new house last week."

"Oh, that! It was so peaceful there, I lay down for a short rest and fell asleep. Surely there is nothing sinister in that?" Jenny poured a second cup of tea and added a liberal amount of fresh cream. "Promise me you won't worry any more, mother. There really is no cause."

"I dare say you are right, Jenny. Once Charles returns, things will return to normal, I expect."

Jenny hurriedly finished her tea. "I shall excuse myself now, mother. If you want me, I shall be in the new house."

"Be careful, child." The words slipped out before Anne could stop them. Somehow the thought of Jenny alone in that house frightened her; Jenny's enthusiasm could be alarming at times. The child was much too intense.

Jenny looked at her oddly. "Careful? Yes... of course." She turned as she reached the bedroom door and added, "I shall not be long, mother."

Anne smiled and nodded, but she could not dispell the sense of foreboding which gripped her.

Jenny entered her house with a light, happy step and walked from room to room as she usually did upon first arriving. It was practically a ritual now. Eventually she would end her little tour in the parlor where she would seat herself on an empty crate and make plans for her future with Charles. She would decorate the house entirely in her head, trying to imagine the effects of various wallpapers she had studied in the large volumes at Tarpley's Store. Or, she would try to visualize what her children would someday look like. Her children and Charles'. Most likely, they would be dark, since she and Charles both had black hair. How she would love to have a little boy with Charles' gentle gray eyes and curly hair. It would be a proud moment indeed, when Charles' son was born.

But where would Charles' son be born? She could never dream peacefully of their future because of the overwhelming unknown. After last week's foray into the twentieth century, she felt a sense of time closing in upon her. She looked around the little parlor and realized that she and Charles would probably never live there, that her children would not be born there, and that her exile would be complete. Oh, Charles would be in his element, there in his own time, and the children would never know anything else, but she, she would always be a stranger, no matter how well she adapted. Charles must never know, of course. She would no doubt enjoy the comforts and ease of living which she had glimpsed in her brief sojourn of last week, but a part of her would always long to return, if only for a visit. A heaviness settled over her, and she began to feel suffocated. If only Charles were here!

Just then, her eyes caught sight of the Chinese vase on the mantelpiece. She stared at it, wondering if she should repeat her adventure or let well enough alone. It was so tempting. Perhaps the more she learned about Charles' time, the more comfortable she would eventually feel in it. It was so vibrantly alive and colorful, and everything moved so fast in his world! She paced up and down trying to recall Charles' words. He had said the town was a museum which had been rebuilt or restored to its eighteenth century approximation; or more specifically, an approximation of the town as it was in the year 1770. 1770 – two years from now! She wondered if the people who flocked to restored Williamsburg were equally interested in other cities such as Boston, or Annapolis, or Philadelphia. Jenny had seen all of these last winter during her journey to Aunt Caroline's, and had found them delightfully different.

One thing was certain, however; travel to the twentieth century was a source of tremendous excitement, and after all, she had come to no harm on her last foray. Why should she not try again?

Emboldened by this thought, Jenny moved toward the vase with a determined attitude. She lifted it carefully and stood there a moment. Nothing happened. She still wasn't sure exactly what triggered the vase into action, but she knew she must try it again. After holding the vase for a good thirty seconds, she began to feel dizzy and lay down quickly in anticipation of the change. She lay on the floor and waited, eyes closed, but again, nothing happened. Irritated by this lack of success, she stood up and began to pace the room. Her hands were shaking in agitation, and she swiftly replaced the vase on the mantelpiece to prevent its breakage. That was all she needed!

Jenny considered how dizzy she had just become after holding the vase. But why hadn't she gone forward? This time, she would hold it more firmly, for a longer time. Perhaps that was all that was necessary. She lifted the vase and clasped it with renewed purpose, little realizing that this time, both her feet were squarely on the hearth. At once she was assailed by the familiar vertigo and knew that this was it! Swiftly, before she could fall, she replaced the vase, then turned and reached out for the floor, but at that moment she blacked out completely and pitched forward, her hands bearing the brunt of her fall. When the world stopped spinning, she realized that she was not lying on the familiar hardwood floor of the parlor, but in the middle of the cornfield. Only now the corn seemed considerably taller than it had been before. She lay there for a moment and looked at the sky. Soon, all her fear was replaced by the exhilaration of success. She had done it again!

FRANCIS STREET

Jenny sat up and brushed the debris from her skirts. It seemed rather quiet as she made her way to the corner of Nicholson Street. This was the place where she had last seen Scott, and she wondered idly where he might be. She remembered him saying something about the college, but she couldn't remember what. Ah well, maybe they would meet again by chance. It was not such a large town, after all.

A sightseeing bus stopped and discharged passengers on the corner opposite the cornfield. The tourists began to follow her toward the main street of town. She glanced back at them uneasily. What if they should speak to her? What would she say? Perhaps the best thing would be to pose as a visitor - from England. Her accent was obviously different, and if these people thought it sounded English, why, so much the better for her story. It was a relief to have some sort of explanation worked out. Now she knew how Charles must have felt when he first arrived in the eighteenth century, alone, and desperate. He, too, had created a background for himself in order to find a job in the print shop.

As she strolled up Duke of Gloucester Street, she became aware of many admiring glances directed not only toward her costume, but to herself as well. Twentieth century clothing was still a revelation, even though she

259

had been exposed to it once already. How comfortable those short-sleeved cotton blouses looked, and those curious cut-off trousers! The day was growing quite sultry, and Jenny was uneasily aware of a prickling under her armpits. How gladly would she remove all those petticoats and don twentieth century attire - if only she dared. The concept was still too revolutionary. Brushing the perspiration from her forehead, she continued on.

In her close observation of the people around her, Jenny could not help but notice that many, even children, were wearing spectacles. They were not like her father's, but then, she would not expect them to be. Did this mean that eyesight had generally deteriorated in the twentieth century, or was it that most people in her day could not afford spectacles? More likely the latter, she decided. She would have to ask Charles.

Before she knew it, Jenny began to feel hungry. There was another need as well. She had had two cups of tea this morning, and her bladder was making itself felt. She had no idea of the time, but it must be at least noon, judging by the sun. Perhaps it would be best to return to the cornfield. She turned back and retraced her steps. Soon she came upon a building with a sign proclaiming "Rest Rooms". Just what she needed - a rest! Before she could enter, however, her attention was arrested by a young woman leaning over the something against the wall of the building. She moved closer, and saw that the woman was drinking. Suddenly aware of her own thirst, Jenny waited until the woman had gone and approached the device, studying it carefully. How did one make the water come out, she wondered. She assumed that the water was coming out of a spring, but in that case, there would be a continuous supply; one would not have to turn it on and off. She backed away and watched carefully. Two little girls in short, ruffled dresses ran up to the fountain and took turns drinking. Jenny crept closer, watching avidly. When the girls had gone, she tried once more. Apparently there was a little white knob which must be turned to release the flow of water. Jenny dutifully turned it and a clear, icy jet of water sprang out right into her face. The coldness shocked her and she gasped.

"Gotcha, huh?"

Jenny wheeled around, and to her amazement, there stood Scott.

"Oh, Scott, it's you!" She was acutely embarrassed. How long had he been standing there?

"Yes, Jenny. I was hoping we would meet again." He tried to stifle his laughter at her predicament. "And, I see that you are in trouble again. What seems to be the problem?"

"I wanted to get a drink, and..."

"Here, let me see." He tried the fountain without incident. "Well, it's fine. Try it again. Better yet, let me buy you a drink at Chowning's. I'm on my lunch break anyway."

Jenny wiped the moisture from her face with the back of her hand. "Oh, thank you. I was just on my way back..." Back to what, the cornfield? She couldn't tell him that! Her face suffused with color. At least he hadn't laughed.

"Come on now. The last time I met you, you were in a hurry to get somewhere, too. Look, if you can't do it now, how about meeting me tonight at Chowning's for dinner? Would that be alright?"

Jenny frowned. Tonight? She sincerely hoped she would not still be here tonight. "Chownings's?" she repeated, to gain time to think.

"Yes, if you like, or The King's Arms?"

"I've heard the Raleigh is excellent." Lud, now what had she said! He was looking at her as though she had just sprouted another head.

"Are you serious?"

"Indeed, yes. I have never been there, of course, but my father and his friends meet there at least once a fortnight for supper and entertainment." What on earth was the matter with him? Surely he had heard of the Raleigh

Tavern!

"Your father...ah. Jenny," he took her elbow in his hand and began to lead her away, "why don't we just make it Chowning's." He was afraid to press the issue, but he desperately wanted to see her again, no matter what game she was playing. "Can you meet me there tonight?"

"I cannot promise it Scott, but I shall see what can be done. Shall we say seven o'clock?"

"Fine, seven it is. I'll be waiting."

"If I am not here by half past seven, you shall know I was detained."

"Okay, no problem." God, she was beautiful. If only he could find out what made her tick. "Please come, Jenny," he said softly.

"I shall try. Good-bye Scott." She turned to go, aware that he was watching her. She really had no intention of returning tonight. Pray God she was able to return home as swiftly as possible. Her mother would surely be frantic by now, and she had promised her to be home early.

Scott's lunch break was nearly over. As he hurried back to work his mind was full of his recent encounter with Jenny. How could she have referred to the Raleigh that way? Everyone knew it was not an operative tavern. But the way she talked, the things she said, it was almost as if....no, that wasn't possible. She certainly

263

did behave oddly, though. Like today, at the drinking fountain. You would think she had never seen one before! And last week, when he first met her, he had thought she was emotionally disturbed, climbing into an empty cornfield like that. She was either putting him on, or she was an exceptionally talented colonial player (as she claimed) acting out a role. If so, she certainly was effective in her wide-eyed innocence.

He walked on, scarcely watching where he was going. No, he thought, something isn't right here, and I'm going to get to the bottom of it if it's the last thing I do!

CHAPTER 22

Charles and Jupiter had already covered more than thirty miles of hot, dusty road since they left the roadside tavern shortly after six in the morning. Charles was determined to reach Williamsburg before dark. The noonday sun had risen to nearly its highest point in the late June sky, and since it had not rained for more than a week, the road was quite dusty. The thermometer had reached at least ninety by his reckoning, and Charles was relieved to be riding through a fairly cool stretch of climatic forest.

Jupiter had taken well to the long day of riding, and had even managed an additional two hours. Of course, Charles made sure to stop often to rest and water the animal. There were only twenty-five more miles to Cole's Ferry as Charles passed the entrance to Shirley Plantation, and he hoped the delay at the ferry would not be long. There had been an hour's delay on the trip out to Shadwell, and Charles remembered reading somewhere that a ferry operator could take more than two hours to take someone across a river, especially when other clients were enjoying a respite in the ferry's tavern. It would take two hours to reach the Chickahominy River, and once across, it was only an hour or so to Williamsburg. He could hardly wait to see Jenny again, and urged Jupiter on to greater speed.

They were galloping along at a fine clip when, without warning, a young buck dashed across the roadway not fifteen feet in front of Charles, and Jupiter reared, sending Charles crashing onto the hard roadbed. Charles landed on his side with such force that the wind was completely knocked out of him. He lay dazed, in considerable pain, and hoped that he had not broken his shoulder. When he was finally able to breathe normally, he eased his way up to a sitting position and looked around for Jupiter.

The horse was nowhere in evidence. Wearily he stood and studied the animals tracks, his back and shoulder protesting vigorously. Jupiter, it seemed, had taken the road back to Richmond. Damn! He hoped that the horse would return on his own. The question was, should he stay and wait for him, or start walking back toward Richmond on the chance that Jupiter had halted along the road to graze? One thing was certain; Charles was going to lose valuable time. At least it was still early and there were many hours of daylight remaining.

Charles began walking in the direction of Richmond.

Jenny clenched her fists in an agony of frustration. She had been trying to return home for what seemed like hours, and nothing was happening. Thank heaven the corn was high enough to shield her from the gaze of curious tourists as she sat, furious, with tears streaming down her face. With each failed attempt, panic had crept closer until now it threatened to engulf her completely. She was trapped in the twentieth century as surely as Charles had once been trapped in her time, and there was apparently nothing she could do about it.

She estimated the time to be mid-afternoon from the position of the sun, and certain physical needs demanded her immediate attention. She had not eaten all day, and the two cups of tea she had enjoyed in her mother's bedroom that morning were now causing her acute discomfort. There was no help for it, she would have to go back into town. Taking several deep breaths, she smoothed her hair and tidied her dress as much as possible, then made her way out of the corn and onto Nicholson Street. When she had refreshed herself, she would try to return home again. Perhaps next time she would be successful.

Just inside the tall brick wall of the Capitol, Jenny came across a man sitting on a small stool painting a sign. Something about him caused her to pause a moment and watch him work. He took great pains with each stroke as he formed the letters one by one. The sign was a modest one, supported one foot off the ground by a small stake.

"Hello, young lady." The painter looked up at her with twinkling eyes. He was an elderly gentleman with a luxuriant white mustache, and was clothed in eighteenth century dress. His long hair was pulled back and fastened with a black ribbon. Jenny felt instantly at home with him.

"Oh, please do not stop on my account!"

"That is a very pretty costume you have on there. Are you a Foundation employee? I don't remember seeing you before, and I certainly wouldn't forget a face as pretty as yours."

Jenny felt herself flush. "Thank you. Actually, I am only a visitor here."

"I see. Well, I hope you are enjoying our town."

"Most certainly. I presume you are a Foundation employee?"

"Yes. I have been painting signs and other things for more than twenty years, just as you see me now." He turned back to his work and added the finishing stroke to an "E".

"I can see that you enjoy your work," she ventured.

"You know, I've never given it much thought, but I take pride in my work, and maybe that's the same thing."

"You are a true craftsman, sir," Jenny returned. His friendliness emboldened her to ask a very pressing question, the answer to which surprised her. So that's what a rest room was!

"Thank you, sir. It was a pleasure speaking with you."

"And with you, young lady. Thank you for stopping by to talk."

Having visited the rest room, Jenny continued her wanderings through the historic area and finally arrived in front of Christiana Campbell's Tavern. There were a great many people on the long veranda, obviously waiting to be seated. She climbed the front porch steps and began to read the menu. Her stomach grumbled longingly, but her lack of modern currency precluded the purchase of even the simplest meal.

A young woman in colonial garb approached her. "Are you having lunch, ma'am?"

Startled, Jenny looked at her uncertainly. "Lunch?"

"Yes, will you be eating lunch?"

"Oh! No...I...ah...was just looking over the bill of fare."

"Fine. Take your time. Gosh, you have the prettiest hair!" she exclaimed, marvelling at the blue-black curls which tumbled like a waterfall from under Jenny's mobcap. "Is that a perm?"

"I'm sorry, perm?"

"Yes, you know, a permanent."

Jenny was completely at a loss. These people certainly were a curious lot. Everywhere she went, they wanted to know about her clothes, and now this....this permanent thing. She was too weary to dissemble any more. Better to confess her ingorance.

"I'm sorry, I don't understand. I am not familiar with the term."

The girl looked at her aghast. "You don't know what a perm is?"

270

"I'm afraid not, should I?" Jenny was becoming irritated.

The girl shrugged. "No, I guess not, not with that hair." People were crowding around, trying to get the girl's attention. "I'd better get back to work. Have a good day!" She consulted her list and beckoned to a group of four hungry diners whom she then led back into the tavern.

Jenny continued her odyssey through the restored area, stopping once to check her footgear. The fashionable leather pumps were extremely light in weight and had never been intended for such punishing use as they were now receiving. With dismay, Jenny saw that they were quite ruined. Moreover, a blister had formed on the side of her right foot and it throbbed more and more with each step she took. Lud, she thought, this would have to happen now!

She walked haltingly back toward the Capitol building, glancing across the front lawn toward Francis Street as she went. There was Mrs. Ashton's town house. Jenny wondered fleetingly what had happened to Mrs. Ashton. Rumor had it that she had retired permanently to England and married an earl. Jenny remembered with a shudder what had happened to her at the hands of this woman, and what had nearly happened. In spite of it all, she harbored no animosity toward Alanna Ashton, for she knew that Alanna had wanted Charles desperately, and she knew what his charm could do to a woman. Oh, why wasn't he here with her now?

Anxious now to reach the cornfield, she tried to pick up her pace, but the blister on her foot threatened to burst, and she limped along as best she could. The sun beat down unmercifully, and perspiration trickled from under her arms and behind her knees. If this continued, she would soon begin to smell. Ugh! Her tightly laced stays enclosed her like a prison, and she longed to throw off the voluminous skirt and petticoat which clung damply to her legs when she walked. Jenny did remove her mobcap, all the while wishing for a few hairpins with which to pin up her heavy mass of hair. Why, oh why hadn't she put it up this morning? She had been in so much of a hurry to reach the house that she hadn't thought of it.

When Jenny finally reached the cornfield, she tried with renewed determination to trigger the process which would take her home, but it was all in vain. Something was not right, but she couldn't imagine what it was. It had worked before - what was she doing wrong? Physical and emotional misery overcame her and she threw herself down and sobbed.

Some time later it occurred to her that she had promised to meet Scott at Chownings that

very evening at seven o'clock. At least she
wouldn't be alone, and he would see to it that
she had a warm meal. The thought comforted her,
and she realized that she had no idea of the
time. According to the position of the sun, it
was late afternoon; she would have to ask
someone.

Soon she found herself seated on the
courthouse steps watching a group of children
at play on the stockade. Across the street near
the Powder Magazine, Jenny saw a soldier
demonstrating the use of a flintlock rifle.
Every once in a while he would fire the weapon
amid a puff of white smoke and a loud blast of
noise. A large group of people gathered to watch
the demonstration. Jenny marvelled at the
crowd's obvious interest in an event she
considered quite ordinary. All the things she
took for granted, they found fascinating.

Head in hands, she sat there wondering what
to do. A middle-aged man sat down beside her and
consulted his guide book. Jenny asked him
politely for the time and learned that it was
six o'clock, a full hour before her rendezvous
with Scott. What to do now? Much as she hated to
walk, there really was no alternative. She
picked herself up and began walking up Duke of
Gloucester Street, conspicuously favoring her
right foot.

Before long, she came to a chain which was

stretched across the road and attached to poles at either end. She limped around the obstacle and found herself at a busy intersection with cars rushing past at what she considered a furious rate. The noise and bustle intimidated her at first, but curiosity won out, and when the line of the vehicles stopped and a group of people began crossing the street, she went with them.

She stepped gingerly onto the road, glancing nervously at the cars as though they were bloodthirsty beasts waiting for an opportunity to pounce on her. The first building on the left corner bore a sign with the legend "Craft House". It sounded intriguing, so she stepped inside. Her eyes widened at the beautifully crafted pieces of eighteenth century furniture - reproductions to be sure - on display inside. She noticed a particularly handsome tall case clock which reminded her of the one in Aunt Caroline's house in Boston. The price on the tag read $13,000. Thirteen thousand something. She wondered what manner of currency was meant, and how much it equalled in pounds. It was bound to be expensive; nearly everything in the store would have been exorbitant, even in her own day. On a nearby table she found a collection of beautifully colored hardbound books about colonial Williamsburg. She picked up several and spent a pleasurable ten minutes admiring the exquisite pictures. The art of photography was not completely unknown to her; she remembered the little black boxes of the tourists and the polaroid snapshot which she had hidden under Charles' pillow. This, then, was a new art form developed in Charles' time, and it produced breathtakingly beautiful likenesses. One book in particular now caught her eye, and she reached for it eagerly. It was "The Williamsburg Cookbook" and purported to have receipts from Christiana Campbell's Tavern, Chowning's and The King's Arms. Here again were the wonderful colored pictures showing various dishes like those prepared by Beulah. She could almost smell the jambalaya, and her mouth watered at the thought of spoonbread.

She wondered suddenly what her parents and Elizabeth were eating this evening. In all probability, they were too worried about her to eat. Her eyes welled with tears as she remembered her mother's words that very morning, "be careful". She had not been careful. She had been reckless and selfishly intent upon her own pursuit, in spite of her mother's pleas and Charles' earlier warnings. If only she hadn't come. If only Charles were here with her. If only...if only....

Surreptitiously wiping her eyes with the backs of her hands, Jenny wandered out of the Craft House and back onto the street.

FRANCIS STREET

A soft breeze was blowing and the air felt somewhat cooler as the sun began to fall toward the west. Jenny looked around her, not sure which way to go. Farther up the street was a large open area on the sidewalk filled with tables and chairs where many people sat eating and drinking at leisure. It looked inviting, especially to one as hungry as Jenny was, and she drew closer. Much of the food looked unfamiliar, and after studying it for several minutes, trying all the while not to be too obvious, Jenny came to the conclusion that people of the twentieth century had very peculiar eating habits. They seemed not to attach too great a significance to the act; indeed, from what she could see, it was a completely casual thing without manner and style. Perhaps it was done differently in the great houses. She had no way of knowing. The sight of so much food sharpened her own hunger to an uncomfortable degree, and she moved on.

Several steps further along she discovered a row of small shops containing ladies' apparel and amused herself by examining the window displays. Marvelling at the differences in the styles of dress, she wondered with growing excitement what it would feel like to try some of them on. In her own time, there were very few items of ready-made apparel, but here, it seemed to be the accepted thing. It would feel downright scandalous to don such skimpy outfits, especially the short trousers, but it was the custom here. Besides, if she were going to make any effort to adjust to Charles' mode of life, clothing would be a good place to start.

But no, it was growing late, and she must not miss her rendezvous with Scott. It must be close to seven o'clock by now, and if she missed him, she would never forgive herself. Should she tell him the truth about herself? Would he believe it? No, surely not. In any case, why burden him with her troubles? Jenny squared her shoulders and picked up her pace despite the burning pain in her foot. At least she would eat tonight, and Scott would know of a place for her to spend the night. Tomorrow...well, perhaps she would fare better tomorrow. Resolutely, she tried to push the thought of her grieving family out of her mind, but it continued to resurface like a bauble cast out upon the waves, and Jenny felt the tears begin to fall once more.

CHAPTER 23

Charles had backtracked for only a short distance when he saw Jupiter approaching him. The stallion appeared glad to see him, nickering and nudging his shoulder - his hurt shoulder - and appearing anxious to apologize.

"Well, it's about time! Where have you been?" Charles stroked his neck and gentled him with soft words. "Everything is alright, boy. Come now, we can go home. Yes, good boy, let's go home." Charles mounted him and started off in the direction of Williamsburg. "I guess it

278

wasn't all that bad. We only lost twenty minutes, and my shoulder feels better than it did. You'll not hear me complain, boy."

He spurred Jupiter on to a gallop, hoping to make up for the lost time. There were about four more hours of traveling time, since the sun would set around 8:45 P.M. The summer solstice had just passed, and these were the longest days of the year. "Thank God this isn't January, boy or we would be faced with pitch darkness within the half hour."

This time their ride was uneventful, and they soon came to the western side of the Chickahominy River. At first, Charles wondered how he should notify Cole of his presence, but then he spotted a pier on which there was a bell mounted on some pilings. A rope hung out of the bell, its purpose obvious. He tethered Jupiter at the head of the pier and rang the bell three times. Almost immediately someone appeared on the east side of the river and signaled to him. Charles acknowledged the signal and settled back to wait. A full twenty-five minutes elapsed before Cole boarded the glorified raft and started across for him. Charles remembered his experience with Cole on the trip out. It would be another twenty-five minutes before Cole moored at the western pier, and then it would be still another twenty-five or so to get across at last. Altogether, it would take more than an hour to cross a river which he could span in one minute or so on the Route 5 bridge in 1987.

"It's nearly half-past seven," Charles observed to Cole when the older man finally arrived on the western shore. He tried to keep the irritation out of his voice.

"So 'tis. Are you goin' on to Williamsburg, or to some other destination, young sir?"

"Williamsburg. I suppose I will have little more than an hour of daylight."

"You'd best step lively then," he observed laconically.

Twenty-five minutes later, Charles led Jupiter carefully off the precarious raft and mounted him, grateful for the summer solstice.

In no time they had passed the fork in the road leading on the left, to Williamsburg, and on the right, to Jamestown. Charles could hardly contain his impatience. "Jupiter," he whispered, "if I ever go away from Jenny again, you can kick the hell out of me, for I swear, I was a fool to have left her."

Rather than accost someone on the street for the precise time, Jenny decided to stop in at the last shop on the corner, The Williamsburg

Drug Company. She had found it delightfully cool, as were all the shops she had visited, and she breathed a sigh of relief. There were a few people browsing leisurely, but the store was not really crowded. She noticed an elderly lady with a pleasant smile serving various customers from behind the long counter in the front, and was struck by her friendliness. The atmosphere put Jenny immediately at ease.

She wandered through the shop, momentarily distracted from her purpose by the variety of strange and wonderful objects on the shelves. There were some familiar things, like long clay pipes and brass candlesticks, potpourri and sweet-smelling soaps and perfumes, but these did not hold her attention long. It was far more interesting to examine the unfamiliar. She enjoyed trying to determine what some of these items were used for, and the colorful pictures on the packaging helped to some extent, but Charles would have a great deal to explain.

Returning to the area near the front of the shop, she heard a voice call out, "Can I help you, dearie?" It was the pleasant woman behind the counter whom she had noticed earlier.

"Yes, actually. Do you happen to know what time it is?"

The woman consulted her watch and replied affably, "Yes, it's goin' on half past six." A note of concern crept into her voice. "You look

281

awfully tired."

"Yes, I am. I have been on my feet all day."

"Just like me, dearie! I put in six days a week, and I'm always on my feet. I'll go home tonight and soak 'em for a while." She studied Jenny quite openly, noting the authentic costume and the pale, serious face. "You know, I don't recall ever seein' you around here before. Are you a new Foundation employee?"

"No," Jenny replied, twisting her mobcap, which was already the worse for having been carried around all day and used to mop her hands and forehead. "I am not an employee. I am...visiting."

"Where on earth did you get such an authentic costume? I've never seen one like it!"

"Oh, I...I made it myself."

"Well, dearie, you did a great job."

"Thank you. I really must go, now, I am meeting someone at seven."

The woman threw her a knowing smile. "I'll bet it's a handsome young man, am I right?"

Jenny blushed at the implication. "He's an acquaintance..."

"And he's a lucky fellow, too. Well, have a good time, and stop in and see me again before you leave Williamsburg."

"Yes, I shall. Thank you."

"Oh, by the way, dearie, what's your name?"

FRANCIS STREET

"Jenny. Jenny Coulter."

"I'm Clara. Everyone knows me as Miss Clara."

"I look forward to seeing you again, Miss Clara. Good evening."

"'Bye now!" Clara watched her go. What a delightful young lady! Manners like that were hard to find nowadays.

His heart pounding with anticipation, Charles walked Jupiter up South England Street. "We're home, boy! Soon you will be in your own stall getting a well-deserved rest and a good mash." Jupiter whinnied. He, too, was anxious to get home. It was just about time for supper, Charles reflected, and Beulah would soon be serving one of her incomparable meals. His mouth watered, and he urged Jupiter forward.

He could smell the stew before he got inside the kitchen. Sure enough, there was Beulah leaning over the fire, her back turned to him. "Can't a hungry man get any food around here?"

She wheeled around and stared up at him as though he were a total stranger. "What yo' doin' heah, Mist' Charles!"

"Why, Beulah, I think it's pretty obvious. I've just returned from Shadwell, and I'm famished. Haven't eaten since breakfast."

"But...but yo' ain't supposed to be heah 'till next week!"

"I know I'm early. I just couldn't stay away any longer."

"Yo' ain't supposed to be heah," she repeated, eyes wide and bosom heaving.

Charles tried not to laugh. "Well, I'm here, and I'm hungry. What have we to eat tonight?"

The cook wrung her hands in agitation, and her voice, when she finally spoke, had risen at least an octave. "First, yo' ain't heah and Miss Jenny is, now, Miss Jenny ain't heah, an yo' is!" Desiree stood as though stunned in the corner, not daring to move.

For the first time, Charles sensed that something was amiss, something to do with Jenny.

"Now calm down. I can scarcely understand you. What are you telling me?"

"I says, Miss Jenny ain't heah!" She was afraid to meet his eyes.

"What do you mean, Jenny isn't here?" He was fighting down his own fear by now.

"Jus' what I says, she gone."

"Where the devil is she?" Charles was nearly shouting.

"No one knows, sir." Desiree stepped forward to impart this bit of information.

Before he could question them further, Billingsley entered the kitchen. "I thought I heard your voice, Charles. You have probably heard that Jenny is missing?"

"Gwan, tell 'im, boy." Beulah urged. She felt he would do a better job of it than she would.

"Word is that Jenny has been missing since mid-morning," Billingsley began. "More than that I do not know, Charles."

"I'd best see Tobias immediately." Charles turned to go, but Billingsley grabbed his arm.

"It's no use, Charles. They are all out searching for her. No one will be home but Mrs. Coulter."

"Dat's right, Mist' Charles. I's takin' tea to her right now. Why doan yo' sit down an' eat?"

Charles ran his hand through his hair distractedly, weighing the possibilities. "I suppose I should eat, I've had nothing since this morning, and who knows how late I'll be up tonight." He sat down and Beulah set a savory bowl of stew before him. "Richard, would you tell Rogers that I have returned and ask him to see to Jupiter?"

"Certainly, Charles." Intent on his errand, Billingsley was nearly out of the door when he turned in sudden excitement and grasped Charles' arm. "I nearly forgot! Miss Jenny left a message for you in the loft. She put it under your pillow and said you were to have it just as soon as you returned!"

Charles stood up so quickly he knocked the chair down behind him. "A message?" He had gone deathly pale. "Have you read it?"

"Most certainly not." He was aghast at the thought. "Come, quickly, Charles, it must be important!"

"Right!" He threw Beulah an apologetic glance and raced off, terrified of what he would find in the loft.

Charles lifted the worn quilt and moved the pillow aside. There it was, a small white envelope of the kind sold in the stationery shop. It was sealed. Without a word, Charles ripped it open and removed the paper inside.

Billingsley watched, stunned, as Charles' face changed from apprehension to comprehension and subsequent horror.

"My God, man, what is it?"

There was a long pause, during which Charles struggled for words, for an explanation of some kind. He looked at the object in his hands, then he looked up at Billingsley.

"Well?" Billingsley urged. "Are you going to tell me?"

"No."

"No! What do you mean?"

"I can't tell you."

"Why not? Miss Jenny isn't...?"

"No, nothing like that." Charles began to gain control of himself and realized that what he held in his hand would mean nothing but trouble. The less anyone knew about it, the better. "It is just something Jenny wanted me to have."

"But Charles, you looked as though the world had come to an end!"

Charles managed a weak smile. "Please, humor me. Don't ask any more questions."

Billingsley, thus appealed to, swore he would not trouble Charles further.

"I must see Mr. Coulter for any intelligence he may have received." He held up his hand to silence the giant. "I know. He's out looking for her. I will find him, and her, too. In fact, I have a very good idea where she is at this moment."

"That's wonderful, Charles. I wish you the best of luck. If you should need me, just say the word."

"Thank you. You are a good friend, Richard. I haven't forgotten what you did for us the last time, you and Dennis. But this is a different thing altogether. I will find her, you may be certain of it."

"Miss Anne will want to know that you have returned, Charles. Shall I tell her, or will you?"

"I'll see her now, Richard." Charles smiled

as he added, "But I'm sure the news of my return
is all over Williamsburg by now!"

CHAPTER 24

"May I help you?"

"I am to meet a young man here at seven o'clock."

The attractive redhead consulted her watch. "You still have about ten minutes. Will it be two for dinner?"

"Yes."

"What's the name?"

"His name is Scott," Jenny replied somewhat apprehensively. These people never stopped asking one questions!

"I need a last name."

"I'm afraid I don't know his last name. Please do not trouble yourself. I shall wait here on the porch until he comes."

"No, wait a minute. You said seven o'clock. Let me see how many reservations there are for two at that time." She scanned the roster quickly and found four. "I have Orlinski, Jones, Taylor and Lambertini. Do you know which it might be?"

"I'm sorry, no. I shall wait outside."

"Okay. Your table will be ready when he gets here."

"Thank you. Please, could you direct me to the ah, rest rooms?"

"Sure. Second floor, top of the stairwell to the right. I love your accent. Are you from England?"

"Yes, well, actually, not exactly. But my grandparents were from Devonshire." Why had she deviated from her story? Oh well, she would never see this girl again, so it probably didn't matter.

"That must be it." Noticing Jenny's hesitation she added, "You can go right on up!"

"Thank you."

Scott stepped inside the front door and looked around, disappointed.

"May I help you?"

"Yes, I am supposed to meet someone, but I don't see her."

"Is your date for seven?"

"Yes, she's a beautiful brunette. Have you seen her?"

"She's here. Are you Scott?"

"Yes, Scott Taylor. I made reservations."

"Your table is ready, and your friend is upstairs. You can wait here if you like."

"Thanks. I will."

"Oh, there she is now!"

Scott turned to see Jenny descending the stairwell like a princess at a gala ball. He rushed forward to meet her. "Jenny! I'm so glad you decided to come!" The smile she gave him was radiant, a mixture of relief, happiness and a renewed sense of security. Now, at least, she was not alone in this perplexing new world.

"Good evening, Scott. You see, I could not stay away," she teased, extending her hand as though it were the most natural thing in the world.

"You look stunning. How are you?"

"Famished!"

He took her outstretched hand and turned to the hostess who stood behind them waiting.

"If you will come this way, please, I'll show you to your table." She led them into the large dining room and seated them against the far wall. Jenny glanced at the table she had occupied with Charles three weeks earlier. She looked toward the doorway, subconsciously expecting her father to enter the tavern and order her out as he did on that first occasion.

They were now asked whether they would like to order cocktails and Jenny looked to Scott for guidance. Scott declined for both of them and Jenny was left wondering what on earth a cocktail was. She did not dare ask, however. This was another thing one was simply expected to know. She turned her attention to Scott. He had changed his clothes and was now wearing a jacket, shorter than she was accustomed to seeing, but very becoming. At his neck was a long narrow stock which hung down nearly to his waist. This change in clothing was obviously in her honor and she was flattered that he should take so much trouble to please her. She wished she could have done the same for him. The long hot day combined with her frenzied emotions had cause her to perspire freely, and now she felt sticky despite the chill in the tavern. Her mobcap rested in her lap, and though she had washed her face and hands in the rest room and tried to neaten her hair, she wished desperately for a comb and a change of clothing.

"Amazing!"

Jenny had turned her attention to the menu and looked up in concern.

"What is, Scott?"

"You are! You are so beautiful. I can't believe you are really sitting here with me."

She squirmed uncomfortably, and her feeling of dishevelment grew despite his enthusiastic compliments. "Do try not to think about it."

"But...I...okay. I'll try." He consulted the menu and announced that he would have the Brunswick stew.

Jenny ordered the same and glanced back at him, mentally comparing him with Charles.

"I love how you look at me like that, as though you are seeing right through me."

"Oh Scott, how you do go on." She lowered her eyes somewhat guiltily. Attractive though he was, Scott could not compare with her image of Charles; but then, no man could.

"And that's another thing..."

"What's that?"

"I love the sound of your voice. It's so soft and gentle. Enticing, that's the word."

Jenny smiled in spite of herself. "Come Scott, you are embarassing me. Please stop."

"Alright then. I'll try, but I can't promise for how long."

The waiter took their order and soon returned with salad and bread. Scott had ordered soup as well, and Jenny turned her full attention to the meal which thus far, was delicious. When they had finished every bite of stew, Scott asked her if she would care for something sweet.

"I think not, Scott, but I should love some coffee."

"What, no ice cream?" In his experience, girls always declined dessert the first time, but were easily persuaded to change their minds.

"Ice cream?" It sounded wonderful, and she suddenly remembered that she had enjoyed this delicacy last year at the Governor's Ball. "Yes, I would love some!"

"Good. I'll order it with our coffee."

"Scott, where do you...live?"

"I'm renting a small apartment on Boundary Street. It's nothing special, but it's okay for the summer. I like the location because it's close to the library and the campus."

"Yes, of course."

The waiter brought coffee and ice cream. Jenny sampled it, curiously at first, then eagerly. "Mmm. This is quite delicious!"

He chuckled. "I thought you'd like it." In this respect, at least, Jenny was like all the other girls he had dated.

"Yes, it is remarkably smooth and creamy. We do not have any..." She caught herself just in time. This was something she could not discuss with Scott.

"Yes, what were you going to say?"

"Nothing important. I was merely rambling

on, as usual."

"Well, please feel free to ramble on about anything you want."

"Scott, there is a matter of particular importance which I wish to discuss with you, but I am not certain how to begin."

He could tell she was disturbed about something. Her eyes had lost their sparkle, and she was twisting that mobcap she had in her lap. Why did she have to wear it in the first place, he wondered inconsequentially.

"I'm listening."

"Actually, there is a favor I would ask of you, if I may?"

"Of course."

"I am...in need of..." She had no idea how to phrase it. "Do you live alone?"

"Yes, I do." This is beginning to sound interesting, he thought.

"Well, I...may I bed down with you tonight? I know it is an imposition, but I shall be off first thing in the morning and... oh, I'm sorry!"

Scott nearly choked on his coffee. He coughed several times and cleared his throat before daring to trust his voice. Finally he managed to blurt out, "You want to sleep with me tonight?"

Jenny was clearly terrified. What had she done? His shocked expression told her that she had made an enormous mistake, and all she wanted was lodging for the night! "I am sorry," she repeated miserably, "please forget what I said!"

He stared at her in complete bewilderment. This was not what it had appeared. There was more to it. "Jenny, you can confide in me. Please, tell me about it."

She took a deep breath and plunged in. "I am unable to return to my home tonight, no, I cannot tell you why, and I find myself without a penny to my name. If that were not the case, I would gladly buy lodging for the night, as it is, however..." She turned her palms upwards, indicating that she had no alternative.

"I see. In other words, you would like to stay overnight with me on a purely platonic basis."

"Yes, if you would be so kind. I really have nowhere else to go."

"Of course, Jenny. You'll find it rather messy, and small, but I can find a place for you to sleep."

Her face brightened. "Oh thank you, Scott. I was afraid...when I asked you earlier..." she blushed furiously. "I'm afraid you didn't quite understand."

"You did give me quite a shock at first. Somehow I didn't think you were that kind of girl. By the way, why don't you have any money?"

"I simply walked out without any. I did not

expect to be away so long."

Was it possible he had been right at the very beginning? Was she emotionally disturbed? At times she made no sense whatever. Perhaps when they were ensconced in the comfort and intimacy of his home, Jenny would tell him exactly what was going on. He sensed that she trusted him, and he would foster that trust as the precious thing it was.

"If I didn't know better, I would say that you were a fugitive from the past - a historian's dream come true."

Jenny blanched. "Scott, if you value my friendship, as I value yours, please ask me no questions."

"Very well. We won't discuss it. Come, it's getting late, and I have to scare up some clean sheets - no easy task for a bachelor, you understand." He was babbling, and it was not solely for Jenny's benefit. Her face, when he made the remark about a historian's dream, told him he was getting close to a full understanding of this mysterious creature, and he suddenly wondered if he was ready for the truth.

Jenny stood up and tried to suppress a cry of pain. She had forgotten all about the blister on her foot, but now she was forced to deal with it in some way. Her shoes were all but useless, and she would certainly not be able to walk very far tomorrow. She hoped Scott did not live too far away, or he might end by having to carry her. In as light a tone as she could muster, Jenny replied, "Yes, let us get home. I must admit I am exhausted!"

Her heart plummeted when he said, "How about a little walk? It's not far, and I left my car back at the apartment." He turned to her expectantly, and she was loath to refuse him.

"Yes, of course." It was going to be a very long walk indeed.

CHAPTER 25

Once outside the bindery where he was alone again, Charles felt the full impact of Jenny's message. It was now too dark to study the picture, but he recalled vividly the twentieth century details. She had found the answer in his absence, and now she was there, in an alien society, with no place to stay, and no one to guide her. He must find the key and go to her at once. He would move heaven and hell to get there and ensure that she was safe. As for now, what on earth would he tell Anne?

Charles followed Bea into the parlor where Anne Coulter sat staring into her teacup. She was remembering two occasions that past year on which she had been certain that Jenny was lost, and in both instances, Charles had engineered her safe return. It was not too late to send a message to Monticello; perhaps she should give orders...

"Mrs. Coulter!"

"Yes, Bea?" She looked up disconsolately and was startled to see two figures. It wasn't possible, but yes, Charles was here!

She threw herself into his arms, weeping with relief. "Oh my dear, we did not expect you so soon! How did you know?"

Charles held her gently. "I didn't know, Anne, but I felt impelled to return as soon as possible. I couldn't stay away from Jenny any longer."

She wiped her eyes on her lace hankerchief. "You have heard?"

"Yes. Can you tell me exactly what happened?"

Anne led him to the sofa and requested another cup for Charles, then she told him everything she knew. She finished with, "Tobias has been riding about looking for her with some of his friends, but they have found nothing of significance thus far."

As if to corroborate her words, Tobias

himself strode in, his face strained with fatigue. Fear lay just beneath the surface of his hearty greeting, but he was loath to show it in front of his wife. Charles inquired as to the outcome of the search.

"Absolutely nothing," he replied with a helpless shrug of his shoulders. "I am at my wit's end to know where else to search, and that's the truth of it, lad."

"Did you question the carpenter and his men? Perhaps they saw her leave the house."

"Yes, yes, of course." He waved Charles' question off impatiently. "No one has seen her. That is what puzzles me. It is damned difficult to go anywhere in this town without being seen. 'Tis as though she'd disappeared into thin air!

Charles knew exactly where she was, and he was anxious to be off. "Take heart, sir. We found her once, and we shall find her again. I'm certain of it. I cannot delay any longer. You would do best to remain here with Anne. She needs you."

"Godspeed, Charles!"

Billingsley was still awake when Charles entered their room in the bindery loft.

"Charles! What's amiss?"

"I am going to search for Jenny. Listen, I am going to leave here now. I will go on foot, and no one is to follow me. Do you understand?"

301

"Of course."

"If I get through, I may be gone for some time. It is impossible to say how long. If I fail to get through, I shall return before sunup."

"I understand. If you have not returned before sunup, I will know you have reached you destination, and that you may be delayed for some time."

"Precisely. I hope to find Jenny without too much difficulty, but whatever difficulties I encounter, it is imperative that I do this alone."

"I wish you the best of luck, as always, Charles, and I know Dennis does too." He indicated the sleeping form of Watson, their roommate. "Here, take these." He fumbled in his bureau drawer and handed Charles two new candles, more priceless than pearls to a man with Billingsley's passion for reading, and several matchsticks.

"Thanks, Richard." They shook hands and Charles set off.

Adrenalin raced through his body as he stood in front of the house on the dig site. Jenny's well-being depended on his getting through tonight. He must not fail!

The door was locked, to begin with. This was something he had completely overlooked.

Damn, he thought, now what? He checked all the windows, but none was open, and he was reluctant to break in. He walked around the yard searching for something with which to force entry, but was disappointed the first time. The second time, he was rewarded by the sight of a ladder carelessly left on the ground near the rear wall by one of the carpenters. He perched it against the wall under a second floor dormer and carefully climbed up, praying that the window in question was open. Once at the top, he found he had about four feet of steeply pitched wood shake roof to traverse. He got down on all fours, stretching himself out to reach for the window framing. At first, he couldn't find anything to hold onto, and stretched himself a bit farther, running his fingers along the front edge of the window casing, then up the sides. At length he found a decorative strip of molding which he could grasp with the fingers of one hand. Hopefully, it would be the same on both sides! He inched and squirmed his way higher on the roof in order to reach the other side of the window little realizing that the more he stretched, and the higher he reached, the more horizontal pressure he was putting on the ladder.

Without warning, the ladder toppled away from the house and crashed to the ground below. Charles' heart stopped. He fell flat onto the wood shakes and made a desperate last effort to grab the molding strip on both sides of the window. His downward slide halted, and he pressed against the molding with both hands to wedge himself securely in place. "God, if you're not too busy, I could use a bit of help!" he whispered, pressing the toes of his shoes outward against the thickness of the wood shakes for more friction. If only he had his sneakers on! His own footgear was worse than useless in an endeavor like this one.

Charles lay still for a moment or two to regain his composure, then he inched his way toward the window until he was in a position to get hold of the whole dormer. Then he stood up slowly, using the dormer for support. Once stabilized, he reached around the front of the window and took hold of the sash. To his amazement, it rose smoothly, with barely an effort on his part.

Charles climbed into the house and carefully lit one of the candles, then he made his way downstairs into the parlor. The vase sat serenely in its accustomed place on the mantelpiece and appeared to mock him. He studied it intensely, as though trying to extract its secret through sheer force of will.

Candle in one hand, he reached for the vase with the other, anticipating an immediate reaction; but the vase was unwilling to relinquish its secret. "Now what is it going to take?" he asked himself patiently. "How would Jenny have used it?"

He replaced it on the mantel thoughtfully. As short as Jenny is, he mused, she would have to stand very close to the mantel to take hold of it. Since it was still on the mantel when he arrived, she obviously didn't have to hold it very long. The trick must be to stand in a certain place while holding it. He looked down, and, with a flash of insight, realized that the hearth might well play a meaningful role in the process. Jenny must have been standing here with both feet on the hearth when she grasped the vase!

Charles was about to test this hypothesis when he realized that the candle was still burning. He doused it quickly. He certainly didn't want the house to burn down; it wasn't supposed to burn down until 1840 or so.

Taking hold of the vase with one hand, both feet planted firmly on the hearth, he closed his eyes and waited, expecting to be assailed by vertigo at any moment. He was not disappointed. The familiar symptoms struck him forcefully, and he began to rapidly lose consciousness. He reached out to replace the vase on the mantel, just as Jenny had done, then he fell into nothingness.

A dim light appeared in the distance and

it consumed all of his attention, serving as a pivotal point on which to center himself. He couldn't remember what position he was in when he fell; now, he knew, or felt that he was motionless, even though the pinpoint of light drew nearer.

As the light grew brighter, he began to feel a cool moisture on his face as though he were outside in the night air. Gradually, the light enveloped him completely, and he was able to recognize the streetlights on Nicholson Street.

He was standing in the middle of a corn field on the corner of Nicholson and Botetourt Streets - the dig site. He had done it! Now, only one question remained; what was the date?

CHAPTER 26

As Scott led the way up Duke of Gloucester Street, his presence conveyed to Jenny a sense of welcome security. She had mixed feelings about this newfound friendship. It was an association born out of need rather than desire, but the more time she spent with him, the more she found herself attracted to him, despite the fact that her heart belonged to Charles. Now, of all things, she was about to trespass into this man's private quarters and stay an entire night with him. This was something she had never done, even with Charles, who had shared the ultimate intimacy, and with whom she constantly longed to share her nights. The plain truth was that at this moment, her options were dismal at best, and she trusted Scott as she would a brother.

"Jenny, what are you thinking about?"

"I was questioning the wisdom of staying all night in your apartments."

"Apartment. I only have one," he chuckled.

"You must know that I have never stayed the night in a man's apartment before, or in any other room in a man's private residence."

"I understand. Are you afraid?"

"Actually, I am a bit unsettled."

He reached out and took her hand in his as they continued walking. "Don't worry about it at all. When we get there I'll make you a nice hot cup of tea and leave you plenty of privacy. I swear, it won't be a problem." He glanced over at her to see how she would react, and for the first time, he noticed that she was walking unevenly, favoring her right foot. "Jenny, why are you limping? How did you hurt your foot?"

"I've got a blister on my foot from walking all day, and I'm afraid it has broken." She regarded him ruefully. "These shoes were never meant for heavy wear."

"You should have told me! I would have gotten the car and picked you up from Chowning's."

"Please do not trouble yourself, Scott. You have done so much for me already."

"Well, it isn't far now. When we get home, I'll fix you up a footbath with Epsom salts, and you can soak it in hot water. For that matter, you can have a hot shower or bath, whatever you prefer. Mine is a pretty classy hotel, you'll find."

"That sounds wonderful," she laughed. "You really are good to me, Scott."

"It's my pleasure. Now, are you still afraid?"

"No, of course, not. I see you are quite the gentleman."

"Yes, damnit," he said, looking down at her cameo perfect profile, "but there are times when I wish I wasn't."

"Well, here we are."

Jenny was surprised to see a small, dimly lit room partially filled with strange-looking furniture placed at irregular intervals. It was quite large in scale and covered with pillows, but most curious of all, it was completely white. How impractical, she thought. How will he ever get it clean? It did look inviting, however, and she sank gratefully onto the largest piece, rubbing her hand experimentally across the Haitian cotton upholstery.

"Go ahead and sit. You need to rest that foot. I'll get a bath ready for you soon. No, just relax."

Jenny had tried to rise, but the deep softness held her prisoner, and in any case, she hadn't the energy to contradict him. "This is wonderful," she breathed. "It's so different... that is; I'm not accustomed to such comfort."

He knelt down in front of her and removed her soft leather pumps. "God almighty! What happened to your shoes? No wonder you have a blister. These are totally worthless!" He raised her right foot and began to massage it, carefully avoiding the open blister.

Jenny blushed scarlet and tried to remove her foot. She should never have let him touch her shoes. She was certain he had never seen any like them before, and now she would have another thing to explain. The massage felt heavenly, though, and at his bidding, she soon lay back and allowed herself to relax again.

"How on earth did you acquire such skill, Scott?"

"Don't worry about it. I promised you a relaxing night with all the comforts, and that's just what you are going to get." He stood and glanced meaningfully at her disheveled clothing. "If that's all you have to wear, I'd better find something for you to sleep in tonight." Before she could open her mouth to protest, he added,

"Don't worry, I won't take your clothes away, I'm just trying to make you comfortable."

"You are so good, Scott. I don't wish to trouble you, but... you did mention a bath..."

"Oh, sure. You'll want to soak that foot. Stay there, I'll get it ready, but hey, don't fall asleep before I come back, okay?" She looked as though she was about to crash any minute.

She smiled sleepily at him. "I'll try not to. Thank you."

The bath was everything she could have wished for. The only problem was that it relaxed her to the point of unbearable drowsiness. Much as she hated to get out, she needed to sleep.

Scott had set out a steaming cup of tea and an old tee-shirt for her to sleep in and turned down the bedcovers invitingly. He had made it clear that he would sleep on the sofa. As she climbed into bed and pulled the cool sheet up to her chin she barely had time to whisper good-night to Charles, wherever he might be, before sleep claimed her.

Scott was not asleep. He had a report to prepare by the end of the week and settled down to do some serious studying. He found it difficult to keep his thoughts on his work, however, and after an hour or so, he tiptoed into the bedroom to check on Jenny.

She was deeply asleep; her tea on the night table was untouched, and her clothes were neatly folded on a nearby chair. As he watched, she began to toss, murmuring something that sounded like a name. What was it? Charles! "Charles, don't leave me!" Poor kid, she was having a bad dream. But who was Charles? An old lover? A current lover? Hell, why should he be surprised - a girl as beautiful as that. Oh well, he'd better get back to work. Still...he was aware of sudden disappointment, almost depression. Whoever Charles was, he was a lucky guy.

Several hours later, Jenny stumbled into the living room, still half asleep. "Scott? What time is it?"

"Just after midnight, why? Shouldn't you go back to bed?"

"I'm sorry I fell asleep, I wanted to...say good night, but I...somehow I was asleep before...."

"Apology unnecessary. Go on back to sleep, you're exhausted."

Jenny went back to the bedroom and lay down, but sleep eluded her. A growing need was making itself felt, and she was unaccountably reluctant to make use of Scott's restroom. What a silly name! One certainly couldn't rest in the ones she had seen. They hadn't even a chair to sit on. She rearranged herself and tried to sleep, but her body continued to draw attention to itself, and she knew she would never sleep until it had been relieved.

The room where she had bathed was now quite dark except for a small glowing light attached to the wall. No matter, she could see what she had to see. Several minutes later she emerged into the darkened hallway and walked right into Scott.

"Jenny! What are you...oh. I thought you were asleep."

"I'm just going. Good night." She rushed past him and into the safety of the bedroom, mortified at having been seen in a garment far more immodest than the nightgown she was accustomed to wearing. Once in bed this time, she sank easily into sleep, grateful for oblivion.

Scott's encounter with Jenny in the hallway had left him with an almost overwhelming desire to touch the luscious body he had just glimpsed. He could not help but notice the exquisite figure under the old tee-shirt, the long and shapely legs, and the small, firm breasts caressed by the clinging fabric. It was too much to take. He tried desperately to remove the image from his brain, but it was damnably persistent. All he could see was her gorgeous face, midnight curls and that sensational figure. Maybe keeping her here overnight was a big mistake. He buried himself in his work

again, determined to control his errant
thoughts.

Just before turning in, Scott checked on
Jenny once again. She lay there peacefully in
the splendor of her beauty, and he could
barely restrain himself from climbing in beside
her. But no, he had made a promise, and he would
keep it if it killed him. He brushed the hair
tenderly from her face and she stirred slightly.
"Charles, please hold me. Charles, where are
you?"

That name again! He stared down at her and
whispered softly as though to himself, "I used
to have a close friend named Charles. I think
you would have liked him. He was a strange one,
like you, but not quite so eccentric. He was
worldly and knowledgeable and dedicated, but the
guy still knew how to have fun. I wonder if your
Charles is as much of a man as the one I knew?"
He pulled the disordered sheet up over her
again and backed away slowly. "Good night, my
mysterious lady, good night."

Charles looked at his pocket watch. 10:45
P.M. Could that be right? Well, no matter,
he could always ask someone. At least he was in
the twentieth century; the presence of numerous
sweatsuited joggers on Duke of Gloucester Street
attested to that. Chowning's was in full swing,

he noticed as he passed; the music and laughter followed him for some way down the street, reminding him of the good times he had had there in the old days, and the time several weeks ago when he had taken Jenny there to her father's great chagrin. Jenny was one woman who would not take women's rights for granted. But where the hell was she?

He walked every restored street from Waller at Christiana Campbell's to Boundary Street and the College of William and Mary. If she was still wandering around, he would certainly have found her by now. She could be hidden in any of the small outbuildings in town, and he would be none the wiser. Damn! It was even possible that she was not alone. With her beauty and charm, it would not be difficult to find someone to take her in for the night. He tried to discourage this particular train of thought, but the possibility rankled. She would be hungry and desperately tired. It was the most natural thing in the world for a kind passerby to invite her in and...damn!

The night wasn't growing any younger, Charles thought, and I might as well bed down myself. He decided to try the Wythe house where he had successfully spent a night last year after first awakening in the eighteenth century. The door to the stable was ajar, but it was pitch dark inside. He decided to leave the door open to let in some light and allow him to study the layout. Finding a secure place in the corner of the tack room behind a carriage, he shut the door and lay down on a couple of blankets he had discovered on top of a storage bin.

He propped himself up against the wall unable to sleep for the moment. He could do no more tonight, the question was, would he find her tomorrow?

CHAPTER 27

Early the next morning Jenny was awakened by the sound of pots and pans in the kitchen. She scrambled out of bed and into the kitchen where Scott was busily preparing breakfast. Jenny glanced around the room with interest. It was filled with objects she had never seen before, and whose use she could only guess at.

Scott greeted her cheerfully. "You can sit here if you like. The bacon's all ready and I'll have the eggs on the table in a minute."

She watched him beat several eggs in a

317

small bowl and pour them into a hot skillet. What she couldn't understand was how he heated the skillet without a fire. There was something red and glowing underneath, like hot coals, that must be the answer. Scott poured coffee into two cups already set out on the table.

"Do you take cream?"

"Yes, thank you." She watched as he opened a large white box loaded with all kinds of food and beverages, and removed what proved to be the cream, though the lettering on the side clearly stated "Half and Half". A sudden popping noise attracted her attention.

"Would you get the toast, Jenny? I've got my hands full."

She examined the small metallic container from which two slices of toasted bread had arisen and quickly pulled them out without thinking. "Ah! These are hot!"

"Good, here's the margarine." He placed a dish of what looked like butter on the table and proceeded to spread some on the toast. "Let's eat while everything is still hot."

Jenny thoroughly enjoyed her breakfast with Scott. The food itself was not unfamiliar, only the preparation, which was marvelously fast thanks to the myriad of contraptions in Scott's kitchen. Did everyone in the twentieth century have such things? If so, the lady of the house must have a wonderfully easy life. She wondered how they washed clothes.

"I'm glad you got up when you did, Jenny. I didn't want to wake you, but I set the table for two anyway. You can go back to sleep if you like, it's only 6:30."

"I wouldn't have wanted to miss you. I know you must leave untimely early this morning."

"What will you do today?"

She took a sip of the hot, bracing coffee, pondering her answer. She had been wondering the same thing herself. "I'm not certain."

"Will I see you tonight?"

"I cannot promise it, Scott."

Something in her eyes warned him not to press her, so he continued in a light tone, "I have to know. I'm going to the store to pick up more food, and I have to know how many I'm cooking for, don't I?"

"Do you do all your own cooking?" She was still trying to evade the main issue.

"Sure. Who else is going to do it?"

She glanced around the room. "I suppose you must."

He reached across the table and took her hand. "Jenny, if you asked me, I would stay with you all day."

"No, Scott, I must be alone. If I return to you tonight, it would be late, but please, do not expect me."

"Can't you tell me what this is all about?

I know something is wrong, you've been acting so strangely. Is that it, is it an act? You told me before you were with the Colonial Players. Are you still putting on an act? If so, you can drop it. I want to know the real you."

Jenny sighed deeply. "Scott, please believe me when I say that you are seeing the real me. I lied when I told you I was a Colonial Player. I am not now, nor have I ever been an actress. The truth is something I can scarcely credit myself. It is possible that I shall be able to tell you the truth some day, but now is not the time." She could tell that he was not satisfied, but she was not prepared to endure the tumult which would result if she told him who she really was. "Do not ask me any more, I beg you."

"Alright. If that's the way you want it. Look, I'm going to do some shopping after a while, and I'll be coming back here. You might as well go back to bed. Nothing will be open this early anyway."

"Yes, thank you for everything, Scott. Some day I hope to be in a position to repay your kindness."

"No need for that. Just having your company is reward enough for me. Well, I'm out of here. See you later, I hope."

"Goodbye."

Left to her own devices, Jenny wandered around the empty apartment examining all the curious devices which she found there. There was, for instance, a large dark box on a stand in the sitting room. She could see her reflection in the glass, but the object was too dark and too low to serve as a satisfactory looking glass. It's intended use was a complete puzzle. She flipped several light switches as she had seen Scott do the evening before and understood that this brightly diffused light had totally eliminated the need for candles. She marveled at the efficiency of this new world, and yet, comfortable as it was, it seemed to have lost a great deal of the charm and romance which characterized her time.

She returned to the kitchen and spent a half hour familiarizing herself with the various knobs and switches she found there. She discovered the sources of hot and cold water and the mechanism for heating the stove. She opened the large white box from which Scott had taken the butter and milk earlier that morning and studied the contents. What would Beulah have given for such a marvelous box! Anyone possessing such a thing need never again worry about the spoilage of food and milk and the highly unpleasant gastronomic disturbances which necessarily resulted. What luxury!

At length, she wandered into the bedroom and sat down on the edge of the bed. She rubbed her bare feet through the thick carpet savoring the delicious sensation it produced. Her blister was much better this morning, and she would do something with her shoes to make them last for at least another day. Hopefully, she would be back home by this time tomorrow. She thought about Scott, and his unfailing kindness. He was a very attractive young man, and a gentle one as well. She wondered why he hadn't married. It must be from choice, since he was a man any girl would be proud to call husband. She might have considered him herself if she hadn't already met Charles.

Jenny stifled a yawn and slid under the covers. It was delightfully cool in Scott's apartment. In fact, it had been quite cool in every building she had visited so far, despite the scorching heat outside. That was something her mother would appreciate, thought Jenny with a smile. Mother had never become accustomed to the summer heat. She must remember to ask Charles how buildings were cooled, and heated for that matter. It was inconceivable that these people relied solely on the warmth of fireplaces in the winter.

Jenny pulled the covers up around her shoulders and drifted off to sleep. Almost immediately, she was joined by Charles and joyfully reached out to touch him, but a dense fog surrounded them and he began to drift away. She ran after him as fast as her legs would carry her, but they grew indescribably heavy, and finally refused to carry her at all. She fell into the swirling fog screaming for Charles, who was now too far away to hear. Finally, the fog began to lift and the sun broke through the clouds. It shone brilliantly down on the cornfield, and there, standing among the tall stalks, was Charles, his arms outstretched to receive her.

Jenny awoke and leaped out of bed. He was here! There was no doubt about it, he had really come for her! She dressed and groomed herself carefully, and fairly ran out of the apartment, remembering Scott's instructions to lock the front door. She floated down Prince George Street, past the Wythe house, crossed the Palace Green and headed for Nicholson Street. Soon she arrived at the dig site, but to her consternation, Charles was not there. She stepped resolutely into the field and tried to find the exact location where she had traveled through time. But she had neglected to leave a marker, and one spot looked much like every other. Ah well, she would simply have to wait here for Charles. There was no doubt in her mind that he was on his way. Pray God he would hurry.

CHAPTER 28

Charles was awakened by the sudden bright light which burst into the dark stable when the door opened. He froze, scarcely breathing, as he strained forward for a glimpse of the person who was sure to discover him any minute. There was a sound of gravel crunching outside the door and Charles knew he was reprieved for a minute, at least. He had to get out of there before the person returned. He stood up and peered over the wall toward the door and wondered if he had time to dash out. No, he'd better wait and hope that the right moment would present itself.

Soon a young woman entered and approached a large feeding bin standing against the front wall. Charles ducked out of sight, hoping she had not seen him. He heard her fill her bucket with grain and close the bin; then, thank heaven, the familiar crunch of gravel again.

He crept stealthily out of the stall and peeked around the door jamb. The yard immediately in front of the stable was vacant, but he could hear the cajoling tone of the young woman's voice. Whatever she was doing, he hoped she was preoccupied enough not to notice his exit.

He brushed himself off and sauntered out into the yard straight toward the girl who was squatting on the ground in front of one of the neighboring outbuildings.

"Good morning!"

She jumped up. "God, you scared me!"

"I'm sorry," Charles said pleasantly, "I was just taking a walk, and I saw you in here working. I wondered what you were doing."

"As you can see, I'm feeding the birds." Her initial distrust was evaporating, but she was still a bit wary.

"Sorry I startled you," Charles said again, "I guess I'd better get on with my walk. See you!"

"Yeah, bye."

In no time at all he found himself at the dig site, hoping against hope that Jenny would be there. But no, the cornfield was empty, and there was no sign of her on the street. Well, it was still early, perhaps she was still asleep. He trudged on, periodically accosting a Foundation employee and showing him Jenny's picture, but it was no use. No one had seen her.

At length he revisited the dig site, but once again, it was empty. This time, he walked into the center of the field and examined the ground. The stalks had been flattened and there were clear signs of small footprints in the earth. So, she had been here, and recently. They must have just missed each other. Buoyed by this hope, he set out again to find her. Sooner or later they would have to meet. The historical area wasn't vast, and there were certain points of interest which he was sure would claim her attention.

For the next hour he visited every site which he had mentally designated as a possible rendezvous, but there was still no sign of Jenny. For want of something better to do, he returned to the cornfield and sat down. It was a beautiful summer day, not too hot and pleasantly somnolent. Before he knew it, Charles was fast asleep.

In the dream, Charles and several of his friends had joined an archeological

expedition in Mexico along the Gulf coast. After
several grueling weeks, they were given a
weekend off and decided to rent a small
sailboat. It was a glorious day, and they spent
it sailing and diving into the warm, blue waters
of the Gulf. At dusk, just as they were about to
head back, they spotted a young woman who was
swimming near a particularly rocky stretch of
shoreline with a strong undercurrent. They found
it odd that she was swimming alone, and in so
dangerous a spot, and so they sailed toward her,
intent on warning her or, if necessary, pulling
her out. As they approached, it was obvious that
she was in trouble. Charles and his closest
friend dove in unhesitatingly and swam toward
her. The current was worse than they had
anticipated, and they found it ever more
difficult to maintain control. Swells were
rising higher than usual and it was impossible
to see very far in front of them, but soon
Charles found her struggling furiously to stay
afloat. When he had come within twenty feet of
her, he gasped in amazement. It was Jenny.
He had no sooner recognized her than she went
under; her strength was nearly gone. When
Charles and his friend reached the spot where
she had last been seen, they dove for her.
Fortunately, the clear water allowed
considerable distance of underwater visibility,
but it was much too rough to stay down for long,

and the undercurrent was a powerful opponent. Charles' partner then saw the girl near the rocks and they both knew that she was in serious trouble since the currents around the large boulders were merciless. She hadn't a hope of getting through. They tried to swim over to her, but she disappeared in a froth of white. Deperate now, Charles swam with preternatural strength, and as he approached, he could hear her calling to him.

"Jack, did you hear that?"

His friend was beginning to struggle himself, and he looked back anxiously for the sailboat which was following them. Everyone on board was motioning frantically for them to get back on board. "Charles, it's no use. Let's...go...back."

"Jack! She's calling me! Can't you hear?"

"That's impossible. We've...never seen...her...before." He was reaching the end of his resources.

"No! I saw her face. It's Jenny! I know it!"

"Who is...Jenny?"

The girl called out to him again, and Charles turned away from his friend. The voice was getting closer now. "Charles! Can you hear me? It's Jenny!"

He felt a hand touch his face, and he opened his eyes. My God, it really was - Jenny!

"Charles, wake up. I've been waiting for you."

"Oh my little darling, I've just had the most awful...never mind. I was so worried about you!" She flew into his arms and he kissed her passionately.

"I knew you would come. I dreamed of finding you this very morning," she told him.

He held her at arm's length, intoxicated by the sight of her. "God, it's good to see you again. I've been in hell since they told me you were missing."

"I, too. Don't ever go away without me again, Charles."

"No chance of that, my love." They clung together fiercely.

"Charles?"

"Yes?"

"We have done it, at last. We are here, in your time." She turned her face up to him with the satisfied air of an athlete who had just won a trophy.

"Yes, love, we have crossed the barrier of time. There for a while I was worried that I might enter a different decade, or even another century, but here we are, still together. It's a miracle."

"But Charles, I must tell you that I have been unable to return home. I tried and tried yesterday, and each time I failed. Suppose we can never go back?"

"You were here before, weren't you? You left the picture for me, and thank God you did, or I would never have known where to look for you. If you returned home after that trip, you can return home now." He corrected himself. "We can return home, if that's what you wish."

"Oh yes. I cannot leave my parents without even a goodbye. They will be desolate."

He remembered his last interview with Tobias and Anne and he had to admit that Jenny was right.

"It can be done. We will find the way."

His voice was drowned out by the roar of a shuttle bus and he pulled Jenny closer. "What do you think of twentieth century life, my love? I'm sure you must have had some interesting experiences."

Her face brightened. "I have seen so many miraculous things, Charles, I can scarcely take them all in! But there is much for you to explain. I have been somewhat reluctant to talk to anyone for obvious reasons."

He chuckled to himself, remembering his own first experiences in the eighteenth century. "I don't doubt that. So, do you want to return now?"

She surprised him by her answer. "Not just yet, Charles. There is so much to do and to see. Give me one more day."

"But you just said..."

"I do want to go home only...not yet."

"Well, in that case, where do you want to go first?"

She threw he arms around him happily. "Everywhere! Take me everywhere, come!" She took his hand and led him down the street toward Duke of Gloucester. "Why did you not tell me about restrooms?" she asked mischievously.

"I...why I just didn't think about it. There was so much to tell you."

"Then show me now." Her eyes gleamed with excitement. All her fears had vanished now that Charles was here, and she quizzed him eagerly on this and that as they walked along.

They strolled through town until mid-afternoon. By that time, Jenny admitted that she was rather hungry. "What will we do about food, Charles?"

He thought about it for a moment. There was the little matter of currency. He had come away with nothing but eighteenth century coins, and they were useless here. "Come, we can go into the drugstore and ask. I have a friend there who may be willing to advance me a small loan."

"Good. I must eat soon, or I shall drop."

"I hope she's in," Charles fretted, as they entered the drugstore. "Last year she got off at three o'clock." He led Jenny up to the front

331

counter which she remembered so well, but Charles' friend wasn't there. "Come, maybe she's at the drug counter."

The mysterious friend was, indeed, at the drug counter, and Jenny caught her breath when she saw who it was. "Why, it's Clara!"

"Hello, dearie, who have you...Charles! Where on earth have you been? Half of Williamsburg's been looking for you this past year!"

Charles looked dumbfounded from Clara to Jenny. "You know each other?"

"The lady was kind enough to introduce herself to me just last night," Jenny replied demurely, amused at Charles' reaction.

"Clara, how are you?" Charles gave her a bear hug fierce enough to crush her bones. "Let me tell you, I thought I'd never be talking to you again!"

"Well," she returned, stopping to catch her breath, "where have you been all these months? We thought you'd dropped off the face of the earth."

"I can imagine. Suffice it to say that I have been away too long. I intend to make up for lost time, though."

Curious, thought Jenny, how Charles' language had changed now that he was in his element. It had lost a good deal of its precision and clarity and taken on a decidedly colloquial cast. It was all she could do, at times, to understand him.

"You sure do have a beautiful girl, there," Clara told Charles. "Where did you find her?"

"It's a long story, believe me. Clara," he began, uncertainly, for him, "would you do me a big favor?"

"Of course, just name it."

"Actually, we are in a jam. We haven't a penny between us. Could you spot me a twenty? I'll pay you back as soon as I can."

"Listen, dearie, if I couldn't give you twenty bucks, I'd say our friendship wasn't worth a damn. Wait here a minute." She soon returned with several bills and handed them to Charles with a smile.

"I really appreciate this, Clara. We haven't eaten all day, and Jenny, here, is on her last legs."

Jenny forebore to mention that she had enjoyed a substantial breakfast. That was a subject for another time, and she was not at all sure how Charles would receive the information.

Clara indicated the luncheon counter and booths at the rear of the store. "Why don't you go on over and grab a sandwich or something?"

He turned to Jenny with a theatrical wink and muttered loudly, "I told you Clara would take care of us."

Jenny smiled at the older woman. "I really

am most grateful, Miss Clara."

"You're most welcome, Jenny. Look, why don't you drop the 'miss'. Clara will be fine."

"Certainly, if you wish it, Clara."

Charles grabbed her hand. "Come on, Jenny, let's eat. Clara, will you join us for a coffee?"

"No, dearie. I'm trying to cut down on the coffee. Better for my blood pressure, you know. But come see me before you all leave."

"Alright, will do."

They sank into a comfortable booth and Charles ordered two bacon, lettuce and tomato sandwiches with lemonade. "This is one of the best places in town to get a quick, inexpensive lunch, or dinner, as you would call it."

"Can I order ham and cheese here?"

"Yes, I suppose so. Where did you eat ham and cheese before?"

"At Chowning's."

"Chowning's!" He looked at her searchingly. "When did you eat at Chowning's, and who were you with?"

"Last week, a very nice young man took me there for...dinner, is it?"

"Yes, dinner. Who was this young man?"

"Just someone whom I met and...well, I was famished, and he offered to take me to Chowning's for something to eat, so I..."

"Jenny, do you know how much of a risk you

took in doing such a thing? You were fortunate that nothing happened." His tone took on a preaching quality which Jenny found mildly distasteful.

"Charles, he was a perfect gentleman. Please credit me with enough sense to discern the difference between a gentleman and a ruffian!"

"Now, now, don't get upset. I simply meant that you must be very careful in this day and age." He felt as if he were walking on eggshells. He must not appear jealous, but damnit, he was.

"You would like him, Charles, and I think that Scott would like you, also."

"Hmm. Just be careful, okay?"

"I know I can trust him. Why, he took me to dinner again just last night."

"He did! Well, I suppose you had to eat," he added, scowling. An extremely distasteful thought flashed through his mind and he tried to dismiss it, but the question had to be asked. "And where did you spend the night?"

Jenny blushed in spite of herself. He had every right to be proprietary, and a part of her appreciated his possessiveness; and yet, another part of her, the independent part, bristled. She looked him straight in the eye and said clearly, "At Scott's apartments."

Her slight mispronunciation amused him and

he nearly laughed, but the matter was too serious, and he wondered if he had grounds to be alarmed. "He treated you with respect, I trust, and did not...uh...Jenny, he didn't touch you?"

She was aghast. "Certainly not! I said he was a perfect gentleman. He drew a bath for me, and made up his own bed for my use while he retired to the sitting room. It was all perfectly innocent. Moreover, he cooked breakfast for me this morning with his own hands!"

Charles reflected with amusement that the latter seemed to impress her the most. "I would like to meet this young man, and thank him myself for taking such good care of you." He was unaware of the irony in his tone.

"That can be arranged."

Their lunch arrived, and they devoured it eagerly, topping it off with a pair of hot fudge sundaes. Jenny was in ecstacies over the concoction and seriously considered ordering another, but Charles distracted her with a list of sights she must see, and literally dragged her out of the drugstore. On their way out, they stopped to say goodbye to Clara, promising to return soon.

"Just where did you go, Charles?" Clara asked curiously. "We were all wondering."

"It's a long and very complicated story which I haven't got time now to tell. Rest assured, someday you'll know everything."

"Take care now, and look after your lovely friend. She's one in a million, Charles."

He glanced down at Jenny's upturned face and squeezed her hand. "Don't I know it? I"ll never find another like her!"

CHAPTER 29

Charles led Jenny by the hand down Duke of Gloucester to the Market Square. "What have you seen outside of the historic area?"

"Nothing at all. I never left the historic area."

"I want you to see more of the modern side of my time." They walked through the half-filled parking lot next to the Craft House at the Wiliamsburg Inn. "See all those cars?"

"Yes."

"Well, try to imagine a lot full of horses,

338

and consider that each car can comfortably carry five or more people, whereas every rider in your day needs his own horse, at least for longer trips."

"It is amazing. I can not understand how so many people can be here."

"The population is approaching 250 million. More than one million walk the restored streets of your Williamsburg every year. The biggest difference you will have to adjust to, is that there is so much more of everything - cars, homes, inns and taverns, roads. I can't begin to tell you everything."

"It will be difficult."

"It will take time." He walked her over to the Abby Aldrich Rockefeller Center on the rear porch deck overlooking a formally landscaped garden of roses with a pool and fountain as the centerpiece. "This is one of my favorite places in town."

She took his hand and squeezed it. "I can understand why."

They seated themselves on one of the benches scattered around the garden. "Jenny, don't you suppose we should return to the eighteenth century? Your family should be told that we are well."

She bit her lip. How could she have forgotten them? On the other hand, they would soon know that she was well, and she must make the most of this opportunity to learn about Charles' time. "Please, not yet, Charles. Suppose...suppose this were the last time we could ever be here together? I mean, if we returned now, and were somehow unable to come back, would you not want to look back on the time we spent here together?"

"I hadn't thought of it that way, but no, I don't agree. I see no reason why we shouldn't be able to come and go at will, now that we have the answer. This is all new and exciting to you, Jenny, I understand that, but you must think of your parents. Think how they suffered last year after Adam's death. They probably fear that something equally terrible has happened to you now."

Jenny was quiet for a long moment. "You are right." She sighed. "Just give us a few more hours. Is that too much to ask?"

Charles capitulated. Later, he was to look back on this moment as the turning point, and regret that he had not been more insistent. But Jenny could be so very appealing when she chose, and never more so than when she wanted a favor from him. "Very well, just a few more hours. But we will not stay the night, you understand?"

"Of course. As you say." Father would understand, wouldn't he? In his place, she would...what? It was on the tip of her tongue to tell Charles that she was wrong, that they must return immediately, when he stood up suddenly and took her hand. "Come this way, please, madame, I have something of the utmost interest to show you." His voice had taken on a comical falsetto reminiscent of one of her mother's most pompous acquaintances.

She giggled. "Oh Charles, you can be silly."

He grabbed her waist and swirled her high in the air. "You want silly? I'll give you silly!" He turned her round and round until she gasped that she was dizzy and begged him to stop.

He lowered her gently to the ground and they exchanged a tender kiss. "Right, now, come this way." He escorted her around the front of the Folk Art Museum, through the oval garden onto the sloping lawns behind the Williamsburg Inn. He turned around and indicated the vast facade of the inn with both hands. "The Raleigh Tavern may have had thirty or so beds. Today, inns of this magnitude might have hundreds of beds, all in separate rooms, or perhaps with two beds in a room, and each room has its own bathroom, or restroom, as you call it."

"I don't call it that, the sign indicated that name. Why are they not all called the same thing?" Jenny was indignant at the vagaries of twentieth century language. But she had to

341

admit that the term 'bathroom' was more appropriate than 'restroom'.

"My funny little dear, let's not go into that right now. There's too much to do."

Jenny was looking out over the manicured lawns with a puzzled expression. "What are those people doing with sticks over there?"

"Let's go see," he replied enigmatically. He led the way to the practice green near the first tee of the Golden Horseshoe Golf Course. "Feel that grass, Jenny!" Several people were putting on the green. Jenny watched for a moment, but she became even more confused at their peculiar antics.

"It must be a game of some kind," she said finally.

"It is. It's called golf."

"I would like to try it. Where does one acquire the sticks?"

"These people buy their own golf clubs in special stores."

"What type of store is it?"

"A store which only sells equipment and supplies intended for sporting activities and games, like this one." Pointing to the tee behind her, he continued, "You see that man?"

"Yes?"

"Watch how far he hits the ball." The man in question struck the ball cleanly with his driver and placed a nice shot near the middle of the fairway.

"I should love to try it. What is the object of the game?"

"At the end of that long stretch of open lawn is one of the greens, as they are called. Your objective is to take the least number of swings at the ball, or strokes, to get the ball into a cup on the green, like one of these." He pointed to the flagged cups on the practice green.

"I think I understand. It seems to require a great deal of skill."

"Like anything else, practice makes perfect."

They strolled back toward one of the swimming pools. There were only a few people sunbathing and several children splashing around in the shallow end.

"Oh, this is like the Roman baths I read about at home! Those must be bathing costumes," she exclaimed, looking at Charles for confirmation.

He laughed at her parallel. "I never thought of it that way, Jenny, but you have a point. Yes, those are bathing costumes. We call them swimsuits."

She wandered over to the edge and put her hand in the water. "It is cooler than I imagined."

"It will warm up with the summer heat. This

is only June."

"Those swimsuits are altogether too revealing, Charles. I could never wear one!"

"Darling, everyone wears them, young and old alike. You'll get used to them in time. Besides, you have a great figure. You'll look fantastic in a swimsuit."

She shook her head. "I'm sorry, but I wouldn't dream of exposing myself to the sun in that fashion. It darkens one's skin!"

He laughed aloud and several people turned to stare. "Well, that's the whole idea!"

She looked askance at the audience Charles' laughter had attracted and moved away, lowering her voice. "Let us discuss it at another time, Charles. I confess I have much difficulty with the concept."

"I understand, darling. Come!" He took her hand again and they made their way into the Inn through the French doors which opened out onto the patio. Jenny saw a very large room beautifully appointed with settings of the finest Georgian furniture, oriental rugs and large vases of freshly cut flowers scattered throughout. There was constant motion as people passed by in both directions, and some departing through the front door which was held open for each guest by a uniformed doorman.

"This is the main lobby where everyone checks in or out of the Inn," he told her sotto voce. "That is the main entrance, and down the hall there, is the main dining room."

"It is very elegant, and very expensive, I should imagine."

"Absolutely. I would have all I could do to stay for even one night." He looked at her with a grave expression. "That reminds me, Jenny. We will have to return home soon. It's getting late."

"Yes, I know. But there is one thing we must do first, Charles."

"What is that?"

"I wish to introduce you to Scott. You said yourself you would like to thank him personally for taking care of me and..."

"Where does he live?"

"I don't remember the name of the street, but I think I can find it."

"Well, if you must go, we will, but remember, we can't stay long."

"Charles!" Scott's face had gone white as a sheet.

"Scott! My God, it was you all along!"

"Come in please." They exchanged warm handshakes as Jenny looked on in unconcealed amazement. Scott turned to her and grinned. "So this is the Charles you talked about last night!"

Jenny was even more perplexed. She had no

recollection of talking about Charles to Scott. What did he mean?

"Scott, this beauty is my fiancée, Jenny Coulter."

"You are engaged?" His face fell, but he collected himself and made the proper congratulatory noises. "Charles, forgive me for asking, but where the hell have you been?"

"It's a long story, my friend. I owe it to you to explain, but I give you fair warning; you won't believe a word of it." He turned to Jenny who was now seated beside him on the sofa. "I should tell you that Scott and I met and became good friends last year while working on the dig site together. That was just before I came to you."

Jenny nodded.

Scott added, "And when Charles disappeared, the Foundation and all of his colleagues had no idea what had happened. They supposed he had just quit, even though that was not at all like something he would do. Nothing made sense, and no one ever heard from him again, most unlike Charles. It was a mystery to all of us."

"I'm sure it was. But wait 'til I tell you what really happened!"

"Go on," said Scott leaning forward attentively, "I'm all ears."

CHAPTER 30

"How did you first meet Jenny?"

Charles glanced at Jenny and they both laughed at the incongruity of the story he was about to tell. "This is going to sound like something out of 'Star Trek', but I swear it really happened. Actually, it all began with visions I had of Jenny while working on the dig site last summer. I didn't know it was Jenny then, of course, I merely saw this incredibly beautiful girl in period costume who seemed to summon me, and I felt as though we belonged together. This was taking place when I unearthed the vase - you remember? It was Ch'ing Dynasty, incredibly valuable, and I had found the first shard. No sooner had I touched it, than I experienced a violent episode of vertigo, dizziness, nausea, the works. I attributed it to the heat, took a rest, and continued on. Every time I found another shard of that damned vase, I felt the same symptoms, only stronger. I'm sure you remember all this. Well, after a particularly bad attack, the doctor ordered bed rest and that was that. I awakened the next fine morning in 1767 instead of 1986."

"It wasn't a dream, or a hallucination?"

"Absolutely not. I thought at first that it must be a dream, but it never ended - I never woke up! To keep from starving I found work with the master printer who happened to be Jenny's father, and that's how I met her. Her father invited me to dinner two weeks later and - there she was! She literally knocked me off my feet, for you see, I recognized in her the girl I had seen on the dig site, in my visions, or hallucinations, call it what you will."

"Wait a minute! You're telling me that you actually went back in time, and that Jenny has come forward?"

"Exactly. I returned to the twentieth century only last night, except for one freak accident back in April when I returned for an hour or so. I had been severely wounded, and somehow the shock must have triggered the time travel mechanism. I still don't understand how it happened."

Scott whistled. "You're right, it sounds just like a script from 'Star Trek'. How did you do it in the first place?" He was totally caught up in Charles' story, but on a deeper level, it was still just that - a story.

Charles and Jenny exchanged glances, and Jenny answered Scott's question. "We are not certain of all the details, but we know that the vase is essential to the process."

"The vase? The same one from the dig site?"

"The very same."

"But how?"

"At some point during my stay in the eighteenth century, I put two and two together and concluded that the vase was largely responsible for my time travel. By April, I knew it was more complicated than that. It was a combination of the vase, Jenny, and the house which Jenny's father had constructed as our wedding present, and which stood squarely on the present day dig site."

"But how did you return last night?"

"It's rather complicated. I was invited to Shadwell for a month, and in my absence, Jenny found her way into the twentieth century, alone..."

"Shadwell! That was Thomas Jefferson's place, wasn't it?"

"Yes..."

"You actually met Thomas Jefferson?"

"Yes, we became close friends."

Scott threw up his hands. "Charles, I'm sorry, but I'm really having trouble with this. Are you putting me on?"

"Every word is true." He sighed. "I knew you wouldn't believe it."

"That is why I could not tell you about myself, Scott," added Jenny.

"But, you're both putting me on! This can't be true. Come on."

"I'm sorry you can't believe it, Scott, but if that's the way you feel, there is no point in continuing with the conversation."

"No, no, wait! Look, tell me the rest of the story. It's just so wild, I don't know how to take it. In my place, would you believe yourself?"

Charles was compelled to laugh. "No, I suppose not..."

Without warning, Charles slumped over, falling onto Jenny. He had been felled by another attack of vertigo more intense than he had experienced. The room swam around him, and he could hardly reach for his aching head.

"Scott! Help him!" cried Jenny as she rose and tried to lift Charles' legs onto the sofa.

Scott made his friend as comfortable as possible under the circumstances and rushed out of the room for a cold compress. By the time he returned, Charles' eyes were open, but he was still as white as death.

"Are you alright? What happened, Charles?"

"It's...going away," he managed with a weak smile.

Jenny hung over him solicitously. She had never before witnessed one of his attacks, but she knew enough to be frightened. "Charles, what are you feeling? Is it the same as...?"

"It feels the same, yes." She looked at him with horror.

"You are not leaving us, now?"

"I think...not." He sat up slowly. "Damn! That is the third time in the last three weeks!. I'm beginning to worry about these recent episodes and wonder what they could mean."

Scott had caught some of Jenny's panic. "Charles, get a grip on yourself, this can't be happening!"

"Now you are starting to sound like me," Charles replied in an ironic tone. He turned to Jenny who brought his hand to her lips.

Scott watched them helplessly. "You were saying that Jenny had found her way here alone..."

"Yes, last week. That was when she met you

for the first time."

"I knew there was something weird about her. There for a while I thought she was a refugee from the local looney bin. Sorry, Jenny," he added apologetically.

Mercifully Jenny had not understood his last reference and smiled sweetly at him.

"At any rate," Charles continued, "when she was here last week, a tourist took her picture, and after she returned to the eighteenth century, Jenny left the picture under my pillow. When I returned from Shadwell, I found the house in a turmoil. They said Jenny was missing, and no one had a clue to her whereabouts. Of course, I knew, as soon as I saw the picture. I understood what she had done and where she had gone. So I set out to follow her at once."

"Tell me more about this mysterious vase. That was the starting point, wasn't it?"

Charles and Jenny exchanged glances, and Jenny continued, "Actually, my Aunt Caroline informed me that the vase came into our family many generations ago. It was apparently a gift from a sea captain who had brought it from China. There were always stories about it, of course, though no one took them seriously."

"What kind of stories?"

"It was said that the vase was cursed. Many who have owned it went insane, or were in other ways victims of tragedies or bizarre circumstances." She paused briefly, and turned to Charles. "It suddenly occurs to me that my troubles this past winter started only after I took possession of the vase upon my return from Boston. Do you suppose there is something to this curse after all?"

His eyes widened. "You know, I believe you are right. You came down with pneumonia during the trip..."

"...not three days after Aunt Caroline had presented me with it!"

Scott broke in somewhat impatiently, "But the time travel thing! I'm still confused as to how the vase is connected with that."

"Well, I had no clue how to escape back to the twentieth century until I saw the vase in Jenny's room last February. It was only after Mr. Coulter presented us with the house as a wedding present that it began to come together. No, wait a moment, actually it was Jenny who discovered it first."

Jenny continued, "It was largely a matter of trial and error. I really had no idea how to make it work, except that it must be handled in front of the sitting room fireplace. I cannot explain the inconsistencies." She turned to Charles for support.

"Well, after studying the arrangement for most of last night, I believe I finally have it.

I am convinced that the vase must be on the mantelpiece in the sitting room, and obviously one must take it in hand momentarily, but...and this is vital...it must be returned to its resting place almost immediately thereafter."

"Why is that?" asked Scott.

"Because our ability to travel through time is contingent upon the presence of that vase on that mantelpiece."

Jenny was aghast. "Are you saying that the vase cannot be removed from its place if we are to return to the eighteenth century?"

"Exactly. Once we return, you may do what you like with it. But if we are to travel back and forth through time, the vase must remain in position."

"Does anyone else know of this?"

"No, Scott, I'm certain of that."

Jenny's lovely face was momentarily contorted with sharp fear. "Oh no! It can't be..."

"What is it?" They both looked at her in bewilderment.

"My...my father did handle the vase once, and he became quite ill, Charles, he actually swooned! Perhaps he won't associate his illness with the vase, though. Do you think it likely?"

Charles looked down at his hands, reluctant to let her see the worry in his eyes. "Let us hope that neither your father nor anyone else will touch it until we return safely, after which a clear and final decision can be made about our future. There is, however, one final condition which must be met if the vase is to work its magic."

"And that is...?"

"I've discovered that the vase only works when you place both feet firmly on the brick hearth while handling it."

Scott shook his head. "That's creepy, Charles. I mean, you sound like something out of H.G. Wells, you know? How can you be sure that you will go back to the exact time in the eighteenth century, though? Suppose you go back too far, or only as far as the nineteenth century? What then?"

Charles and Jenny exchanged glances, both momentarily at a loss for words. Then Charles took a deep breath and replied slowly, "I have asked myself the same questions over and over, Scott. The answer is I simply do not know. It is possible, I suppose, but so far it hasn't happened. That is a risk I...we simply must take." He reached out for Jenny's hand and cradled it in his own. "I'm not even sure two people can make the trip at the same time."

"I won't go back without you, Charles."

They stared at each other, weighing the possibilities. Then Charles said, "You must try it first. At least we know that you succeeded on two previous occasions."

"But I failed yesterday!"

"Yes, you did. I had forgotten, but I know one thing for certain. You must return, and as quickly as possible. We cannot take a chance that you will be trapped here."

"And why not, if you are here?" Her voice betrayed her agitation and a hint of annoyance as well.

"I have been thinking about that very seriously. If you were to come into my time permanently, all your family's history subsequent to the year 1768 would be changed, and somehow I don't feel we have a right to tamper with history and all the future generations of your family, do you?"

She stared at him in shock. "But that would mean that we..."

"I know what we said, but think about it seriously, Jenny. It is not a decision to be made lightly."

Jenny wanted to scream that she would remain with him whatever the cost to future generations, but her throat was constricted with unshed tears and she could only stare at him in silent disbelief.

He knew his words had momentarily disarmed her, and longed to take them back. He loved her more than ever, but could they possess each other at any cost? He turned to Scott. "You see what I am up against! As I said before, I just don't know if two people can safely make the trip. We could both end up in the Dark Ages for all I know!" He ran his hands distractedly through his hair.

Scott was watching Jenny, mesmerized by the fiery brilliance of her eyes. What a woman! If Charles was fool enough to want to part with her, she would not find herself alone for long.

"Just how physically dangerous is the time travel experience, Charles?"

"That's another thing that concerns me. It could actually be life-threatening. The experience drains the body of a great deal of energy. I'm not sure it couldn't cause cardiac or respiratory arrest."

"I am perfectly willing to remain here with you for the rest of my life. You know that, Charles. There is no need for us to attempt it again!" Jenny urged vehemently.

He sighed. "Perhaps that would be the best thing for us, personally, but have we the right to change history?"

She bit her lip. It was all too complicated. She had thought they were in complete agreement never to separate again, and now Charles had found a seemingly irrefutable argument against her remaining in the twentieth century. Was he really willing to live with her in her time? Wouldn't that change history as well? Of what significance were the lives of two people within the vast complexity of space and time? Did they dare flout the cosmic plan - could they? Perhaps Charles was right. In that case, there was nothing for her to live for.

"There are altogether too many unknowns involved here. Jenny, you must make the trip back, and you must go first. I'm not even sure I can go back unless you are already there. I suspect the vase won't transport me anywhere away from you."

"Good! And that is precisely how it should be." Jenny looked up joyfully through tear-filled eyes. "You know we are meant to be together!"

"I do know, darling." He sighed. "We must discuss this at length when we return to the eighteenth century. Perhaps we should tell your father. His advice would be most welcome at this juncture."

A tear rolled down her cheek. "I have dreamed of losing you so often, and now it almost seems inevitable. I pray God it is not so." She threw her arms around him. "I would not hesitate to sacrifice those unknown generations to live out my life with you. Would you not do the same for me?"

Pain engulfed him and he held her close, kissing her hair tenderly. For a long time he remained silent, then he said. "Yes, Jenny. God forgive me, but I would do the same. Only I cannot help thinking that nature will demand a great price from us."

Epilogue

Richard Billingsley couldn't sleep. He tossed restlessly from side to side for two hours before he finally got out of bed and got dressed. This was the second night with no word from Charles. Although he had complete faith in his friend, he couldn't help but sense some threat of danger looming over him and Jenny. It was frustrating as the devil to be unable to help, and to relieve his pent up emotions. Billingsley took himself out of the loft and into the cool night air.

His wanderings inevitably took him past the little house on Nicholson Street which was soon to be occupied by Charles and Jenny. Where were they now? Were they together? And what was it about that letter which Jenny had so lightheartedly placed under Charles' pillow, and which Charles had regarded with such horror?

He was standing in the middle of the street staring up at the stars as though the answer to his questions might be written there, when something drew his attention to the house itself. There was something mysterious about it there in the moonlight. He felt that if the walls could speak, they would tell him of Jenny's whereabouts, and Charles' as well.

As he gazed, Billinsgley noticed a flicker of light inside the house, in the parlor to be exact. He watched it intently, unsure of what he was seeing. Damned if it didn't look like a candle. But who would be in the house at this time of night? Coulter? He moved closer to the front of the house, careful not to make any noise. If it was indeed Coulter, the man obviously wanted to do his grieving alone.

Consumed by curiosity, Billingsley crept up to the parlor window and peered inside. He was astounded to see the unfamiliar figure of a man, candle in hand, standing before the fireplace, while a second man carefully concealed what looked like a vase inside his coat. Scoundrels! Well, they wouldn't get away with it, he would see to that! He backed away from the window as the front door opened. The two men stepped out of the house and had already descended the stairwell before Billingsley could react. In desperation he yelled after them, "Stop! Stop, thieves! You'll pay for this!"

They turned in alarm, then without a word they took off in two different directions, and Billingsley lost more valuable time deciding which one to pursue. Unfortunately, running was not one of his strong points, though in hand-to-hand combat he was invincible. His size worked against him now, and the thieves slipped away before Billingsley could cover more than a few yards in pursuit.

A loud groan escaped him. Damn him for a fool! He had ruined everything. Realizing that it was pointless to continue the chase, Billingsley turned and ran down Nicholson Street to give Coulter the news.

If you have enjoyed reading

"Williamsburg's Francis Street"

and wish to be notified when the third book in the Williamsburg trilogy is published and available, please send your name and address to:

Colonial Publishing, Inc.
Trilogy Info.
P. O. Box 233
Timonium, Maryland 21093-0233

For additional copies of "Williamsburg's Francis Street," send $7.95 plus $2.00 for postage and handling (total $9.95 for each book, check or money order) to:

Colonial Publishing, Inc.
Mail Order Dept. F
P. O. Box 233
Timonium, Maryland 21093-0233

For a Special Gift

For a personally autographed copy of "Williamsburg's Francis Street," provide the name of the recipient and send $7.95 ea., plus $4.00 ea. for postage and special handling (total $11.95 for each book, by check or money order) to:

Colonial Publishing, Inc.
Mail Order Dept. F
P. O. Box 233
Timonium, Maryland 21093-0233

Allow approx. 4 weeks for delivery